The Doberman Wore Black

Other Novels by Barbara Moore

HARD ON THE ROAD
THE FEVER CALLED LIVING
SOMETHING ON THE WIND

The Doberman Wore Black

Barbara Moore

ST. MARTIN'S PRESS
New York

Design by Kingsley Parker

Moore, Barbara, 1934—
    The doberman wore black.

    I. Title.
PS3563.057D6 1983 813'.54   83-2978
ISBN 0-312-21474-X

First Edition

10 9 8 7 6 5 4 3 2 1

To Anne Woodruff, who
gave us Gehli and taught
us to love Dobermans

The
Doberman
Wore
Black

AS GORDON CHRISTY, D.V.M., left Denver's smog below him and gained the mountains, his spirits climbed faster than his aging car, but that's the way mountains affected Christy. After spending four years at the Colorado College of Veterinary Medicine at Fort Collins, Christy couldn't fathom how anyone could bear settling down in Colorado's Front Range cities. It had driven him a little crazy to sit on the plains looking up at the great wall of mountains just west of him and thinking that only an hour or so away there were the icy streams, the moss-covered rocks, the aspens, and, yes, the eagles.

He felt crazy again that October afternoon, but it was the craziness of anticipation. The first two jobs Christy had tried out after finishing vet school were in Denver suburbs. This one, at last, was in the mountains. The car seat beside him was lined with cages containing two cockatoos and a chameleon that his new employer had asked him to pick up from specialists in Denver, and the back seat was crammed with large potted plants that Dr. Potter had phoned back and asked him if he could bring. Christy's own possessions were stuffed in the car trunk, but the bulk of his gear waited with a friend. If Christy decided to stay after Dr. Potter's vacation, and if Dr. Potter agreed with his decision, he would collect his belongings, especially ski equipment, the first time he drove back over the mountains.

Skis were important. His destination was Vail, the number-two ski resort, after Aspen, in the nation. Vail, playground of ex-presidents, the occasional film star, and the monied Midwest. To Christy, the Vail area meant basically the high country that he loved, but since he enjoyed skiing in a bumbling sort of way, he regarded Vail's ski runs as a pleasant bonus. Vets were in short supply, and Christy knew he could go just about where he pleased. But mountains were mountains, and Christy harbored the hope that his newest temporary job might become permanent.

The cities he had left behind tried to invade the mountains with freeway traffic on a six-lane interstate highway, but eventually the divided lanes narrowed to four and traffic thinned. Christy began to whistle tunelessly. It was his best effort, as he had never been able to carry a tune, but one of the cockatoos stirred restlessly. He smiled at the bird's implied criticism and reached to feel the hot-water bottles in both birds' shrouded cages. While he was at it, he stretched to the far edge of the seat to the chameleon's cage so he could check its hot-water bottle. Although autumn sunshine bathed the mountains, Christy knew he had to take care. Tropical creatures couldn't stand much cold.

So he was already distracted, even before he heard the simultaneous blast of two horns. He jerked both hands back to the wheel. Though still in the right-hand lane, he had drifted toward the center line, just as an Oldsmobile was overtaking him. And a black MGB had chosen that moment to cut in front of the Olds and pass them both.

As in all accidents and near accidents, Christy found the

events of the next few seconds happening so rapidly that he was left with only a confused mosaic of impressions by the time he was off the shoulder of the highway in a clump of willows, ears buzzing, listening to the faint popping of metal as his car commented on its sudden stop. He knew he had yanked the steering wheel automatically to the right, but he knew nothing else for sure, and it seemed important to know.

The top had been down on the black sports car. He distinctly remembered a black Doberman grinning in the wind beside the MG's muscular, blond driver. Illinois plates on the Olds. Braking hard to lose speed before he met the willows. Seat belt cutting into shoulder and stomach.

He might have remembered more, but he realized he was contemplating the golden leaves of the willows through his open car door. The other door and the trunk had also popped open. Where were the birds and the chameleon?

Both cockatoos were secure in their cages. At first Christy thought they had escaped the hard stop without harm, but then he saw slow drops of bright blood welling from a broken claw on the smaller cockatoo. The chameleon had apparently slipped under its hot-water bottle. No, oh, God, its tiny cage door was open, and it was nowhere to be seen.

The need to attend to both creatures at once rattled Christy, but the bird's bleeding toenail took precedence. Even big birds had only a few cc's of total blood volume, and birds could bleed to death in short order. Clip the broken claw, that was it, then cauterize. But with what?

Like any medical man, even a beginner, Christy had his own collection of favorite instruments. They didn't include anything as ordinary as nail clippers, and Christy grimaced as he realized that his new Metzenbaum scissors, though they might get sadly blunted, would have to do. He carried no cauteries. Who would? Oh, for a simple silver-nitrate stick.

Christy recaged the bird and leaped from the car to rummage in the trunk for his instruments. A young man with a military haircut thudded up behind him. Christy glared at him, thinking of the sports-car driver, until he remembered the man in the MG was a blond, with much longer hair. He smiled abstractedly and turned back to the trunk.

"Anybody here hurt?" the young man asked. "That darned fool in the MG ran us onto the median, and I saw you fly off down here. It looks like your car's all right, but are you okay?"

It was the Illinois driver, then. Christy's hand closed on his instrument case, and he turned and said, "What do you use for shaving cuts?"

"Well, uh, a styptic stick."

"Do you have it with you?"

The young man said uncertainly, "It's in my suitcase."

"Great, get it, will you?" The man's cautious expression sank in on Christy, and he hastened to explain. "I'm a vet. One of the cockatoos I have with me got banged up a bit. I've got to stop the bleeding. Oh, and listen, keep an eye out for a chameleon. One got away. It might still be in the car, but they can really move if they feel like it. It's bound to be scared, so it's probably bright green by now."

The young man from Illinois didn't look very reassured, but he obediently turned back toward the highway. Christy used the next couple of minutes to check his car and make the cockatoos as comfortable as he could, then he made an unsuccessful search through the potted plants in the back seat for the chameleon. By the time Christy's would-be rescuer appeared, a young woman and two little boys following behind him, Christy was sitting in the front seat with the injured cockatoo tucked under one arm, trying to stop the bleeding with pressure from a sterile gauze pad.

The rescue party was obviously entranced by the sight of the cockatoo, which struggled and squawked indignantly. Christy caught a relieved expression on the man's face, as if he thought Christy might really be sane after all.

"Where's he bleeding?" the older of the little boys asked.

4

"It's his toenail," Christy explained. "It's broken back to the quick. You know how that can hurt."

"Oooo," said the child.

Christy tucked the bird more firmly under his left arm and reached for the Metzenbaum scissors with his right. "Now, what we have to do is cut this tough old nail the rest of the way off," he said, "and then your dad is going to lend me his styptic pencil to stop the bleeding. Do you think you'd better not watch?"

"No, we can watch," the child said confidently.

Christy grasped the bird's foot. The bird grasped back with all the claws on its good foot. It found ribs and dug in as Christy neatly severed the broken claw. It wasn't the most antiseptic way of conducting minor surgery, but feeling he had little choice, Christy jammed the styptic stick tightly to the bird's claw. He tried to smile at the two blond boys. "That's it," he said. "Ah, now, that's already better. See?"

The younger child seemed shy, but he started asking questions. What was the bird's name? Could he and his brother touch it? Was the other bird hurt, too? Christy knew he was just being self-important, but he chatted briefly with the kids before checking the cockatoo one last time and caging it. A chill west wind began to blow, and the young mother rounded up her brood before Christy thought to ask again for assistance in finding the chameleon. He anticipated little trouble, but once the Illinois family left and he was alone by the willows, he began to feel dismayed about the chameleon's chances.

Poor damned reptile. Christy had never been able to overcome an aversion for snakes and their fellow creatures, but the chameleon had been given over to his care. Small sunlover, it was now lost in an alien environment, a granite-walled canyon in which somber stands of pine whispered of the deep hush that on still days filled these mountains. The wind was gaining strength, and cloud shadows ate black holes in the sunshine. The chameleon surely wouldn't survive long. But how to find a seven-inch-long creature in all these miles of wilderness?

Christy started searching along a tiny creek that watered the willows. An hour later, after searching in widening circles, he was back at the creek again, worrying that he would be late into Vail. Dr. Potter would be waiting. Should he go without the chameleon? Abandon it? But how could he just leave it here to die?

The creek tumbled and chattered at his feet. Tall grass edged the banks, and a wild rose, its leaves sporting autumn shades of red, nodded and dipped in a wind that steadily grew colder. A willow branch nodded, too, drooping down into the current, and Christy's eye, alert for any movement, followed it to a great pad of emerald moss that grew in the icy spray of the water. He had checked it before, just because it was green, but now his glance caught on a dull gray object at the rim of the moss. It was the color of stone and as immobile, and Christy had to lean close before he saw that this stone had a tail.

The chameleon at last. He scooped it up hurriedly. Did it move in his hand? He didn't wait to find out. He unzipped his jacket, unbuttoned his shirt, and slid the little creature in next to his skin. It was the warmest place he could think of. He hurried to his car to start the motor and get its heater working.

At least the car still moved, and its radiator seemed intact. Christy jockeyed it back onto the highway in time for cold rain to start hitting the windshield. The rain soon turned to sleet as he drove deeper into the mountains. It was as if he were traveling into winter.

Sleet gave way to light snow, which danced on the west wind so prettily while it lasted that Christy found himself feeling cheerful again. Then the sun came back out, announcing the end of that particular mountain shower, and, miracle, Christy suddenly felt movement inside his shirt. He was glad that the chameleon was obviously still alive, but his skin crawled when, after a while, the chameleon's gripping toe pads began to move cautiously across his stomach, then up toward his neck.

Christy stopped only once before reaching Vail, pulling into a roadside rest stop to check the wounded cockatoo and to peer squeamishly inside his shirt. The chameleon, now a deep brown, peered back. It must have resented the intrusion, because its brown hue took on a golden look as it started a new color change. It expanded its throat pouch as if it were getting ready for combat. Christy hastily rebuttoned his shirt and drove on.

It was two o'clock in the afternoon when he reached Vail Pass, though he had confidently planned to be at Dr. Potter's clinic by noon. Pine trees crowding the highway soon gave way to near-leafless aspens, a valley opened up, and then to the south of the highway he spotted the first cluster of Vail's ubiquitous condominiums. He had been to Vail before, but the town looked different without snow. For one thing, he had never before noticed the big golf course east of town, and Vail itself looked smaller somehow.

Vail's official population was only twenty-two hundred people, although how census takers arrived at any figure at all was a mystery to Christy. The big blocks of four- and five-story condominiums had a population almost as transient as the lodges and motels, and land was so expensive that condos outnumbered by far the kind of single-family house in which most permanent residents would be expected to settle down, raise families, and collect pets. "Downtown" was more condominiums and tourist-oriented businesses scattered from south of the highway to the foot of the ski slopes, brown now and barren, noticeable only because of the wide swaths cut for them through the aspens. Somewhere in the main section was Dr. Noah Potter's own condo that came with Christy's temporary job, and somewhere south and west was Dr. Potter's clinic. Christy dug into his shirt pocket for the directions Dr. Potter had sent to him, and the chameleon scurried up from his stomach to investigate the movement.

Exit to south frontage road. West past LionsHead. Follow road alongside Gore Creek past Chevron station. Road will dip. Log building on south side of road.

It was a large log cabin, a handsome anachronism after all the modern buildings Christy had passed. Although it looked more at home in the mountains, Christy had a moment's pause, wondering what sort of antiquated equipment he might find inside. Three cars and a bright red pickup were parked out front, a red Jeep and another car to the side. It looked as if Dr. Potter had a busy practice. Christy parked next to the Jeep, checked his shirt buttons to see that the chameleon couldn't escape again, then picked up the cockatoo cages and hurried inside, for the skies were gray and the west wind still spoke of winter. His passengers would finally be out of the cold.

A short corridor led to the reception room. Christy liked what he saw. Sand-colored tile, easy to clean. Skylight cut over the corridor, and hanging baskets of begonias, too high to provide fodder for four-footed patients. Voices in the reception room. The moment he appeared, one woman shrieked, "Fritzie! Gus!" and grabbed for the cockatoos. Another woman—small, delicate-looking, dressed in old jeans, a torn corduroy shirt, and cowboy boots—said in a loud, deep voice, "Thank God!" The receptionist, an iron-gray woman somewhere in her fifties, said, "Dr. Christy? You're late." A woman holding a camera in one hand and a big male Siberian Husky by a slip-collar with the other hand only muttered and looked disturbed. The last person in the room, a girl holding a calm Siamese cat on her lap, said nothing at all.

"Where's Alfred?" the woman now in possession of the cockatoo cages demanded. "And did you bring Mr. Knight's plants?"

But the deep-voiced woman in cowboy boots drowned out

everyone else. "We've got to hurry," she said. "I'll drive you, but you've got to come right away. Mark Niemeyer said the dog won't even let them in the apartment, much less near the body, and before we know it those damned fools will shoot the poor thing. Do you have a Kapchur gun? You might need it. From what Mark says, that bitch is mighty upset."

Christy chose arbitrarily. "Ah, Miss, um," he said to the iron-gray receptionist, "does Dr. Potter have a Kapchur gun?"

"I've never seen one," she said.

"Could you ask him, please?" Christy said.

The deep-voiced woman interrupted. "Potter left town this morning," she said. She took his arm in a strong grasp. "Hurry!"

She started him out the corridor, calling instructions back over her shoulder as the receptionist watched blankly. "You with the Husky, leave him. Dr. Christy will look at him later. You with the cat, it can have its shots tomorrow. Alicia, take Mr. Knight's cockatoos home. Dr. Christy will phone you later. Come on, Dr. Christy, *move.*"

Christy succeeded only in discovering his driver's name, Bev Farrell, and that he still had the chameleon inside his shirt before the woman hurled her red pickup truck back to the highway. She headed for the north side of Vail, where new buildings were going up on the steep south face of the valley. It was a short trip, and she made it a fast one, pulling to a halt in front of a burnt-orange condo whose builder surely hadn't had that particular color in mind when planning the structure. Two green Saabs had preceded them. Police cars, Christy realized in growing confusion, since one of the sedate little vehicles sported a tall antenna and a light-bar on its top. But it was a third car that riveted his attention. Pulling out of an underground parking area as they nosed the curb was a black MGB with its top down.

"Hey!" Christy yelled. The driver turned one startled glance at him, and the car took off fast down the slope. It wasn't the blond man. Christy couldn't even be sure it was the same car that had run him off the road earlier, for there was no black Doberman, and this driver was definitely a girl.

"This way," Bev Farrell barked. Christy blinked and followed. On the second floor rear, four men stood in the hall peering through a crack in the door. Two were policemen, young and as muscular as Christy's missing driver, while a shorter man in mufti tried vainly to peer, too. He was blocked by the elegantly tailored shoulder of a dark-haired man dressed in brown tweeds. The police and the short man all wore side arms, and the sight of their guns set Bev Farrell to sputtering.

"My God, have you shot her?" she said. "Mark, I told you I'd bring the vet! Bastard was late. Get away from that door."

The police officers hastily closed the door. The tweedy man Bev had called Mark stepped in front of them. "Oh, settle down, Bev," he said. "They haven't shot the Dobie yet. Of course, I believe I did mention it would be over my dead body."

"Nobody wants to shoot anybody," one of the officers said. He turned to Christy. "All right, it's all yours. But if you didn't bring a dart gun, we're going to have two bodies on that floor."

Christy felt the chameleon stir. Or maybe it was his stomach doing flip-flops. "Are you trying to tell me a dog killed someone?" he asked.

"Not unless it's got a revolver," the officer said. "But it damned well won't let anyone come in. You did bring a dart gun, didn't you?"

Christy sighed. "We didn't wait to look for one," he said. "I just got into town. But maybe I can do something. Let me have a look."

Bev Farrell may have appeared delicate, but neither she

nor her friend was a coward. "Let me go first," she said. "A lot of dogs are afraid of men."

"No, let me go first," Mark said. "You've got to be calm with strange dogs, and you've never been calm in your life, Bev."

"No, you don't," the other young officer said. "I told you, it has to be a vet or an animal-control officer, and Herb here hasn't been too anxious to go in."

"It'll be all right," Christy said, although he hadn't the faintest idea why he said it. "Maybe you should all stand back."

He opened the door. A deep growl warned him to open it no farther. The original blond driver of the black sports car lay crumpled beside a coffee table. And staring at him, all forty-two teeth bared, was the MG's black Doberman.

2

THE DOG SNARLED so fiercely that it sounded as if it were choking as Christy took his first step inside the apartment. He was impelled, but only by Bev Farrell's weight as she leaned against his back trying to see. The dog was not near the body. It had stationed itself between a white couch and matching chair. The brightest touches of color in the room were the dog's red gums and the blood that seemed almost to cover the blond man's body. The dog took a step backward, but the growl deepened. From childhood, into Christy's mind came a line from Kipling's *Jungle Book*, the krait whispering, "Be careful. I am Death."

"She's afraid," Mark whispered in back of Bev.

And fear biters were the worst, Christy thought grimly. The dog wore a black leather collar but no tags. Not that he was eager to get close enough to her to read a name tag. Aloud he said, "What's her name? Does anyone know?"

There was no information forthcoming, only chatter behind him, and the talking made concentration difficult. In a quiet voice, Christy said to the dog, "All right, girl. It's all right now. No one's going to hurt you." He forced himself to take another small step. The dog backed up. Her rump collided with the chair, and her eyes widened, showing white all around the pupils.

Christy froze. After a moment, he said over his shoulder, "Be quiet out there." He grabbed from his memory the name of the only female Doberman he'd ever met, Gala, a show specimen he'd treated for myositis during the first of his temporary jobs near Denver.

"Good Gala," Christy said. "She's a worried girl dog, Gala is. You don't like all these people, do you? We'll just close them out. All right now. All right."

The dog he'd named Gala planted her back feet wider and tensed, but Christy eased through the door and shut it behind him. There was a muffled exclamation, probably from Bev or her friend Mark, but Christy had no time for bystanders. "Go-o-o-o-d Gala," he crooned. "Pretty girl, Gala. Just quiet down. Everything's okay. No one's going to scare you anymore."

The quiet crooning seemed to help. As if she had gained courage, Gala moved, but only to sidle around the chair. She watched Christy carefully for another second, then trotted a few feet toward an inner hallway.

"*Good* girl," Christy sang. It was time for courage of his own. Taking care not to crowd the dog, he stepped toward the hall himself. "Okay, Gala, go lie down," he said briskly. "Hurry up. It's time to go lie down."

Gala scuttled. She ducked into a bedroom off the hall, and Christy followed her at a medium pace, taking care to keep his arms from swinging and his movements calm. The Doberman, looking less formidable now, had paused a few feet inside the bedroom, and when he came down the hall she growled again, but the growls were less menacing, as though they were hiccups she was unable to control.

To make a dog respond to a command was a good way of

gaining the upper hand. Even if the Dobe wasn't obedience-trained, she probably knew the simplest order of all. "Gala, sit," Christy said, testing her, and he was gratified at her quick response. He glanced around the room. There was a big dog basket in one corner. Probably why she'd chosen this room as her refuge. The basket was cushioned, but Christy spotted a man's old sweater that apparently served as additional bedding, a red ball, a black leather glove, and what looked like an old sock, evidence that she also used the basket as a place to hoard her treasures.

"Bed, Gala," Christy said. The dog only looked up at him, so he tried again. "Lie down, Gala. Lie down. That's good. What a good girl she is. Okay, stay. That's good. I'll get you out of here in just a minute."

He noticed that his hands were shaking when he stepped back through the door and closed it, leaving the dog curled in her basket. Inside, she grumbled once, but softly, and Christy paused long enough to take several deep breaths, trying to adjust to the lunatic confusion that had engulfed him since the minute he had arrived in Vail. Motion inside his shirt reminded him that he had once again forgotten the chameleon, and he grinned as he turned away from the door. He lost the grin as he crossed the living room. He had seen dead animals before, but never a dead human. The young man, locked in Christy's mind as a face seen through a rear-view mirror, now lay sprawled on his back looking like the victim of a massacre. Or a firing squad. God, there was so much blood. The fists were clamped tight, and the heels appeared to have dug into the off-white rug in a last paroxysm, as though the body were in violent protest. A blurred, bloody pawprint by the head told that the dog had approached closely enough to get her feet into the blood that had soaked into the carpeting. There were other blurry prints, at least one departing. Well, any animal would be drawn to investigate, and it surely would have been profoundly disturbed at the result. Christy discovered that he, too, was disturbed. A new image would dwell in his memory now. He hastened to the front door and opened it.

"The dog's shut up in a bedroom," he said. "Do you want me to take her out, or do you need to, er, deal with things here first?"

One of the officers asked, "The dog can't get out?"

Bev Farrell shouldered past the officers, followed by Mark. Mark flinched at the sight of the body, and so did Bev. "Who is he?" Mark said. "You can barely see his face for all that blood."

"I've never seen him before," Bev said. She coughed and seemed to choke, and she backed up a step.

"I have," Christy said. "He ran me off the highway a couple of hours ago near Dillon. The dog was with him. Listen, a girl drove away in his car just as we pulled up. A black MGB."

"Who was the girl?" the shorter of the officers asked.

Christy shrugged. "I just got here, remember? I don't know a soul in Vail."

"You say this kid ran you off the road. Did he stop? Did you quarrel?"

"Hell, no, he just kept going."

"If that was hours ago, how come you just got to Dr. Potter's clinic?"

Christy didn't like the way the officer looked at him. "I was searching for a chameleon," he said. He unbuttoned his shirt and groped inside. The chameleon skimmed around his belt to his back, and Christy felt idiotic as he grabbed for it. The chameleon was upset at being dragged from its warm quarters. White dots appeared on its back as it began a color change from contented brown to nervous green, and it nodded its head rhythmically, looking for something to bite. Christy held it carefully in one fist. "See?" he said.

"That's Alfred," Bev Farrell said. To the officer, she said, as if explaining everything rationally, "It's Cletus Knight's Alfred. He burned himself on a light bulb, and Dr. Potter

sent him to some specialist in Denver. You know Knight—
nothing's too good, even for a chameleon. He sent his cockatoos to another specialist, just because they got bored and
plucked a few feathers out."

The police officer seemed interested. Bev seemed glad to
look at something other than the corpse on the floor, and
Christy was happy to discuss topics other than his whereabouts at the time of a murder. But the other officer at-
tended to business. He rose from a visual inspection of the
body and said to the shorter officer, "Better call Chief Fellows, Dave. No, not that phone. Somebody in the building
will loan you one. Tell Fellows we've got something nasty
this time. It looks like someone emptied a revolver into this
guy. He's Philip Schumacher, Peter Schumacher's brother.
Tell Fellows."

Christy's knowledge of police procedure was meager, but
he suspected it would take time. He said to the businesslike
officer, "I have cases waiting for me at the clinic. If everybody will just stand back, I'll take the dog through."

"Better fill me in on things first," the officer said. He introduced himself as Nat Shannon. Christy expected to see
him whip out a notebook, but Shannon only listened, questioning Christy about seeing the now-dead youth on the
highway and about the girl who drove away in his car.

The dog in the bedroom started barking, and Shannon
turned his attention to the animal-control officer, who had
refrained from moving more than four feet away from the
front door. They consulted quietly, and Christy caught only
snatches of words: ". . . dog . . . the shelter or . . . ?" Shannon finally turned back to Christy and gave him permission
to take the Doberman to the clinic. He was concerned that
the dog be locked up and held safely, which Christy was
willing enough to promise. Mark Niemeyer found a leash in
the kitchen, and only then did it occur to Christy that he'd
have to confront a frightened, probably snarling Doberman
again, this time at close enough quarters to snap a lead to her

collar. Christy didn't give himself time to get antsy. He strode to the bedroom door, announced, "All right, Gala, we're going now," and went in.

The dog rose from the basket, and although she didn't growl, her hackles rose. "Come, Gala," Christy said briskly. He took care to show the dog the leash. "Good girl, now sit, stay."

It worked. The Doberman seemed eager for the leash, standard signal that she was going somewhere. She didn't even growl at Bev when Bev walked past her to scoop up the dog basket, commenting, "Better take her gear. She's bound to be more comfortable with familiar things around her."

At the sight of Officer Shannon standing near the body in the living room, Gala's hackles rose fully, a stiff ridge all the way down her back. She growled, but she stayed close to Christy's legs. The animal-control officer hastily left his post near the door, and Mark Niemeyer, with both eyebrows raised to the heavens, stationed himself in front of the man as if to protect him when the dog passed. Christy barely had time to close the door behind him before the Dobe was tugging him down the hall. Bev Farrell and Mark Niemeyer flew out. Bev called, "Wait!"

The Dobe growled some more when Bev and Mark joined them, but both had sense enough to ignore her. Downstairs, Bev indicated the back of her fire-engine-red pickup and said, "Just tell her to jump up. I don't think you'll have to lift her."

"Not on your life," Christy said firmly. "I've heard about too many animals that have fallen from the back of pickups. She rides up front with us."

"Whatever you say," Bev said indifferently. "Mark, are you coming with us, or do you have your car?"

"How do you think I got over here?" Mark said. "Listen, Dr. Christy, I know how Dr. Potter is about board bills. I'll pay for the Dobie. Just put her on my account."

"Don't worry about it," Christy said. "I guess the cops will pick up her tab."

"Hadn't you better walk her around a little?" Bev said. "No telling how long she's been shut up in that apartment. Poor old girl. All alone with a dead person. What do you suppose she thought?"

Christy had no answer. What animals thought was a mystery to him. He had no doubts that they did think, but he suspected that if he could change places with a dog or a cat for five minutes, the workings of their minds would be so different from his own that it would be like taking drugs or going insane. Yet, in a doggy way, the Doberman seemed sane enough, even after what was surely a traumatic experience. She did her business after he walked her around the building a few minutes, then jumped timidly into the front seat of the pickup. "Gala, sit," he commanded her, and she did. They waved good-bye to Mark, who pulled away in a blue Mercedes, and Bev started them back to the highway.

"How did you and your friend get mixed up in all this?" Christy asked her. "Did the police try to reach Dr. Potter, or what?"

"No, Nat Shannon called me," she said. "Herb Johnson's the county animal-control officer, but it always takes him forever to get down to Vail from Eagle, and Nat knows that Mark and I can usually handle animals. He got really scared about this bitch, though, so he insisted on a vet, too. They got a barking-dog complaint, you understand, from a couple time-sharing downstairs. Honeymooners, I think. You know the kind. They come to a gorgeous place like Vail, then they draw the drapes, lock the doors, and never go out. Well, the Dobe's apartment was locked, but she just kept barking, and the couple kept complaining, so Nat got the keys from the rental agent and started to go in. But the Dobe wasn't about to let him."

"Why would the couple complain about a dog barking but not report hearing shots right above them?"

"Dunno. People are crazy. I'll take dogs any time. But you know how some people hate dogs."

Gala the Doberman leaned a little against Christy, and he put an arm around her to steady her. The dog didn't seem to object, and when Christy relaxed so did she. Alfred the chameleon snuggled against Christy's belt. Although their driver continued to talk, Christy stopped listening. He and the creatures all had had quite an afternoon.

Bev obviously knew her way around Dr. Potter's clinic, for she took them to a rear entrance. The Doberman let Christy lead her in, balking slightly when Bev guided them into a large back room lined with wire crates. A Labrador puppy was the sole resident of the kennel. It barked enthusiastically, and the Dobe said she had no desire to go near him. Only at a sharp "Gala, come!" from Christy did she allow him to put her into a big crate on the other side of the room. Bev bustled out and returned with the iron-gray receptionist. "Water and food, do you think?" Bev asked. "Or let her settle down a little?"

For the first time, Christy was able to look at the dog as just a dog. She was underweight. Dull coat. It looked as if she hadn't been eating too well. "I'll give her a half-hour to get used to things, then water her," he said. He turned to the receptionist. "We haven't even had a chance to say hello," he said. He put out his hand. "I'm Gordon Christy."

The woman gave him a smile of rare sweetness and a firm handshake. "Millie Carroll," she said. "I know you'd like to have a chance to look around, and Dr. Potter was adamant that you read a bunch of notes he left you, but the lady with the Siberian Husky is still waiting. A new patient, but she says the dog is severely depressed."

Christy smiled back. "Then we'd better have a look at it," he said. "The examination room is . . . ?" Miss Carroll gestured, but Christy had an afterthought. "Just one thing," he said. He unbuttoned the bottom of his shirt and brought Alfred out to the light of day. Alfred squirmed in Christy's hand, but Christy found that he was getting used to it. "If he was supposed to go home with the lady who took the cockatoos, maybe she'd like to come for him," Christy said. "He's had a long day."

Freed of Alfred, Christy accepted a crisp, green jacket from Miss Carroll, waved off Bev Farrell's thanks and waved her a farewell, then went to meet his patient. There appeared to be two examination rooms, and Christy's eyes opened widely when he saw that each was equipped with a brand-new Elsam examining table, the kind the animal walked on at floor level and was automatically weighed before the table lifted hydraulically to the vet's preferred height. Dr. Potter's log-cabin clinic obviously lacked little in the way of modern equipment. Christy hoped he could find all the proper buttons.

Miss Carroll provided a new chart for the dog, quite blank except for four entries: "Mrs. Carolyn Read, Holiday Inn," and "Dandy, severe depression."

The big Husky did look depressed. He glanced around the examination room only briefly, then huddled next to his mistress's legs when Miss Carroll ushered them in.

"Sorry you had to wait," Christy said. "We had a little emergency."

"I know," Mrs. Read said. She put her camera and purse on the floor and stroked the Husky. "How's the poor Doberman? They didn't really shoot her, did they?"

"Oh, no," Christy said. "We got her under control without much trouble. She's back in the kennel now. Let's have a look at this boy, shall we?"

He found the right buttons after all. The movement of the table appeared to frighten the dog, but that, too, was to be expected. He spoke to the Husky soothingly as he checked the eyes, oral mucous membranes, and heartbeat. Depression was symptomatic of many things, among them poisoning. But the dog was happily free of convulsion, poison's general symptom. Heartbeat and membranes were normal, and the eyes looked more anxious than ill.

He located a thermometer to check for fever and asked the dog's owner, "Has there been any vomiting? Diarrhea?"

"Well, he threw up last night in the motel, but he does that all the time. Dandy eats things. He's terrible about it. I have to watch him all the time at home or he eats rocks. Since we've been traveling, he's been specializing in motel soap. And, well, toilet paper. He just reels it off and eats it by the mouthful. Some ladies I play bridge with here told me I should have him psychoanalyzed, but I say no, he's sick."

Christy checked the thermometer. A little low. Through the Husky's thick coat he thought he could determine that the skin felt a little cool. Feet, too. Christy washed his hands and went back over the membranes of the mouth and eyelids. Maybe a little pale? He started shooting questions.

No, Mrs. Read and Dandy had been in Vail almost a month, and Dandy hadn't been around any poisonous yard plants. No, certainly no castor beans or Virginia creeper, no, no, no, no, he hadn't even had a stick in his mouth except maybe a little aspen twig when Mrs. Read and he had gone hiking with their friends. No, back home in Seattle he'd always lived in the house, Mr. Read had loved him so, certainly he hadn't been a yard dog, even though Mr. Read had kept the house so cool for Dandy's comfort that Mrs. Read was chilly all the time. No, it was almost a year since Mr. Read had passed on, and Dandy seemed to have gotten over his loss long ago. Mrs. Read had just decided she didn't want to be at home for the, well, anniversary, so she decided to bring Dandy and come to Vail for the aspens, but it was strange, as the McAfee sisters said, they'd all turned black this year instead of the glorious colors they were supposed to be. Yes, Dandy seemed happy enough staying in motels, although he did get miffed and ate the toilet paper when she went up to the Lodge some afternoons to play bridge. No, she hadn't missed any panty hose. Well, yes, as a matter of fact his favorite rubber elephant had disappeared. She had missed it two days ago. Or was it three? No, it was quite small. He liked the small toys, and, besides, he always had the squeakers out of the big ones within ten minutes.

Christy carefully went back over the Husky's stomach, palpating, watching the big dog's reactions. A little tender? A bit of pain there?

"It's possible he swallowed the elephant, Mrs. Read," Christy said. "Dogs often pass things like that without any problem, but once in a while the stomach juices will start working on something like a swallowed ball, and the ball swells. Mind, I don't know that it was the elephant."

"What can we do? Can you X-ray?"

Textbooks were less helpful there than Christy's memory of a conversation of the first experienced vet he'd worked with. "If it were a nail or something metal, sure," Christy said, "but we see so many latex toys now that we can't count on the result. Unless . . . Was the squeaker metal or plastic?"

"Plastic, I think. Oh, Lord."

"Mrs. Read, I'd like to keep Dandy under observation overnight and try to figure out exactly what we've got here. If there's actually an intestinal obstruction, well, I'll be right here to take care of it. If there's not, I'd just as soon not have to tranquilize or anesthetize him. We usually have to do that, you know, to X-ray. Dandy seems depressed enough as is. But not actively uncomfortable, if you see what I mean."

"You mean, maybe the elephant would, ah, pass on its own. If he actually swallowed it, that is?"

"That's just what I mean. Now, I'm going to give Dandy a few teaspoons of strong coffee as a stimulant, and then I'll just watch him. Nothing complicated."

"But you'll call me if he gets worse. At any hour?"

"If you'd like."

The Husky's mistress reached for her purse. Sensing that his person was about to leave, Dandy whined nervously. The proper procedure, Christy knew, was to whisk the dog back to a crate, but Mrs. Read detained him.

"The Doberman you rescued today, I suppose she's ownerless now," Mrs. Read said. "If she and Dandy got along together, maybe I could give her a home. They'd keep each other company. I'll be happy to pay the Doberman's bill."

That made two offers in a single afternoon. The expense surely belonged to the Vail police, Christy thought, but maybe there was a real opportunity here to place the Dobe in a decent home. Christy didn't say it. He only promised Mrs. Read he'd keep her posted on the Doberman's fate, then took the Husky back to the kennel.

Christy noticed a sign on the kennel door, WARD ONE. He wondered where Ward Two was. Now there might finally be time to find out. Gala the Doberman got to her feet expectantly when Christy entered with Dandy, and the Lab puppy started barking again. Surrounded by the three animals, Christy felt almost normal. He whistled in his tuneless way as he tended them. Each big wire crate had a plastic resting bench in it. He removed Gala's and put in her own basket, then gave her water, which she lapped politely before trying to dash out the crate door. He settled the Husky, checked the pup, and started out before remembering something his eye had registered back in the dead youth's apartment. Gala watched him nervously as he came back to her crate.

"Move back, girl," Christy said, reaching in. "Where's that ball? Yep, there it is. Now let me have it. It's too small to play with without supervision. You could swallow it, you know. End up like poor old Dandy, couldn't you?" Though the Dobe showed interest in both ball and basket for the first time, Christy succeeded in fishing the small red ball from her belongings. "Just play with your glove," he told her, "at least until I find something better." He wrestled with her a moment to keep her from dashing out of the crate while he shut the door. She sat down and made a small, sad noise in her throat.

At the door of the ward a human throat was cleared, and Christy turned to see Miss Carroll smiling at him.

"You're just like Dr. Potter, always talking to the animals," she said. "You really like them, don't you?"

"Sure," Christy said. "Don't all vets?"

"I'd hope so. Though some seem, you know, cold."

Christy nodded at the puppy. "What's the matter with this little guy?"

"Round worms. Dr. Potter dosed him before he left, and he's all cleared out by now. His people will come for him before five. Would you like a little tour of the facilities now that things are quiet, or would you rather go on over to the condominium? I can feed the Husky before I go home."

"He's not to eat," Christy said. "I'll take him on to the condo tonight just to watch him. But I'd like to give him a little lukewarm coffee now. Could we start that tour at the coffeepot, assuming there is one?"

"Oh, yes. Dr. Potter lives on coffee. But, Dr. Christy, I'm afraid you can't take the dog to the condo. It's one of those no-pet buildings. I've often wondered if that's why Dr. Potter chose it."

"Oops," Christy said. He looked at the clean cement floor of the ward and grimaced. "I'll need to observe the Husky through the night. It looks like a hard floor to sleep on."

"There's the little cabin," Miss Carroll said. She gestured at the back door. "But it hasn't been redone like the clinic. That's where Dr. Potter puts all his relatives, if they insist on visiting. No one's ever come a second time."

"If it's got a bed, I'll settle for it for one night," Christy said. "Let's get that coffee, shall we? I think I'll join Dandy in a cup."

Miss Carroll led Christy down another hall. "You missed lunch, didn't you?" she said. "This is Dr. Potter's office. Oh, dear, he said he'd clean it up. Maybe he did. Maybe these are just some of the notes he left for you. Let's see if he left anything more worthwhile in his refrigerator."

A refrigerator-freezer shared an alcove with a coffeepot and a half-gallon bottle of vodka and another of Scotch. Vaccines occupied part of the refrigerator. Propped in front of them was a note saying, "Be sure and order a carton of D.A.2P.L. when the Norden rep comes by." Miss Carroll pocketed the note and pulled out cheese, a hard Italian salami, and a bottle of pickled sausage before Christy said he would settle happily for cheese and salami. After dosing the Husky with coffee as a stimulant, he munched salami while looking about. Ward Two was an isolation room, and there was a small Ward Three especially for cats. There was also a fine surgery, a separate X-ray room with unusually good shielding for a vet's setup, and eight or ten spacious outside runs, each with its own insulated doghouse, for either boarders or convalescents. The phone rang while Christy and Miss Carroll walked to the outside runs, and she went back to answer it. Across a small meadow was a sagging log cabin. Dr. Potter obviously hated his relatives.

Christy wandered back into Dr. Potter's office and picked up the first sheet from a toppling pile of notes. It said, "Be sure Erica Sinclair puts her Peke on Filaribits a week before leaving for Florida." Filaribits were heartworm pills. But who was Erica Sinclair?

He put the question to Miss Carroll when she reappeared, but she looked puzzled. "I'll check the records, but I don't think I remember a Sinclair," she said. "Of course, she might be one of Dr. Potter's lady friends."

"Does he have many?"

"Heavens, yes. Sometimes I think every widow in Vail is out to catch him." Although they were alone, Miss Carroll lowered her voice. "If you ask me, he's gone off on his vacation with a lady. I think that's why he left early."

"Where did he go, anyway?" Christy asked.

Miss Carroll looked at him thoughtfully. "Didn't he tell you? He said he'd told you where to get in touch with him if anything came up that you couldn't handle."

"He didn't tell me a thing, except how to get here and

where to pick up all those potted plants. Hey, I'd better get them out of my car. They'd freeze overnight, I'll bet."

"It's all right. Alicia Johnson collected them when she came for the chameleon. They're for Mr. Knight's aviary. Every time the cockatoos eat them, he just buys more."

"Who's Bev Farrell, Miss Carroll?" Christy asked. "One of Dr. Potter's lady friends?"

"No, more of a friend-friend. She's one of the Vail pioneers. Bought a lot and built when it was first developing, the lucky thing. She's retired now. Military. A major, I believe. And now she breeds German Shorthairs. But she loves all dogs. And cats. Dr. Potter gives her special rates, you'll discover, since she runs sort of an informal animal-rescue service."

"And her friend Mark Niemeyer?"

"The same. Only he breeds Whippets. They go to dog shows together when they're not busy rounding up strays. Is there anything special you'd like this evening, Dr. Christy? Otherwise . . ."

Christy looked at his watch. It was well after five. The tolerant Miss Carroll awarded him another of her charming smiles as he tried to apologize, but she refused to leave until she'd found him the cabin keys and all the clinic keys and assured herself that he knew where to find restaurants for dinner.

Christy knew he would stay with the Husky instead. If Dandy went into shock or started vomiting heavily, immediate surgery for intestinal blockage would be indicated. Dr. Potter's office refrigerator seemed promising enough for snacks. In fact, Potter's Scotch bottle didn't sound so bad, either.

Before raiding the Scotch, Christy put Gala the Doberman in an outside run and fixed dinner for her, choosing canned Science Diet for his initial offering. Potter had a supply of good kibble, including Wayne and Iams; Christy could work out a standard diet for the dog starting with breakfast. She was hungry enough to leap at the food bowl when it appeared. Christy had to put her on sit to keep her from spilling it. She didn't want to turn her back to him, so Christy put the bowl in a corner where she wouldn't have to scoot it around too much, then left her alone in the run. She gobbled. The bowl was licked clean within seconds and polished brightly within a minute. Glad to see her in appetite, Christy left her to get some exercise, and he didn't put her back in the ward until he was ready to take Dandy the Husky and explore the cabin. The Doberman didn't want to enter her crate, and once inside, she stood right by its door making low moaning sounds again as Christy put the Husky on lead and left. As an afterthought, he stepped back inside and turned the light back on. It was foolish to think of animals in human terms, but after what the Doberman had been through that day, he thought she might not like the dark.

There was a marvelous snap in the air. Although the temperature was probably no lower than forty, cooler currents drifted from the shadows. Given the dryness of the mountain air, anything over thirty degrees was shirt-sleeve weather to Christy, but he was happy to put the rough door of the cabin between him and the out-of-doors. He felt for a light switch and was mildly surprised to find one. For Potter to condemn his unwanted guests to candles would have seemed more natural to the image of the man that was slowly building in Christy's mind.

The cabin was primitive enough. It was one big room. Stone fireplace for heat. Old iron bedstead for sleeping. Iron cooking stove. Closet-sized bathroom with no sink, so apparently the kitchen sink doubled for washing both dishes and faces. A phone extension. Odd that Dr. Potter would bother having an extension in the cabin. Maybe he sometimes entertained his lady loves here while remaining on tap for emergency calls.

A shabby blue couch looked inviting to Dandy. The big

animal climbed onto it and lay down with a groan that Christy knew was contentment but which sounded like complaint. Complaint began in earnest from the clinic as Christy fetched things from his car. It was the Doberman crying. He called out to her cheerily, dug a copy of Archibald's *Canine Surgery* from the car trunk, and went inside the cabin to bone up on surgical technique, in the event Dandy took a bad turn. At least the cabin was clean, the chimney drew well, and wood was stacked high outside the door. He would set the alarm on his travel clock for two hours hence, then every two hours through the night. That way he could feed the fire while checking on Dandy.

He propped up on two pillows with the big book, but instead of opening it he stared at the flames. How alive fire was. He blinked away the memory of red blood on a white rug. So much blood. And the way the dead fists— No, think of the flames. Listen to Dandy, who was whimpering in his sleep. But the legs were jerking. Just a running dream. Was a dog hunting or being hunted when it dreamed that way? He'd never know.

Then the saddest, most mournful sound filtered to his ears over the hiss and whisper of the flames. The Dobe, still crying. Oooh, she said. Oooooooohhh. I am forsaken. I am frightened. Oooohhhh, I am all alone.

She wouldn't stop. Christy called reassuringly to the Doberman through the window, then finally shouted, but she kept moaning. Christy told himself the dog's agonizing cries would keep Dandy awake, though he could plainly see that the Husky roused only when he shouted. Eventually, sheepishly, Christy put down his book and went back to the clinic. Gala the Doberman must have been listening for his footsteps. She quieted instantly, and when he looked through the ward door she was on her feet, ears alert and eyes expectant.

"Oh, all right, damn you," Christy said severely. "You can spend the night with Dandy and me, but you'd better be nice to him, not one growl, do you hear? He's sick, and if there's anything I can't stand anyway, it's dogfights."

Gala started jumping, little straight-legged hops, when he opened her door, and she came instantly to his side, staying so close that she brushed him repeatedly as they crossed the yard to the cabin. She gave the Husky a glance, and she stayed very still as he climbed off his couch to sniff her. Then she jumped up on Christy's bed.

"I sleep on the right side," he told her. "Don't crowd."

But she did. She crept to him after he turned off the light, and he could feel her warm, bristly presence against his legs. It was comforting somehow. They slept.

3

THE PROBLEM WITH Dandy's bill, as far as Christy could see, was that he'd done absolutely nothing to the dog, so how could they charge the Husky's owner forty-five dollars?

"Maybe fifteen," he suggested to Miss Carroll. "About the price of an office call?"

Miss Carroll put down her coffee cup. "Dr. Potter's policy is based on the fact that no one who isn't rich can survive long in Vail," she said patiently. "And he says if they're rich, they can darn well pay enough for him to be able to afford Vail."

"Are you rich, Miss Carroll?" he asked.

She smiled her lovely smile. "No, but I live out in the county," she said. "Of course, it's getting expensive, too, but my family has ranched near Eagle for three generations, so we're pretty well set. The way land prices are going up, I guess if Dad ever decided to sell the ranch, we'd be millionaires."

"I don't think Mrs. Read is a millionaire," he said. "The

only thing I did for Dandy was give him three tablespoons of coffee. He got rid of the elephant all by himself."

"Ah, the coffee," she said. "I'd forgotten."

Christy leaned over to watch. She neatly added four dollars and fifty cents for medication to the Husky's bill, then totaled it. Christy gave up. It was Dr. Potter's practice, so he had the privilege of setting policy. And to do nothing for a dog with a possible intestinal obstruction took some small amount of skill, Christy supposed. Knowing when to wait was part of what he'd spent a total of eight years learning. The big Husky was romping joyfully in an outside run. Mrs. Read would be happy. Christy might as well be happy, too, that a night's fasting and the dog's normal functions had done the trick.

Thinking of the bills, he felt a little sorry for the girl whose Siamese cat needed its annual shots, and for the next patient, a gerbil with pneumonia. Despite the fact that the two women who came next both wore cashmere sweaters and drove a new Buick station wagon, he felt sorry for them, too.

Mrs. Read had come just a couple of minutes before for Dandy. Salving his conscience about her bill, Christy gave her a little advice about Dandy's chewing habits: no more tiny toys, but the addition of a ham-flavored nylon bone to his gear, please, so he'd have something good, not damaging, to chew on. Then he went to the outside runs to get Dandy. Gala barked from the next run when the Buick station wagon pulled up. It came to an instant halt. Both women stared at the Doberman. One asked timidly through the window, "Is this where we park?"

"Quiet, Gala," Christy said. "Sure, it's fine. Don't be afraid of the Dobe. She's just yappy."

Their apprehension seemed indeed misplaced. Before Christy could warn them, they opened a car door, and a large, unleashed Old English Sheepdog tumbled out. "Stay, boy," one of the women called. But the Doberman began to roar threateningly at the sight of the dog and the women, and the women's eyes were all for the barking Dobe, not the Husky. Christy got a firm grip on Dandy's leash and prepared himself to try to ward the Old English off with his foot. Huskies had no great tolerance for other males. But the Old English only rushed to a frost-bitten bed of petunias and squatted. "Boy"? Didn't the women know their Old English was either a very young male, which was unlikely from its size, or a female?

A short Keystone Kop routine ensued. The Old English seemed to choose a direction at random, then simply took off, limping on its right front leg but trotting rapidly. Gala flung herself at the gate of her run, as if trying to chase the Old English. The two women did chase after it, still calling, "Here, boy. Come, boy!" Christy hurried into the clinic with Dandy, turned him over to Miss Carroll and a beaming Mrs. Read, and grabbed a slip-lead before rushing after the Old English and its owners. They caught the dog by the creek. It apparently didn't want to get its feet wet, so it stopped, allowing Christy to collar it. The two women panted heavily. Neither was young, and Vail's eighty-two-hundred-foot altitude tired even Christy quickly. The dog was out of breath, too. All panting together, they achieved the front door of the clinic just as Mrs. Read was leaving with Dandy. The idiocy almost began all over again when the Sheepdog's owners stopped to pet Dandy and greet Mrs. Read, who was obviously a friend. Christy managed to tug the Sheepdog into the clinic, and there he finally got a good look at it.

It was unquestionably the most matted dog he'd ever seen. Its long, thick coat was snarled into fist-sized clumps in which there were dead leaves, clods of mud, dried fecal matter, even a tangle of what looked like weed stems. Someone had clipped a long strip on its back, then must have given up, leaving the rest of the coat neglected. Christy put the dog up on the examining table, and from pure curiosity he felt under the stomach for the genital region. He wondered more about the two women who had brought the dog. It was definitely female.

Miss Carroll preceded the women with a chart. It was as new and empty as Dandy the Husky's had been. Listed as the owners were Miss Harriet McAfee and Mrs. Jean McAfee Ditton, with the Lodge at Vail as their address. It appeared that Dr. Potter's practice got its fair share of transients. The space for the dog's name on the chart had been left blank, and the entry for "History/Owner's Instruction" read, "Right front-leg injury." Christy smiled a hello at the women and examined the foreleg. Hide ripped completely away from the vertical wound. But no swelling. Inflammation, yes, but no other signs of infection. "When did she do this?" he asked the women.

He glanced up to see identical worried expressions on the women's faces. Although one woman had reddish hair and the other dark hair, they strongly resembled one another. Sisters, their names indicated. Hadn't Mrs. Read mentioned some sisters named McAfee? They also shared rather flat, broad noses and small hands, as well as a broad-in-the-beam-and-bust tendency that middle age had done little to enhance. But if they were indifferent to plumpness in a lean age, they obviously weren't indifferent to animals. Christy added quickly, "It's not nearly as bad as it looks. You might say the skin has been torn away from the flesh. That's why it looks so ugly. But the wound isn't really serious."

The women looked scarcely less disturbed, but the red-haired sister tried to answer his question. "We saw a car hit it yesterday morning. The poor thing was wandering across a road, and the car didn't even try to stop. The dog didn't seem to be hurt and it ran into a ditch and a little boy caught him. I mean, the boy said it was a he. We couldn't find anything wrong then, and the boy said she was a male dog that belonged to some people who lived near the volleyball courts, you know, by LionsHead Centre. So we drove the dog and the boy to the house, but we went to check on her later, just feeling uneasy somehow, and it wasn't the same dog. Oh, dear, what I mean is, the people said the dog the little boy thought she was had been safe in its yard all the time. So the people and the boy just turned her loose, and we've been looking all day for her."

"You've made it completely confusing, Harriet," the other woman said. "What it comes down to, Dr. Christy, is that she's apparently a stray, and now we've discovered that she's injured and we'd like to help her."

Christy was hampered in examining the dog by the extraordinary shagginess of her coat, and he had to take clippers to her to discover the source of a dried bloodstain he found near the anus. At that, she'd been lucky for a car victim. She'd apparently been bumped, a glancing blow sending her back hard on her bottom, with the rupture of one of the small blood vessels in the anus as the only result. But the condition of her rump, when the shag came off, was bad. Bright red urine burns, from urine held tightly to the skin by the matted coat.

Christy paused before explaining his findings to the women. "I'm sorry, I guess I was looking at the dog, and I didn't get your names straight," he said.

The dark-haired woman said, "Just call me Jean. She's Harriet."

It was a dilemma Christy hadn't had to face before in his brief professional career. The women were older than he, and he feared it would sound patronizing for him to call them by their first names while they called him Dr. Christy. He suppressed an inner qualm. He'd worked hard for the title of "Doctor," but he junked it in an instant and said, "Everyone except my mother calls me Christy."

"Then Christy you are," Jean said. "What's wrong with the dog's bottom? Why is it so red?"

"It's her coat. If you want to try to keep the dog, it would be a good idea to do something about all those mats. Shaggy dogs can get really bad skin conditions when their coats are neglected like this. I can ask Miss Carroll if there's a grooming parlor in town, but if there isn't, you might have to take her to Denver."

He waited delicately. He'd already learned that many would-be good Samaritans would rush an injured stray to a vet, but they could have second thoughts when they realized that consideration had to be given to the dog's future. So few people were willing or able to provide homes.

"Oh, we want to keep her, Christy," the red-haired sister, Harriet, assured him. "The poor dog keeps staring around and whining. It's as though her people dumped her, and she wonders how to get home. We can't keep a dog at the Lodge, I suppose, but we've been thinking of renting a chalet for a while anyway. There are several available, between seasons like this. We could get a place with a yard. Then later we could take her back to California with us. Can you keep her for us for a day or two? And after you've treated her leg, do you think you should just go ahead and clip her coat?"

Vets weren't dog groomers, but the dog's condition pleaded for help. Christy said, "Good idea. She might not look like an Old English after I'm through with her. All those mats will have to be sheared out, I guess. But hair grows back. You'll want basic shots, too, of course." He finished examining the dog while he talked, palpating lymph and mammary glands to rule out abnormalities, listening to her heart, but it was only when he checked the eyes that he found cause for disturbance. Peering from a shaggy waterfall of hair, one eye was clear, normal, and a glamorous shade of pale blue, but the other was gray and abnormally enlarged. "Trouble here," he said. He held the hair back so Jean and Harriet could see. "Could be an old, untreated puncture wound."

Christy found that he was holding his breath. Taking in a healthy stray was one thing, but even these concerned and charitable women might draw a line. Christy wouldn't know much until he had time to find where Dr. Potter kept his ophthalmoscope, but the iris looked severely inflamed, with much fibrin in the anterior chamber.

Jean only said, "Poor, poor dog. How could anyone neglect a dog so?" Harriet added, "You'll do what you can, won't you, Christy?"

"Of course." Christy thought he'd tamp things down a bit. An unnamed dog was somehow a different being from a named one. "What are you going to call her?"

Harriet smiled at Jean. "Agatha," she said. "She reminds me of Great-Aunt Agatha, doesn't she you? Aunt Agatha, that's your name, doggie. Isn't it? Yes, you like that, don't you?"

Agatha the dog wagged her bottom, in lieu of a tail, as, being an Old English, she lacked one. She seemed a good-tempered beast, and Christy felt optimistic about her prospects. He felt even more so when Harriet asked protectively, "That Doberman Pinscher you have won't frighten Agatha, will she?"

Ignoring the fact that he'd let Gala and Dandy spend the night loose in the cabin together, Christy said, "We always keep the dogs strictly separate. Besides, you mustn't believe everything you've heard or read about Dobermans. They're basically just as good-natured as any other breed. They only look fierce."

"Well, she certainly barked enough when we pulled up to park," Harriet said. "But, then, I suppose she's terribly nervous after that shooting and all. Do you have to keep her here, or will you be sending her home to her family?"

"You've heard about the shooting?"

"Vail is a very small town," Jean said. "It seems to shrink even more between seasons like this. So naturally everybody keeps up with everybody else. Besides, we're friends of one of your patients. Carolyn Read's Dandy. We've hardly had a minute to ask, but is he feeling better? He certainly looked bouncy enough when we saw him outside."

"I think he'll do just fine now," Christy said. He let Agatha down from the examination table, his mind turning to priority of treatment. The leg wound, then a look at that bad eye, then the coat. Maybe a mild tranquilizer between the eye exam and the coat, because he'd be a long time clipping. But something the women had said pinged in his brain.

"You mentioned the Doberman's 'family,'" Christy said. "Do you know whom she belongs to?"

Agatha's new owners were vague on the question, but, yes, if the dog lived with the dead youth, there was a family. A mother and father living in Vail. One of their bridge friends had said something about Dr. and Mrs. Schumacher only this morning. Christy assured them again that he wouldn't let Gala intimidate Agatha, and it was after morning office hours when he noticed, to his mild astonishment, that Gala really did seem to dislike Agatha. The dislike appeared to be mutual. He crated them on opposite sides of the ward, but when he called Agatha from her crate to take her to the surgery, she ducked away from the slip-lead with which he tried to lasso her and, stiff-legged, uppity antagonism bristling from her shaggy hide, rushed Gala. Had the Dobe not been safely crated, blood would have spurted.

Gala's grudge grew while Agatha was being worked on. It was as though she suspected Agatha was out walking or playing with Christy, having a wonderful time, while she, Gala, simmered in her crate. The sight of the roughly clipped Agatha, slightly woozy from the tranquilizer, returning to the ward over an hour later, spurred Gala to a bouncing charge against her crate door, with appropriate sound effects. Then it was Agatha's turn to challenge, as Christy took pity on Gala and took her outside to enjoy the fresh air in a run. Once there, Gala seemed morose and sullen. Christy studied her.

"Do you really have a family right here in Vail?" he muttered to her. "Do you want me to take you home?"

He pursued the question more fruitfully with Miss Carroll. Yes, there was a Dr. Elliott Schumacher in town, a psychiatrist with offices in a little medical complex on West Meadow Drive, and a house on Forest Road. Dr. Potter occasionally referred patients to him, both dogs and cats, when their illnesses seemed beyond the normal physical problems. Dr. Potter had no faith whatever in four-footed psychoanalysis, but it seemed to reassure his wealthier clients, and Dr. Schumacher was always grateful for the extra business, since Vail was really too small to keep a full-time resident psychiatrist working around the clock. It was past lunchtime, and Christy hadn't eaten a real meal in more than twenty-four hours. Vail's restaurants were good, he remembered from his earlier ski trips. He decided to take the Dobe to her family, then treat himself to a proper lunch before office hours resumed at three in the afternoon.

Village ritual, Miss Carroll explained, called for a daily stop at the Vail post office. A Jeep was the most fashionable means of getting there, with a pickup truck second, and Dr. Potter had left the keys to his Jeep expressly for Christy. Christy took directions, Gala the Doberman, and the outgoing mail from Miss Carroll and went out to the red Jeep. A handful of notes were Scotch-taped to the steering wheel. Dr. Potter's last-minute instructions? The first two read, "Get payment in advance from Russ Richards if he wants to board his Golden, as the clod always has some excuse not to pay his bills," and, "If anyone comes asking about a Siamese, Thelma & Rex Jenkins have a new litter." The next read, "Would you mind pinching back the semperflorens begonias in the corridor?" The next, more hastily scrawled, read, "And please pinch back the coleus on Miss Carroll's desk. She's always too tender-hearted to do it." The next, in capital letters, instructed, "PINCH BACK ALL THE PLANTS, ESPECIALLY IN MY CONDO." The last said, "*Don't* pinch back the ficus."

What was a ficus? Christy put the question aside and set

off in the Jeep along the south frontage road, Vail's substitute for Main Street. It was good to be out. Even between seasons, Vail seemed a bustling place, although the bustle was different in the ski season. Today, delivery trucks and construction trucks created small traffic jams everywhere, and it looked as if every other building was being remodeled or enlarged. Cars with out-of-state plates were plentiful on those streets that allowed traffic. Christy slowly realized that if a person wore a coat, he or she was probably a tourist, and if the garb was parka, sweater, or blue-jean jacket, he was probably looking at a resident. Gala failed to discriminate between the two, and she barked at every pedestrian, drawing a scowl from a young woman crossing to the post office with a toddler in a stroller.

Government in Vail stayed off to itself on the north side of the frontage road. The post office and the Vail Municipal Building both were white buildings with brown trim, sitting side by side. Of the two, the post office enjoyed the greater popularity, and Christy had to wait a couple of minutes for a parking space. Gala stopped grumbling at a trio of deer hunters in International Orange jackets and stared hard at a young, bearded man, who stared back with a curious, interested expression. He looked as though he was about to speak, then returned his gaze to a big stack of mail that threatened to slip from his arms. He hurried past.

Anticipating a fresh spate of barking, Christy said, "Gala, quiet! Sit!" He congratulated himself for catching her attention before she started roaring, but her silence didn't last long. He could hear her barking all the time he was in the post office, and when he came out he saw that despite the crowd driving in and out for mail, no one had parked on either side of him.

Golden aspens lined the streets, though they had already dropped their leaves on the ski slopes above the town. Maybe the shelter of the valley in which the town lay gave the town's trees a longer season. And what had Dandy's owner said? The bulk of the aspens had all turned black this year instead of lemon-yellow, pumpkin-orange, flame-red. An early freeze must have killed them before their time, Christy decided. He puttered slowly south in the Jeep, peering around. Vail was a walker's town, not a driver's, and the streets Christy knew best were closed to traffic. The center of Vail was relentlessly cute, in a mock-Tyrolean way, with cute shops and cuter bars. But in its own strange way the town worked. An unlikely blend of New York's Eighth Street and Los Angeles' Rodeo Drive, with a mean little dash of Puerto Vallarta's touristy charm and a heavy lacing of Rocky Mountain purity, Vail had unique energy. With snow on the streets and sun sparkling on the snow, it pulsated. This time of year, snow could fall any time. Christy found himself whistling happily again.

In three blocks he was above the town looking for the Schumacher home. It turned out to be big but undistinguished. The house looked like a two-story box made of brown wood, with no windows on the street side. Gala exhibited no eager excitement, no joy, at the sight of it. She jumped out readily when Christy parked in the driveway, then seemed to think she'd earned a short walk. Christy urged her to the front door instead and rang the doorbell. After a long wait, he backed up and studied the house and saw that stairs led to an upper deck with another front door. He climbed the stairs with Gala and rang the top doorbell.

At the sight of the maid who answered the door, Christy felt an oafish smile spring to his face. She had long Titian-red hair. A short girl, she avoided being plump, but she was so well curved that she resembled a cupcake-sized fruitcake packed with goodies. She looked undisturbed by the Doberman and let Christy and the dog in through a narrow hall. Then splendor opened up before him. The entire north wall of the house was windowed, with Vail stretching below the house and the Gore Range looming on the north side of the valley. The house was upside-down. The kitchen and huge living, dining, and breakfast rooms were all on the upper floor, no doubt for the view, and stairs from the living room led down to what Christy assumed were bedrooms. A blond youth in the living room glanced indifferently at Christy and the dog, then turned his eyes back to a television game show, ignoring both the glorious redhead and all the glory outside the windows.

"Where's your dad, Peter?" the maid asked the youth.

"How would I know?" he said.

She seemed unsurprised. She invited Christy to sit and went down the stairs. Gala stayed beside Christy and made no move to go to the youth.

"Uh, you're, uh, Peter Schumacher?" Christy said awkwardly. "I'm very sorry about your brother."

The youth raised keen, speculative eyes. "Why?" he said over the drone of the television set. "Philip was a rat. He always was a rat. Ever seen a rat older brother bully a little brother? That was Philip. I don't see any sense in forgetting that kind of treatment."

The maid peeped through the banisters at floor level. "Shut up, Peter, your mother might hear you," she said. "Come this way, Dr. Christy. Dr. Schumacher's down here."

He followed her gladly. Peter Schumacher's speculative gray eyes had bored holes through him, and Christy had no idea what he could have replied to Peter's calm profession of posthumous hatred. At the foot of the stairs, Christy found himself in a big family room in which a wispy-looking blond woman sat weeping, with another woman patting her hands. Here was someone who grieved. The mother, no doubt. Another hallway, and they fetched up at a corner room, a snug study. A tall, white-haired man rose from behind a desk as the maid murmured, "Dr. Christy, Dr. Schumacher." Schumacher's face looked pale and very sad, but he shook Christy's hand and was the first person in the house to show any interest in the dog.

41

"I'm sorry to seem abrupt, but I don't usually treat dogs in my home," he said. "My wife's allergic to them. I'm afraid I won't be holding office hours until after my son's funeral, but I'll be happy to see your bitch later."

"Of course," Christy said. "I'm terribly sorry to barge in at such a bad time. But the dog— She isn't yours?"

"God, no," Schumacher said. "You don't have dogs when there are allergies in a household. Sue said 'Dr. Christy.' You're. . ."

"Veterinary medicine," Christy said. "I'm filling in for Dr. Potter while he's on vacation. I'm sorry about the dog. You see, she was, ah, with your son when he, ah, and, yes, I'm afraid I must have assumed that she belonged to him or to the, uh, whole family."

For a moment, the younger son's speculative look stared through the father's sad brown eyes. "How very strange," he said. "Philip hated dogs. His mother's aversion to them affected him, I suppose. He certainly never had a dog. What is this about the dog being with him? The police never mentioned a word about that. But see here, the dog really should leave now. Rosamund comes in here from time to time." He seemed to bethink himself and added with what sounded like automatic geniality, "I'll be very glad to see any of your patients in my office, Dr. Christy. I've gotten some really fine results with a recent case of separation-anxiety syndrome, for instance. But now isn't the time to talk about that. You'll excuse me, I hope?"

Christy stuttered his way out. The maid intercepted him in the hall and took him out a downstairs door. She lingered in the doorway smiling at the Doberman. Christy was not sorry to look at her again.

"I'm new in town, and I guess I'm a little confused," Christy said to her. "Would you mind my asking, does Dr. Schumacher really have many four-footed clients?"

"A few," the girl said. "He'd like to have more. He's always hustling for patients." In the clear gray light of the afternoon Christy could see that she was one of the lucky redheads—no freckles. She continued: "I hear he's got a terrier-type that won't go to sleep at night unless it licks its master's toes for twenty minutes. Odd, hm? And someone told me about a cat that keeps getting false pregnancies. Is that physiological or psychological?"

"Darned if I know," Christy said, "though we see a lot of false pregnancies from purely physiological causes. As long as I'm being nosy, can I ask you a personal question? What in the world is a girl like you doing working as a maid?"

She laughed. "You really are new, aren't you? Let me be the first to tell you that unless you're loaded enough to afford a couple of thou a month for some sleazy studio apartment, you can't ski Vail all winter without a job that comes complete with room and board."

"Is it really that expensive here?"

She pursed finely cut lips. "So much so that I stayed on all summer with the nutsy Schumachers rather than try to find a new job just for the winter. It's a big house to keep clean, but fair Rosamund only sighs and takes over the cooking when I declare I'm going skiing. She doesn't cook much better than I do, and they can't afford to pay very much, but a private room with bath is everything."

"Congratulate me, then," Christy said. "My job came complete with a condominium."

A voice called from within the house. The girl cocked her head, listening. "Duty," she said. "They've got relatives flying in from Maryland for the funeral, and I'm assigned the funereal baked meats. That's the trouble with a made-up town like Vail. There aren't any old family friends or neighbors to drop in with a ham or a few loaves of banana bread. Some lady did bring a big bakery cake, but we gotta do most of it ourselves. Philip would have been overjoyed at causing so much trouble, though I must confess I'd rather go to dear little Peter's funeral than Philip's."

The voice called again. She smiled, waved, and closed the

43

door. Gala pulled on her leash, wanting to go to the Jeep, and Christy reluctantly followed her. That hair. That skin. And, he confessed to himself, all those intriguing little remarks about the Schumacher family. While the Schumachers were no business of his, the Doberman who leaped into the Jeep beside him almost seemed to make them that way. Christy scratched the dog's throat, and she closed her eyes and stuck her chin out, enjoying it.

"So you're still homeless, girl," Christy said. "I guess you'll have to stay on in the clinic for a while. Now, I'll tell you how things are going to be. I'll pick up hamburgers for lunch, since I can't take you into a restaurant, but after office hours I'm finally going to see my very expensive, highly desirable condominium, and you're going to sleep in Ward One in your own little basket. Got that? You're darned right you've got it."

Gala also got a McDonald's hamburger, which she treated as though it were both exquisite and excruciatingly expensive. Christy unwrapped one of his own cheeseburgers to munch as he drove back to the clinic, and he opened the paper wrapper of Gala's burger and put it on the seat beside her for her to consider. First she nosed the hamburger apart, appearing to find the bun and the wrapper more interesting than the beef patty. She licked all the onions off the bottom half of the bun. Then she tested the patty with one big bite, and, liking what she found, swallowed the rest whole. She licked the pickle but didn't care for it. Slowly, but with evident pleasure, she ate the bun, liberally smearing the car seat with catsup, chewing each mouthful twenty times, like a well-brought-up child. With nothing left but the pickle, she mouthed it, shredded it, ate two-thirds of it, and spat the rest out. She then turned excited, pleased eyes to Christy. It obviously made her feel special to be given a whole hamburger of her very own, and she hardly bothered to growl at Agatha the Sheepdog when Christy took her through the back door of the clinic and crated her in the ward. Miss Carroll found Christy there, giving both Agatha and Gala bits of his second cheeseburger, and presented him not with a three o'clock patient but a three o'clock cop and Bev Farrell.

The police officer was Nat Shannon, the more businesslike officer at yesterday's scene. They talked in Dr. Potter's office, where Potter's biggest stack of notes, still unread, had become overlayered with Christy's morning charts. Bev still wore blue jeans, possibly the previous day's, and cowboy boots, and she went straight to the coffeepot as though she had raided it before, pouring for all of them as Shannon went carefully over the information about Philip Schumacher and the MG that he had gleaned from Christy the day before, this time writing it down.

Bev refilled Shannon's cup before he finally gave an explanation for his interest.

"You might say we're retracing Philip's steps right before he was shot," Shannon said. "We're assuming he'd been to Denver. The Denver police are helping us out, but it'll take time. It's time that's the essential thing. Can't you remember just when it was you say he ran you off the highway?"

"For the sixth time, no. Not exactly."

"You didn't have the car radio on?"

"I don't have a car radio. I just got out of school, remember? I've been on a tight budget for so long that I wouldn't know how it felt to spend money unnecessarily."

"And you didn't even glance, just barely glance, at your watch?"

"Not that I remember. I was watching the scenery. And the road."

"And these people from Illinois—they didn't happen to mention their names or anything?"

"I think the mother called one of the little kids Michael. Does that help anything? Of course not."

"Well, I don't know. Short haircut, two kids and a wife,

Illinois plates, one kid named Michael. We'll check on it. Maybe a military family, a new transfer or something."

Bev Farrell said, "Oh, hell. Maybe the guy just liked short haircuts, or maybe he didn't look at his watch either."

"Yeah, but this car thing. Are you certain it was a black MGB? Philip drove a Scout. A white Scout. He wrecked it about three weeks ago, and it's over at Hughson's body shop in Breckenridge being repaired."

"Come on, Nat," Bev said. "Christy can surely tell a black MG from a white Scout."

"I'm sure it was a black MGB," Christy said. He put his coffee cup down. The brew had gone stale and bitter. "I had an MGA once, so you kind of look at them. Would it be so hard to check on? There can't be all that many MGB's in town."

"That's enough," Bev said. "For God's sake, let's go see the Dobie."

Nat Shannon rose from his chair. He, too, seemed to know his way around Dr. Potter's clinic, for he led the way to Ward One without asking directions. Gala growled when the two people entered with Christy, and Agatha the Sheepdog got to her feet and wagged her bottom at them. Bev rushed to Agatha's crate. "The darling!" she said. "What in the world has happened to her coat, Christy?"

But the police officer was interested only in the Doberman. "A little problem has come up about the Dobe," Shannon told Christy. "No one seems to know who she is. We're making pretty good progress interviewing Philip's friends, and they all claim he didn't even have a dog."

"That's what his father told me, too," Christy said. He described his attempt to deliver Gala to the Schumacher family, and the officer looked concerned.

"It's a good thing they didn't take her," Shannon said. "I thought I warned you, Dr. Christy, that the Dobe had to stay in tight custody. After all, she's a witness."

Christy grinned. "What kind of courtroom testimony do you think you'll get from a dog?" he asked.

The officer grinned back. "Yeah, it sounds silly. But the Dobe obviously knew the murderer, because she let someone just waltz right into the apartment, shoot Philip, then waltz out again."

"How do you know she didn't try to defend Philip?" Christy asked. "Maybe the murderer did all the waltzing, but with twenty bite marks on his legs and arms."

Shannon said, "We're checking on that. Since you took her outside the clinic, tell me this: Has anyone tried to avoid her?"

"Just about everyone," Christy said. "But a lot of people are that way about Dobermans."

"That's no help," Shannon said. Bev Farrell stopped cooing over the Old English and rejoined them. The officer addressed both her and Christy as he added, "We keep coming back to the point—Whose dog is she? If she wasn't Philip's, how come he was keeping her? I've asked Millie Carroll to check Dr. Potter's records on all female Dobermans, and the other vets in the area are doing the same, but our animal-control officer tells me I might be wasting everybody's time. He claims all Dobes look alike, unless one's black and one's red. Do they all look alike to you, Dr. Christy?"

"I never thought about it," he confessed. "Maybe, unless they have some kind of distinguishing marks or scars. Or a tattoo. Gala isn't tattooed, but a lot of purebreds are, I guess."

"Well, take good care of her," Shannon said. "Eventually she'll have to be put to sleep, I suppose, if no one shows up to claim her, but right now she's a witness."

Christy found that he felt stricken. Put Gala down? Maybe she had a reserved and grumbly temperament, but she was a young, basically healthy animal, and it seemed a terrible waste. He warned himself not to start feeling attached to her.

Bev stayed behind when the officer left. She made a face at his departing back and muttered, "Dumb cops. I saw the way your face fell, Christy, when he started talking about putting the Dobie to sleep. What foolishness. We'll find her a good home. Mark and I placed three Vail Specials just last week. We're getting darned good at finding homes for dogs."

"What's a Vail Special?" Christy asked.

"Sort of a Lab-Husky cross. They're usually big, black, and shaggy. Seasonal people take them in as pups, then just turn them loose when the time comes to leave town. We get a lot of purebreds abandoned that way, too. We've got a pretty good humane society going now, but we never run out of abandoned dogs."

"You're a good person, Bev," Christy said.

"Nope. I'm mean as the devil to people. I'm only kind to animals. Mark says I'm an animal junkie. But, then, he says the same thing about himself."

"Have you ever had any dealings with Dr. Schumacher about animals?"

"Psychoanalyzing them, you mean? No. The animals we help are usually just starved, not loony, and my own dogs are pretty good kids. Schumacher is a neuropsychiatrist, somebody said, and treating dogs and cats is just a sideline. He seems to know what he's doing. Gets the whole family in for about a three-hour session and studies the people as well as the dog that's having a problem. Aggression, usually. I hear he can get results. I've always suspected he's treating the people more than he is the dog, which makes sense. Vail is full of nuts. Ask anyone in town, and they'll tell you I'm one of the more renowned nuts, just because I like dogs."

"How many do you have?"

"I decline to answer on the grounds that I might tend to incriminate myself," Bev said loftily, and she left.

Christy understood. Colorado counties all seemed to be setting limits on the number of dogs a person could have, and he knew of at least one couple in crowded Denver who had bought the house adjoining theirs just so they could thumb their noses at a law that limited dogs to three per household. They had five dogs, and two officially lived at the next-door house. Bev was apparently over the Eagle County limit, but mountain communities were too relaxed for many neighbors to get excited about minor city or county ordinances, as long as a family of dogs was quiet and well cared for.

But after the afternoon's routine cases Christy discovered that Vail would have one less canine resident by nightfall. Miss Carroll came to him quietly with the report that the last patient of the day was a euthanasia case.

"Mr. Jackson says his Nellie had another mini-stroke this afternoon," she said, laying a well-filled chart on the examination table for Christy to look over. "He thinks it's time now. Poor Mr. Jackson, he's out in the waiting room crying."

From the chart, Christy could see that Nellie was an old, old Collie who had surely had many fine innings, but to have to euthanize a patient after hearing the threat to Gala's life made him groan to himself as he prepared to help the dog down the long, last road.

4

THE BAD THING WAS that the old Collie was so frightened. As Christy came into the waiting room, Nellie's weeping master rose and tried to lead the dog toward Christy, but she balked and huddled next to her master's legs, saying clearly that she was too terrified to go. Christy thought of the two syringes loaded with Sodium Pentothal and T-61 that he'd left waiting in the surgery, and he instantly changed his strategy.

"Just let her stay with you a minute," Christy told the red-eyed older man with the Collie, and he ducked back into Potter's office, grabbed a bottle, and shook several yellow Valium 5s into his palm. But Mr. Jackson was apparently too distraught to have registered Christy's words, and he stumbled to the door after Christy, dragging the frightened dog.

Christy stopped him. He knelt beside the dog and stroked her. She was trembling so hard that her stiff old legs could barely hold her up. "All right, Nellie," he said, "you've got the wrong idea. This is just routine, old lady, just like all the other times you've been here." He stood and brusquely shoved a Valium at Mr. Jackson, thereby violating law and ethics, but not conscience. "Here, take this. You're upset, so she knows something's up. In a minute or two we'll give her a tranquilizer, too. I promise you, Mr. Jackson, she can just slip happily away in your arms if we go about this right. Just a minute, I'll get you a glass of water for that pill."

"What is it?" the grief-stricken dog owner asked faintly. "I can't take just anything. My heart—"

"Then how about a couple ounces of Scotch? Is it okay if you drink?"

"God, could I ever use a drink," Mr. Jackson said.

The level on Dr. Potter's Scotch bottle was considerably lower than it had been upon Christy's arrival. Even so, he briefly thought of joining Mr. Jackson, but he decided against it. While Mr. Jackson sipped at the Scotch, Christy outlined his battle plan.

"Now, the minute you're feeling a little better, we'll go ahead and put Nellie up on the examination table and kind of go through the motions. She'll calm down once she gets the idea everything's normal. And I'm going to tranquilize her pretty good, so she'll start feeling euphoric. Then, well, then let's take her for a nice walk. Do you think you're up to it?"

"Yes," Mr. Jackson said. "Yes. But I don't know if I could stand being here when you . . . when you . . ."

"That's all right. As soon as she's calm, we can talk about it."

Mr. Jackson asked for a second Scotch. The aged dog still trembled, cowering next to him, but Christy gently slipped two of the Valiums down her throat, not wanting to alarm Mr. Jackson with the sight of a syringe. He asked Mr. Jackson to coax her to the examination room. The Collie still looked around wildly, obviously hoping to escape, but her master was now under better control, and Christy began a soothing hum of remarks addressed to no one but himself while pretending to listen to her heart and look into her ears. She calmed a little. Ancient veteran, with the milky-gray haze of cataracts clouding her lenses. Graying muzzle, and bones feeling so queerly light and fragile between his soothing hands that he wondered she was able to walk at all. She'd had three previous strokes, Mr. Jackson told him in a stronger voice. With nothing but misery before her, it was indeed time.

Nellie's tranquilizers seemed to be taking effect. He lowered the examination table so she could step off it, and although she staggered a little, she seemed to perk up immediately, all but asking aloud, Is that it? Is that all we came for?

"How about that walk now?" Christy asked Mr. Jackson. "It's nice and level until you're almost to the creek. I think she's up to it, and I'll bet she'll enjoy it."

"Yes," Mr. Jackson said. "I'd like to give her that. God, I'm so sorry that I frightened her."

"It's fine now," Christy said. "You'll see, it's going to be fine." In the waiting room, he summoned a smile for Miss Carroll in exchange for her sympathetic look. "I'll close up this afternoon, Miss Carroll," he told her. "Don't worry about feeding Gala or Agatha. I'll look after things after we take Nellie for a nice walk."

He got Mr. Jackson and Nellie swiftly out of the reception room. Miss Carroll looked on the verge of tears, and he was afraid they'd be catching. The sun had come out for a late afternoon peek, after being hidden by gray clouds all day. Nellie tottered as she stopped to examine a bushy potentilla by the front door on which canine patients had obviously lifted their legs, but the old Collie sniffed earnestly, then squatted and relieved herself near the same spot before continuing on with a sort of tottering briskness. She went to her car. Mr. Jackson's knuckles turned white on her leash, but he called her on in a steady voice, and she opened her mouth in a shaggy smile and trundled along with him and Christy.

They let her stay out a full fifteen minutes. Nellie ambled from ponderosa pine stump to clump of dried grass, dutifully smelling everything she encountered. She wanted to go down to Gore Creek, but Christy could see that the tranquilizers were working on her balance, and he knew that if she fell it could undo Mr. Jackson all over again. Eventually she was staggering pretty badly, and Christy gestured toward the clinic. "I think she's getting pretty groggy now, kind of a three-martini high. Maybe we'd better start back."

"I wish I'd asked for a tranquilizer for her to give her at home," Mr. Jackson said. "Then she could just have passed out in her own surroundings, couldn't she? Before I took her on to you?"

"Sure. It's a good way to go about things. But her walk has had about the same effect."

"Dr. Christy, Nellie loves her car. An r-i-d-e is ecstasy for her." Automatically, Mr. Jackson spelled the magic word. "Couldn't we do it in the car? Start the motor, maybe even drive a couple or three feet? The stuff doesn't take long, does it?"

"No, just a few seconds."

"Does it hurt?"

"There's a tiny sting of the needle, but she's used to that after years of shots. She'll hardly notice it. They just slip painlessly away."

"Then let it happen while she's happy. Please, Dr. Christy, let's put her in her car."

Christy prayed that he wasn't doing the wrong thing. Nellie was underweight, being such an aged dog, but she was still heavy enough to require eight or nine cc's of the standard anesthesia with which he'd planned to inject her. It would put her to sleep in seconds, then he would finish the job quite painlessly with the T-61. He'd seen an injured Dalmation, too badly injured to save, turn and seriously bite a fellow student in clinical practice at vet school when a large, lethal dose went into the vein. Christy was willing enough to risk a bite, but he didn't want that last-second panic for Mr. Jackson and old Nellie.

Mr. Jackson's eyes reddened again, and Christy hastily agreed that car it would be. He found himself swallowing most unprofessionally as the man fought back sorrow, but then, as long as he was behaving so unprofessionally, why let a lump in his throat bother him?

"She can sit on the front seat beside me, can't she?" Mr. Jackson said. "That's where she always likes to ride."

"Why not?" Christy said. Nellie stumbled, and he stooped, thinking he might have to carry her, but she recovered her balance and ambled on again. "Just walk her toward the car. I'll be right back with you, and we can drive her around the parking lot a tiny bit."

When Christy returned with the loaded syringes, Mr. Jackson chirped, "Ride, Nellie? Do you want to go for a *ride*?"

Mr. Jackson's words were the last thing Nellie heard. Unless Mr. Jackson had a private whisper for her while he helped the old dog climb into the car. Christy slipped into the seat and leaned over, holding his breath while he felt for the cephalic vein, then he counted to three to himself as the car started. Nellie stopped glancing to see what he was doing and looked eagerly through the windshield. Then Christy plunged the first needle home. She didn't gasp. She didn't even jerk. She let out a long, quiet breath and within seconds slumped against Mr. Jackson's shoulder. He braked the car and put his forehead on the steering wheel, and Christy injected the second syringe unnoticed. After a moment, Mr. Jackson raised his head and said in a quiet voice, "Lucky Nellie. Why don't they let people go out that way if they have to go? I wonder what I'd choose instead of a car ride? Maybe the Denver Broncos on the ten-yard line. But they'd fumble and lose the ball, damn them. You can always count on the Broncos to goof at the wrong moment."

Sliding the dog's body from the car took Christy a minute or two, but he didn't let Mr. Jackson help. He cradled her in his arms and said good-bye to Mr. Jackson, but of course it didn't end there. It seemed as if it never did. Mr. Jackson came back to life with the dog's death and had the usual pet owner's anxious question: Is she really dead? Are you absolutely positive that she's dead? Christy solved that by taking Nellie's body back to an examination room and checking the silence of the heart with a stethoscope, then letting Mr. Jackson listen. It was as if every pet owner secretly feared that veterinarians were body snatchers whose object was to pretend to put an animal down, then bring it back to life and rush it to a vivisection lab.

Then there was the disposal of the body. The Jacksons naturally lived in a condominium. They naturally planned to move soon to a Sunbelt state, having found the Colorado winters unpleasantly cold and icy. They naturally preferred that Nellie's body be cremated, and could Mr. Jackson have the ashes, please, so Mrs. Jackson could decide what she wanted to do with them later? Mrs. Jackson was at home crying her heart out, but she'd be very consoled when she learned how Nellie went.

Everything was natural, including the fact that Mr. Jackson forgot to request his bill, and Christy was too chicken to remind him of it. He rashly promised cremation and ashes, knowing that he might face driving down to Denver with Nellie's body in the trunk compartment to accomplish the deed. He let Mr. Jackson listen a final time to the unbeating heart, and he controlled another choking feeling of his own when Mr. Jackson gave the dog's dead body a last, loving pat. When Christy finally locked the clinic door after Mr. Jackson, he positively fled to Ward One and to the living— Gala the Doberman and Agatha the Old English Sheepdog, both eagerly on their feet at the sound of the door opening and both eager for their dinners.

Gala knocked her food bowl from Christy's hands again out of anxiety to reach her dinner. He forgave her without fussing, happy with her company and with that of the zanily bouncing Agatha. He put them in outside runs for exercise, then contemplated the remnants of the afternoon. After Nellie, there was no question that he would leave Gala in the clinic so he could spend the night at some silly condominium. But an excursion for supplies seemed due. He'd see if the iron cook stove in the cabin worked. Christy was no cook. His mainstay was grilled-cheese-and-bologna sandwiches. He could manage hamburger meat in a dozen different ways, though, and anyone could put together a good salad. It even sounded pleasant, to spend a quiet evening in front of the big fireplace with a dog snoozing at his feet.

The dog in question seemed to have enjoyed her earlier Jeep ride. She'd like going along to the grocery store. Agatha probably would, too. But Agatha had prospective owners, and Christy knew he shouldn't be tooting around the town with every animal brought to the clinic for treatment. He gave Agatha her evening antibiotic and checked the stitches he'd taken on her ripped leg. Everything was going well. Wasn't it? Once he got her crated, he studied her for a while, troubled by the careful way she lay down. Arthritis? He shelved the question for the following day and put Gala in the Jeep.

Traffic was busy on the highway. Even Vail had its evening rush hour, he supposed. Several cars pulled in after him when he turned in at the village's Safeway parking lot. The store was crowded, but Christy's purchases were few, and daylight lingered when he returned to Gala and the Jeep. The mountains called.

"What do you say, Gala?" Christy asked her cheerfully. "Shall we see if we can find some quiet little road and give you an off-leash run?"

He had to look closely. Gala's tail had been docked so short that she could scarcely be said to have one, but he could have sworn he saw a little wagging motion.

Continued traffic on the interstate pushed them westward more rapidly than Christy wanted to go, but he tried a turn-off at a crossroads named Avon and was soon happy to spot a trail that climbed easily enough beside a rushing creek. He left the Jeep at road's end, and once they were well up the path, he unsnapped Gala's leash. She didn't hesitate. She shot off ahead of him and was quickly out of sight. Soon he heard her crashing through willows, circling back. When she intersected the trail in front of him, she flashed him an excited look, with wide eyes and open mouth, and dashed into the creek. She obviously liked to wade as well as run.

Christy followed the path more slowly than the dog, the altitude working on him. Once he lost even her crashing, splashing sounds, and he tried "Gala, come!" She came promptly, checking in before dashing off again. He stopped worrying about her after that, and allowed himself the luxury of simply existing for that moment in the private place he always thought of as The Mountains.

Heavy scent of pine on the wind. Bitter smell of fallen willow leaves underfoot. How wonderful it must be to be a dog, with a dog's scenting ability, rambling by a mountain stream. Christy cleared a granite outcropping and entered a meadow. He saw Gala, a black shadow, leaping through the grasses. She doubled back. Mouse? She dashed onward. Beaver? Surely there were beaver in the vicinity. The dams on the creek looked tidily kept. The light changed abruptly, as it always did with mountains to measure the sun's passage. Shadows would deepen quickly and the night would be cold, but Christy loitered. He had never once seen a beaver, only countless beaver dams proving that they lived and thrived. Perhaps at twilight one could see them.

Of course, given Gala running in eccentric circles in the meadow, no beaver would pop its snout above water. Christy finally turned to call her and was interested to see sudden movement in a wild raspberry bush she had just charged past. Surely she'd spooked some creature, although it probably wasn't his beaver. She whirled and looked at the bush, then put on speed and ran toward him. There was a *fizzzz* that stopped her short. A dried wild-flower stem broke off and fell to the ground. Gala cowered for a moment, then ran the rest of the way to Christy. She ran behind him and sat in her best obedience pose. Another *fizzzz* kicked up a small geyser of earth near Christy's left shoe. He couldn't believe it, but he had to—someone was shooting at them.

Christy found that his body had already acted. He hit the earth, hugging it, and he felt one leg touch Gala as she wriggled closer to him. What did you do for cover in an open meadow with only grass and dried Jacob's ladder and a few raspberry bushes to hide behind? Christy grabbed Gala's collar and pulled her into the relative shelter of his arms. With the dog beneath him, he began to wriggle toward the granite outcropping that marked the edge of the meadow. He blessed the quickening twilight.

If more shots were fired, Christy didn't hear them. His heart was beating too loudly in his ears. Gala hated the hovering protection of his body, and she struggled to squirm out from under him. It didn't occur to him that the panicky dog might bite him. He maneuvered her to the far side of the outcropping, and only then did he notice that his face was within inches of her teeth. Christy kept crawling until he could drag her into a willow thicket by the creek. She struggled to stand, but he rasped, "Down, Gala. Lie down." She subsided. Then there was only the gurgle and plash of the creek and the swift coming of darkness.

Christy waited until he could breathe easily. Then, holding Gala's collar, he waited some more. When it was so dark that he couldn't tell willow from rock, he leashed Gala and started downstream. He hoped she would be able to find the trail and follow it. But if, with some extra animal sense, she knew it was there, she wouldn't go near it. Christy gave up and waded the icy creek, slipping on boulders, falling into outreaching undergrowth, and both he and the dog were sopping and shivering by the time they regained the Jeep.

Christy approached the Jeep with all the caution he could

muster, despite a howling impatience to climb inside. He wanted the little warmth it would give his chilled body. He even wanted its vinyl seats, its smell of gasoline, after the cold darkness and wetness of his beloved out-of-doors. He held the shivering dog, trying to listen, worrying that their assailant might be hiding there in the dark. At last they made a run for the Jeep. The dog seemed as glad to be inside it as Christy was. He started it quickly and drove as fast as he could, not to the clinic and its cabin, but to the Municipal Building and its police department. Christy's destination was chosen by pure selfishness—the building would have a furnace, and he and Gala could get warm far quicker than they would by waiting through the fumbling it would take to gather firewood at the cabin and light a fire.

One green Saab and a bicycle were parked outside the entrance marked by a discreet sign, POLICE. Christy parked the Jeep sloppily and hurried Gala up a short flight of steps through the door. Then he stood shivering and blinking while a young woman at a counter blinked back at him.

"Nat Shannon," Christy stuttered. "I need to see Shannon. Oh, please, don't tell me he's gone home for the day. Someone just shot at his witness."

Christy had plenty of time to think, retracing the small sights and sounds that told him it was Gala, not he, that had been the sharpshooter's target. Shannon refused to hear a word until Gala had been toweled off and Christy changed into dry jeans and a flannel shirt, Shannon's own off-duty clothes. David Lincoln, the officer who had been with Shannon at the apartment when they found the body of Philip Schumacher, seemed to lose all fear of the Doberman—wet, cowering canine lady that she'd become—as he dried her without seeming to think of killer Dobermans, then settled her on a borrowed sheepskin jacket next to Christy. The dog's teeth clacked audibly. Lincoln fussily buttoned the jacket around her, creating a wooly sausage with a black head sticking out, and Gala let him do it with no signs of a snarl.

"Some protector," Shannon said after he had heard Christy's tale. "Ran right in back of you, did she?"

"Unhesitatingly," Christy said.

"But you're absolutely sure someone shot at her?"

"I was sure at the time," Christy said.

"It is hunting season, you know. Is there the faintest possibility—"

"That some mighty hunter mistook a middle-sized black dog for a big old mule deer? Come on, Shannon."

"Yeah, but we've gotten some weird complaints about hunters," Lincoln interposed. "Gun-happy, people call them. Was it last year or the year before, Nat, when that Lakewood fellow shot those two Great Dane puppies in the lady's yard? Damned near shot the lady, too," he explained for Christy's benefit. "At least that's what she charged. The hunter claimed the pups had been up on the mountain killing a young stag."

"Did they?" Christy asked.

"Well, there were two dead pups in the yard, but no dead stag on the mountain."

Shannon said, "Look, Christy, maybe you should keep the dog in for a while. No more runs in the mountains, okay? If somebody wants to kill her, that's all the more reason for us to want her alive. Are you at all expert on attack training? Can you tell if she's been trained for that?"

They all regarded the dog. She had worked her front feet out of her sheepskin sausage, but she lay quietly, looking content. She certainly didn't look dangerous at that moment, but Christy felt a new shiver in the vicinity of the back of his neck. "I wouldn't know," he said honestly. "They use special code words for attack, don't they? Something innocent, like 'cotton candy' or 'marmalade.'"

The dog didn't stir. Shannon and Lincoln both looked relieved. Shannon said, "Well, here's something else that's going to sound a little peculiar. Can you tell if she's been trained to steal things? The chief read somewhere about a special kind of dog in England—Lurchers, he said—that the gypsies bred or trained to steal clothes off clotheslines. So he asked does she steal?"

"Good Lord, she's shown no signs of it," Christy said. "What's this all about, anyway?"

"Can I trust you to keep your mouth shut if we fill you in a little?"

"Sure. I guess I'm just like everyone else. I blab everything I know unless somebody tells me to keep something to myself. Then I do."

Shannon looked dubious, but David Lincoln apparently had more trust in his fellow man. "We found all kinds of goodies in Philip's apartment that are on our swipe sheets," Lincoln said. "If you ask me, that's why he kept the Dobe there, to guard the loot. Cameras, stereos, that sort of thing. We've had break-in after break-in during the spring and summer seasons. It looks like good old Philip might have gotten himself mixed up with a burglary ring."

"We don't know that for sure," Shannon said. He turned to Christy. "It turns out the apartment wasn't really Philip's. It belonged to somebody named Stan Bell. So Bell's missing, and we haven't got a line on him yet. The loot could have been his. Philip could have been an innocent party. The stuff was all stacked in one closet. Maybe Bell's. So maybe Philip went in to borrow a tie and saw all the stuff and said, 'Uh-oh, call the cops,' and maybe that's why he got killed."

"Yes, and that sounds like a pretty nice whitewash job," Lincoln said. "Just the thing you'd expect from his dad. Try Philip's little brother. You might get a different story. Not that you could believe it either. Tell him what else Dr. Schumacher said. Tell him about the suicide."

"You mean Philip shot himself?" Christy said.

"Hardly," Shannon said. He sighed. "How did we get into this anyway?"

"Go on, tell him."

"Oh, it's just Dr. Schumacher's comment that Philip was going through the post-adolescent blues or something. I wrote it all down, but I can't swear I understand it. Schumacher didn't even believe it himself. Or didn't want to. I guess it was Mrs. Schumacher who was worried that the boy killed himself. But he didn't." Shannon sighed again. "You see, the medical examiner found six shots from a thirty-eight-caliber pistol. According to the grooves on the bullets, it was probably a revolver, maybe a Smith and Wesson. That's a lot of gun. It looks like somebody stood there and emptied it at a boy who was probably good and dead after the first couple of shots."

"My Lord," Christy said.

"Amen," Shannon said. "If the dog really got shot at tonight, I'd guess the weapon was a rifle, but—"

"Where do you get the 'if'?"

"Well, deliberately shot at, not accidentally. But damn it, I want you to be careful with her. Keep her safe. Keep her alive. And watch her, will you? If it turns out she's an attack dog, or even if the chief's crazy theory is right and she's a thief, I want to know about it. Okay?"

It was fine with Christy, there in the warmth and bright lights of the police station, but he discovered while driving home with Gala that life had taken on a new dimension. A highly unpleasant dimension at that. Every car, Jeep, or pickup that appeared in his rearview mirror was suspect. Why had he left so few lights on in the clinic and, blast it, none at all in the cabin? Having the Doberman at his side when he unlocked the clinic and went inside the shadowed building to check on Agatha the Sheepdog was a definite plus. Just hearing Gala's toenails clicking down the hall made him feel a little bigger, a little more confident. It also reminded him to clip her overgrown nails the next morning. The normality of the thought made him feel better yet. It wasn't until he got the lights turned on in the cabin and started unloading the groceries that his benign feelings toward Gala turned sour.

"I can't believe it," he scolded her. "Here the police are already suspecting you're a member of a burglary ring, and what do you do?"

At some point during their evening ride, she'd gotten into the grocery sack. She'd stolen and eaten the hamburger meat. Christy soon had the roaring fire in the fireplace that he'd planned, and he had the dog sleeping at his feet, but he only got salad for dinner.

5

CHRISTY WAS STERN with Gala the next day. He kept her crated in Ward One except for supervised outings in the runs. He allowed no visitors. When Jean and Harriet came to visit Agatha, he brought the Sheepdog out to them rather than let them stroll casually into the ward. Agatha jumped up and down on her two saviors. Christy had noticed that she jumped up on everyone, but it pleased the two ladies, and that pleased him. They took Agatha for a walk, then patted and petted her for a few minutes in the waiting room. Christy was on the verge of discussing with them the problem of Agatha's injured eye when a hearty pat on Agatha's back brought a yelp of pain from the dog. Harriet apologized to Agatha for patting her too hard, and Agatha bounced some more. Christy worriedly kept silent. What could possibly be wrong with the dog's back? He'd do some more clipping when he had Agatha to himself and see if he'd overlooked yet another problem.

The morning went fast. A young cat named Schopenhauer, refusing food and in obvious discomfort, complicated things. The gray tiger-stripe had swallowed a needle, X rays clearly showed. So Christy performed necessary surgery, with Miss Carroll assisting, as soon as the last of the morning's patients departed. The heavens blessed Schopenhauer, and the needle had not been threaded. Otherwise, probing for the thread in its intestines could have taken hours, and Christy doubted the young cat could have withstood so much stress. Minus one needle, it was sleeping off the anesthesia when Christy came out to Miss Carroll's desk with freshly scrubbed hands and found her holding the outgoing mail. "And if you don't mind," she said, "we're low on distilled water. Could you pick some up at Safeway while you're out?"

"Sure," Christy said. "Thanks to Gala, I need more groceries anyway. Any appointments before three o'clock? If not, I'll eat lunch after I run the errands. I'm starving. I never seem to get anything to eat in Vail."

Miss Carroll fished a brown paper bag from a desk drawer. "Half a tuna sandwich and some carrot sticks?" she said. "I'll gladly share."

"Thanks, but I'm going to splurge. I think I'll go to the Red Lion and eat veal parmigiana. Want to come with me? My treat, and I'd love the company."

Miss Carroll declined, and Christy ignored Gala's loud moans as he went out the back door of the clinic without her. Agatha moaned, too, but only because she'd obviously figured out he'd been taking Gala for rides, and she wanted one for herself. He'd get to Agatha later. This particular afternoon break was dedicated to his own selfish pleasure.

The sun was out today. With no Doberman barking from the Jeep, Christy discovered that people smiled at him, and he smiled back, beginning to feel less a stranger. He parked the Jeep in what Vail called its transportation center—which afforded intelligently planned parking space for a town that forbade cars on many streets—and trotted down steps into the original development, Vail Village. The approach was broad and parklike, narrowing as Christy neared one of Vail's landmarks, a covered bridge over Gore Creek. A kiosk north of the bridge fluttered with notices: "Wanted: ride to Chicago." "We would like to rent a room for the winter. Call Linda at . . ." "Afternoon Happy Hour, Ladies' Drinks 50¢."

The town was peculiarly quiet. An unleashed black dog appeared to be the only customer at a sportswear shop south of the bridge. Only one couple, honeymooners perhaps, sat huddled in sweaters in lawn chairs outside a normally busy inn. Christy thought he might have the Red Lion all to himself, but a few couples occupied its black leather banquettes. Although he discovered that the restaurant's off-season menu didn't run to veal parmigiana for lunch, he contented himself with bratwurst and German potato salad. It was served so promptly that after he'd finished he decided he had time to gaze into a few shopwindows and consider a birthday present for his mother.

Christy's mother wasn't easy to please with presents or anything else in life, but Vail, he thought with a sharp nip of foreboding, would be just her kind of town. All those gift shops with sunflashers in their windows wouldn't catch her glance, but that elegant boutique three doors down with the display of imported sweaters, the one across the street with the crimson parka in its window, those would soon know Louise Christy's easy smile and pirate's eyes. She didn't ski, but trifles never stopped her. A New Yorker with the typical East Coast opinion that nothing existed beyond the Hudson River, she had calmly moved to Denver after a then-youthful Christy confided that his choice of vet schools was Colorado State. She established residency in the state, and thereby gave him a good edge on admission. She left as efficiently and quickly as she came, moving back to Manhattan, but exposure to the West had changed her. B.D.—before Denver—she'd gone to the Bahamas for winter vacations. Last year it had been Tucson, and the two years before that Mexico. She disliked cold weather. Maybe Vail wouldn't appeal to her after all.

But that crimson parka might. She'd look smashing darting into Balducci's, a little plump, a little breathless, for leeks and gorgonzola, or popping into Vito's for freshly baked bread.

As Christy gazed, a hand reached into the window and removed the crimson parka. He felt his mouth drop foolishly. He frowned at his rival, a girl with long blond hair to whom a clerk was handing the parka. Then he caught his breath. He'd seen that particular mane of blond hair leaving an apartment building across the valley in a black MGB. Christy wondered for a moment if he should phone Nat Shannon, but in the meantime the girl might buy his mother's parka, then disappear. He entered the shop.

The girl had shrugged into the parka and moved to a mirror, her eyes uncertainly inspecting her reflection. There was no reason for her uncertainty. Christy saw immediately that the crimson garment would never suit his mother. It belonged on this tall, graceful girl. She appeared to be somewhere in her early twenties, with a look of energy and vibrant good health about her. Summer jogger, winter skier, Christy would have bet. Her face, framed by the shiny hair, was so rosy that her cheeks looked like delicately tinted apples. She wore jeans and an old sweater and scuffed hiker's boots. The parka carried a price tag of nearly three hundred dollars, Christy was appalled to see, so he inferred that she dressed as she pleased, not as she was required. His own reflection emerged in the mirror, and she gave him a polite, pleasant smile and moved over, as if not to hog the mirror.

Christy wanted to smile back, but he told himself he had crucial business with this young woman. He said, "I beg your pardon?"

She laughed at his stuffiness, a warm little laugh. "What

have you done?" she said. She had an accent, not pronounced but distinctly Southern.

"The very question I'll put to you," Christy said. "Would you prefer talking about it privately?" He gestured outside.

She began to look alarmed. "No thanks," she said.

"I really think you should," Christy said. "I want to talk to you about an MGB. You see, I chanced to notice it a couple of days ago in front of a certain apartment building."

Christy saw that he'd secured her attention thoroughly with that one. Hazel eyes stared at him. She gave the parka back to the clerk, nodded at Christy, and went outside.

"Now—" she began.

But Christy prefered his own starting point. "My name is Gordon Christy," he said. "I'd like yours, please. Or better yet, just wait and tell it to the police."

"I'm Karen Hamilton," she said quickly. "It's my car. I was just getting it back again."

"Don't you know the police have been looking for it?"

"Please, do you have to tell them?" she asked. "It's got Texas plates, so I popped it down to a friend's garage in Colorado Springs. I'll take it home one of these weekends, and that'll be the end of it. Don't say 'police' again. My dad hates for me to get mixed up in that kind of thing."

"Sorry," Christy said.

"I didn't shoot Philip, if that's what you're thinking. You don't go around shooting somebody over a mere car."

"Then why worry about talking to the police?" Christy asked. "Surely you know that the Schumacher boy was driving your car before he was killed. He almost ran into me on I-Seventy. The cops know that, and they're interested in all the wheres and whens of what he'd been up to."

The girl looked decidedly upset. "That's all I need, for Philip to have wrecked my car," she said. "Listen, do you think these local cops would feel just utterly, absolutely compelled to tell my dad that my car got swiped?"

Christy said, "Unless you're under twenty-one, or the car

is in your father's name, I can't think of any reason why they would. They seem like pretty decent guys."

"Of all the rotten messes. Well, I might as well go see them," she said. "But if they tell my dad, you're on my list, Gordon Christy. Are you planning to escort me to the cop shop, or am I on my honor as a citizen? An innocent citizen, I hasten to emphasize."

"So am I," Christy said, "but I'm not a very trusting one. I think I'll just walk you up to the police station. Better yet, we'll pick up my car, and I'll drive you."

She seemed to expect it. She fell in with Christy without protest and asked only, "Aren't you going to ask me any questions? Don't you care why Philip swiped my car?"

"Is a cat curious?" Christy said. "But really, you don't have to tell me anything."

"Maybe I won't," she said.

Twenty minutes later, while Christy watched the minute hand of his watch creep closer to clinic hours, they were still sitting on a sunny rock wall below the parking area, and Karen Hamilton was deep into a denunciation of Philip Schumacher. They'd dated during the summer, she said. It wasn't a serious relationship, especially for Karen. A lot of tennis, the occasional dinner date. But Karen soon decided she didn't like the people Philip ran around with.

"Especially Jerome," she said. "Every time we went out, we seemed to end up at a party at Jerome's condo, though what Philip found amusing about Jerome's parties was more than I could fathom. Nothing ever happened. Jerome has to be the most boring guy in the world. He just sat, night after night, smiling in a sort of nasty way. A Cheshire cat smile. I thought at first he must have been on some kind of heavy stuff, but they never did much except smoke a little pot. I don't know. Philip's gang was like frozen TV dinners. All bland and okay on the outside, but unhealthy somehow."

"Philip's gang," Christy mused. "Did he ever say anything to you about, oh, checking out any of your other friends, telling him where they kept jewelry or cash or the like?"

"Good grief, no," Karen said. "Are you implying they were actually robbing people? For money?"

"I don't know," Christy admitted. "Maybe some people do it for kicks."

"I certainly wouldn't. Even Philip would have known that. Although, you know, talking about other friends, he did ask questions sometimes."

"Did any of them ever get burgled?"

"No." Karen was silent, thinking. Christy glanced at the clock tower this time, not at his watch, and he knew he had to get cracking. He still had to go to the grocery for the distilled water they used in the autoclave to sterilize instruments.

But Karen wasn't through. "Boy, I think I really am going to be in trouble," she said. "Remember the car, Philip swiping it? He tried to rape me. Oh, maybe you'd call it just a heavy pass, but when a guy starts putting muscle on you, rape is rape in my opinion."

"I'm with you," Christy said. "How did it happen?"

"He came by my place late, really soaked. They'd been boozing it up at Jerome's, he said. We weren't seeing much of each other by then. He wanted another drink, and then he wanted to play muscleman. I slugged him with a Boston fern. A big one. It broke the pot. Oh, how I laughed. There was Philip with potting soil and indigo blue pot shards slowly oozing off his forehead. I guess I shouldn't have laughed. That made him even madder. He bad-mouthed me a while and left, but the bastard picked up my car keys while I was laughing, I guess, because the next thing I knew I heard him tear out in my car. An MG motor is pretty unmistakable, you know."

"That's the moment you should have called the cops."

"I suppose so. But, oh, dear, since my mom died two

years ago there's been the daddy problem. He remarried pretty fast. I didn't mind. He was lonely as all get-out. But it was as if he had to prove even harder that he was going to keep on looking out for me. I'm perfectly welcome to stay in Vail at the condo as long as I'm on my best behavior. Otherwise, it's nothing but lectures. And the thing now is, if I tell the cops, they're going to say I had a motive for murdering Philip, aren't they? Attempted rape, car theft, the female of the species' revenge, all those things?"

"Karen, I only know they're looking for the MG, and they're bound to get a line on it. And you. Won't it look worse if you keep on waiting?"

"Oh, boy," she said, but with resignation. She stood, and Christy started her up the steps toward the Jeep. Before they reached it, she brightened. "I'm safe," she said. "They're saying around town a Doberman Pinscher was at Philip's place when somebody shot him. Everybody who knows me knows I'm scared stiff of dogs. Especially big brutes like Dobermans and German Shepherds. Seventy-five or a hundred people can vouch that I'd never go into an apartment with a big old dog standing there. Why, I even turned down an invitation to Cletus Knight's house because of his Dobermans, and you know how often you get invitations from Knight. Well, you don't know, you're new. I would have loved to have seen his house, but who can look a dozen Dobermans in the teeth?"

"This Knight person has a lot of Dobes?" Christy asked. "Does he breed them?"

"Breeds them, shows them, I don't know."

"Maybe he knows who Gala is," Christy said.

"Who's Gala?"

"The Doberman Philip was keeping."

"Philip sure didn't have a dog as long as I knew him," Karen said.

"How about the guy he shared the apartment with? Stan Bell?"

"No. Or you can be sure I would never have set foot in the place. I really am phobic about dogs."

"Darn, and I was going to ask you a favor," Christy said.

"Ask," Karen said. "Surely I owe you one for dragging me to the police."

"You'll turn me down."

"Maybe."

"Well, it's about Mr. Knight. I was hoping maybe you could introduce me to him. I'd like to take Gala to him and ask if he's ever seen her before. Maybe this afternoon after the clinic closes. Then we'd take Gala home and maybe we could have dinner together."

Karen beamed at him. "You lovely man," she said. "You actually think the cops aren't going to throw me into a cell ten minutes from now, don't you? Just for that vote of confidence, I'll do it. You won't let Cletus's Dobermans eat me, will you?"

Christy managed to post Miss Carroll's mail during the afternoon break, but he flunked distilled water and postponed the look he'd promised himself at Agatha the Sheepdog's back. Officer Shannon had to be called into the police station after he arrived there with Karen Hamilton. Christy waited with her, no longer to be sure that she actually talked to Shannon, but to give her moral support. He would cheerfully have stayed with her while she told her tale to Shannon, but he was already ten minutes late for clinic hours.

It was a day for cats. Another gray tiger-stripe, this one named Mildred, awaited him, feeling lethargic and refusing to eat. A black cat with ear mites was next in line. Then it was a catfight victim with the usual deep puncture wounds. Miss Carroll stayed thirty minutes late helping with the feline flood, and the clinic doors were still unlocked when Karen Hamilton arrived. She was in jeans and sweater again, but the sweater was the color of cream, the jeans sleekly fitting, and high heels had replaced her hiking boots. She also wore the crimson parka. Thinking of its price tag, Christy figured he could find a gift more in keeping with his income for his mother's birthday.

"It's all set," Karen announced. "Knight's expecting us. He's going to Denver tonight, so he said early-ish. Okay?"

"And you're not in jail?" Christy said.

"Certainly not."

"And Shannon's not going to tell your dad?"

"Tell him what?" Karen said. "I'm not to leave the state for a while, but I hadn't planned to anyway. Knight said cocktails. You ready?"

Christy wasn't, but he found himself leaving anyway, shooed out by Miss Carroll. Christy caught a merry look in her eyes, as though she thought she had yet another ladies' man to look after. He fetched Gala from Ward One and was delayed several minutes by the dog's glee. Gala jumped, little, short, stiff-legged jumps, laughing in the direction of Agatha the Sheepdog. Then she danced in tight circles, demonstrating her pleasure. Christy realized that he had the Jeep keys in his hand. He'd have to be more careful about setting her off. He finally calmed her enough to risk introducing her to a person who was afraid of dogs. There was a touchy moment. Gala jumped into the front seat with him and Karen. Karen gasped and looked genuinely frightened. Christy ordered the dog to the back and was gratified to see Gala stick her nose out the window, prepared to ignore Karen and enjoy the ride.

"Now tell me," he said to Karen, "how did you and Officer Shannon really get along?"

"Well enough," Karen said. "He seemed to believe me. He wouldn't have let me leave if he hadn't, would he? I got a little lecture about not reporting the theft of a car, but like I told Shannon, it wasn't really theft, just an ex-friend borrowing it without permission. Thin line and stuff. I think he understood. Even about Philip's muscle job. Then he wanted to know all about Philip's friends. It took forever.

73

But he was a gentleman and took me home after the third degree so I could change and drive down here."

"What're you driving?"

"A junker I rented in Denver. Want to take me to Colorado Springs early tomorrow morning for the MG? Shannon's dying to go over it, even though tomorrow's Saturday and I guess they'll all have to be paid time and a half. He wants to send a cop named Dave Lincoln down with me to pick it up. I'm sure I could talk him into letting you go instead. Save the city a buck."

"Sure. I'm free at noon."

"I don't think Shannon wants to wait. Let's get the Knight visit over with. It's this way. Come on, Christy, you offered me dinner, and I'm getting hungry."

Cletus Knight lived on the same side of town as the clinic, above LionsHead, and within five minutes Christy was looking at a house that didn't whisper of money but yelled it. It sat high above the village on Rock Ledge Road, and whereas pine and aspen were the natural growth on Knight's particular slice of the mountain, his house nestled in its own little forest of Colorado blue spruce, surely brought in and planted, and surely, given the size and symmetry of the trees, planted at large expense. The house was T-shaped, of stone and redwood, and great windows of tinted triple-paned glass stared smugly out at the inferior world. The heavily carved front door was eight feet high and almost as broad. When Karen rang the doorbell, a frenzy of barking greeted them. Karen cowered. So did Gala.

"Courage," Christy said to both of them.

A voice inside spoke sharply. The barking stopped at once, and the door opened to reveal the biggest, most powerful-looking man Christy had ever met.

Cletus Knight was black. He was also getting on toward seven feet tall. Christy had to look up, then higher, then higher, to look the man in the face. Knight effortlessly looked over the top of Christy's head at Gala, who had gone into a sit in back of him, then said in a low, pleasant voice, "Ah, you brought your little bitch. Dancer, Velvet, go to the living room."

Staring at Knight, Christy had neglected to register fully the heaving wave of Dobermans that jostled and shoved next to Knight's legs. There were five, no, six, no, eight full-grown Dobes. Karen stood stiffly and apprehensively, and with reason. She raised her hands to the top of her head, obviously afraid of touching one of the pack. Yet the dogs seemed well-behaved. None growled, not even at Gala, al-though Christy saw that two bitches, one red and one black, were giving her the kind of look Count Dracula reserved for his victims. Knight said more sharply, "Dancer. Velvet. Liv-ing room." The vampire-eyed pair turned and trotted quietly down the hall.

Knight greeted Karen, then didn't wait for introductions. He engulfed Christy's hand. He also offered his knuckles, fingers tucked in, for Gala to sniff. "Bring her on in, Dr. Christy," Knight said. "The rest of the mob are pretty good-natured. She'll be okay. I'll just put Dancer and Velvet away. They're both a little sassy until they get to know someone. They'd probably behave themselves with your bitch, but why take chances?"

Karen looked as though she preferred not to take the chance of stepping inside, but she made the effort, hands still carefully held out of the dogs' reach. The big, splendid man and his six remaining Dobermans preceded them into the big, splendid house. Everything was oversized. Paintings and mirrors hung at Knight's eye-level, not that of common mortals, and three leather couches that lined the walls in the big den in which he left them were all ten feet long. A moss-rock fireplace looked large enough to burn whole trees. A vast desk with only one object on it, a glass paperweight, sat next to French doors that went into an adjoining room. Christy gazed through them into an aviary in which two fa-miliar-looking cockatoos sat nibbling potted plants that also looked familiar. Somewhere about, Christy figured, there was probably a chameleon named Alfred.

Christy's eyes snagged on the paperweight on Knight's desk. It was a snow scene, with a miniature red house set among tiny pines. He shook it, and the snow fell. As he put it back on the desk, six Dobermans suddenly erupted back into the den, and both Karen and Gala looked alarmed. Christy felt uneasy himself. He was goosed by at least three different Doberman noses. From Karen's little cries, he knew that she was getting her share of the attention, but Gala got goosed by all six. Gala roached her back and tucked her short stub of a tail and tried to whirl away as the Knight pack nosed around her, then she appeared to give up. She stood very still as she was thoroughly sniffed, and she was thereby assured of her status as an inferior interloper, as she wasn't allowed to sniff back. Then five of the Knight dogs arranged themselves comfortably on the leather couches, and a young bitch remaining made a play bow to Gala and invited her to wrestle. Gala declined. She was edging back toward Christy and Karen when Knight came in with two women, one black, one white. He provided only first names. The younger, black woman was Lucille, and the older woman was the Alicia whom Christy had glimpsed upon first arriving in Vail with the cockatoos. After introductions, drinks mixed by Alicia, and a few minutes of polite conversation from Lucille, both of the women meandered away.

"Doggy talk. It bores them," Knight said. "Now tell me, Dr. Christy, how can I help you with your bitch?"

"No one knows who she belongs to," Christy said. "Since you're a Dobe expert, I wondered if you'd ever chanced to notice her around town before."

"I don't know how expert I am, but, sure, I've noticed her. She belongs to Jerome. I don't think he's had her long. Maybe a few weeks."

Karen shot a look at Christy, and one and one became two for him. Jerome. That was the fellow she'd mentioned meeting through Philip. Jerome, the Cheshire cat.

"Great," Christy said. "I'll get right in touch with him and tell him where his dog is. But I have to wonder—surely he's heard about the murder and the Dobe being on the scene. Do you have any clue why this Jerome wouldn't have already come around looking for his Dobie?"

Knight was silent, so Karen replied. "With Jerome, everything is a mystery," she said. "Come to think about it, I don't even know his last name. Or is it his first name? Is he Jerome Somebody, Cletus, or Somebody Jerome?"

"Maybe Alicia knows," Knight said. "Excuse me just a moment." The six Dobes followed him, but a moment was apparently all it took, for they reappeared and started to sniff Gala all over again. Knight loafed through the door and called Gala to him. She went quickly. He hunkered down and quietly looked at her eyes and her teeth, just as though he were a vet conducting a physical exam. He then slid her collar high on her neck, right below the ears, told her, "Stand, stay," and positioned her effortlessly so that her stance was suddenly noble and beautiful, with front feet planted firmly, back legs slightly stretched out, head high. Then he let her relax, absently massaging her neck.

Knight's general demeanor was aloof, but Christy found himself feeling friendly toward the man. "You obviously know just where it feels good," he said, nodding at the contented Dobe.

"You're not doing so badly with her yourself," Knight said. "She's filled out since I first saw her. Getting a little shine to her coat. Watch her toenails, though. She's flat-footed enough already without overgrown nails to throw her onto the backs of her feet."

"Is she flat-footed?" Christy said. He was taken aback, almost as though he were a parent whose cherished child had just been called cross-eyed.

Knight nodded. "Poor nutrition when she was a puppy, maybe. Soft topline, too, but that might firm up. She's got a round eye, but it's good and dark. Lousy tail dock, but, then, she's no show specimen. Which is not to say she won't make you a grand pet, Dr. Christy."

Christy decided maybe he didn't like Cletus Knight after all. Nor did he like the amiable Dobermans who sprawled on the carpet and couches. There was one big black male, the young black bitch who had wanted to play, four red bitches. How their coats gleamed. How short their nails were. And there was something . . . hmm, yes. Gala had whiskers, but these Dobes all looked as if they'd seen a good barber that day. Gala also managed to look oddly shaggy beside them, despite her naturally short Doberman coat, but Christy couldn't quite detect what the difference was.

As if he had read Christy's mind, Knight said, "Bring her over some afternoon, Dr. Christy, and I'll show you how to groom her. It only takes five or ten minutes. We're lucky to have Dobes, aren't we? Think what Poodle people have to go through."

Alicia appeared at the doorway. "He doesn't answer, Cletus," she said. "Shall I keep trying?"

"Jerome," Knight explained succinctly. "What about it, Dr. Christy? Do you want to phone him later tonight, or would you rather I speak to him?"

Karen intervened. "You do it, Cletus," she said. "Jerome would probably hang up on a stranger. You know how he is."

"No, I don't. I've never met him. But maybe he won't hang up on me."

Christy would have laid odds on it. He couldn't see anyone crossing Knight unnecessarily. Lucille reappeared to smile at them as they finished their drinks. She didn't seem to object to bird talk, and Knight thanked Christy for bringing his cockatoos home from Denver, then chatted about an outdoor aviary he hoped to build for them for the warmer months. Christy found himself liking the big man again before they left, but Gala may have had a different opinion of the Knight household. As soon as she hit Knight's driveway, she relieved herself, as if to say to Knight's superior Dobermans, Now that I'm not in the same room with you, here's what I think of you. Karen also seemed glad to be away from the Dobes.

"We'll just take Gala back to the clinic, then think about where would be good for dinner," Christy said.

"Want to go by my condo for another pre-dinner drink?" Karen said. "People new to Vail usually like to see how we natives live."

"Grand," Christy said. "And how about an after-dinner drink at Dr. Potter's condo? He left it for me to live in, but I haven't managed to get by there yet."

"Love it," Karen said. "What did you think of Knight's place?"

"I was overwhelmed," Christy said. "What does Knight do, anyway?"

Karen looked at him with mild surprise, and Christy realized that such questions apparently weren't asked in Vail. It was like the resorts his mother enjoyed. People didn't do things; they just were. But Karen obligingly delved into her memory and reported, "I've heard a rumor: Mafia. Now, when you hear someone's connected with the Mafia, it's usually a rumor that the person's started himself. Just to seem important. But with Cletus, I wonder."

Mafia connections or no, Christy figured that in Knight he had seen power. No, Power. With a capital *P*. Once started, Karen chatted on about Knight. He was so exclusive that he didn't date Vailites. He seemed to prefer blacks, and a succession of gorgeous young black women appeared, then disappeared, and Knight himself often disappeared. Off to dog shows, Alicia Johnson said, but who knew? Alicia? She was officially Knight's secretary, and she hired and fired houseboys and gardeners and did the grocery shopping, and she dog-sat when Knight was away. Wouldn't it be lovely to have someone to attend to all of life's junk: answer the phones and renew the car insurance and stuff like that?

Christy agreed. That evening, eager to get on with a

happy night out with Karen, he would gladly have assigned an underling to exercise Agatha the Sheepdog, leaving him free only to check the two cat patients that were staying overnight. He crated Gala, put Agatha in an outside run, and looked in on the cats. Schopenhauer, now minus a needle in his stomach, felt lively and interested in a human hand to scratch his chin, but the other gray tiger, Mildred, even after an IV that afternoon, was still lethargic. She had ignored the basket Miss Carroll had put in her cage so she could feel private and protected, and huddled instead in her litter box. She still refused food. Christy cleaned Mildred up and patiently stuffed Nutri-Cal into the roof of her mouth, stroking her throat until the little cat swallowed enough to give her some nourishment. No temperature. He put Mildred in her basket and called to Karen that he'd be only another couple of minutes, then went to bring in Agatha.

The Sheepdog was her usual bouncy self. Gala jumped up when Christy brought Agatha into the dog ward, claiming that it was her turn to go out again, but Christy ignored her. He stayed with Agatha briefly, petting her, letting her bounce. A black, oozy fluid left a stain on his hand. He looked closer. Agatha had gotten something on her back. Oil? How could that be?

She wouldn't stop her joyous bounding, so he led her into an examination room and raised the table. That always quieted her. He looked closely at her back, parting the clipped-off locks of hair, parting, parting, and then he felt sick. How in hell could he have overlooked this? The apparent hair growth on the dog's back was just long locks from her sides and neck. No hair grew on the back at all. It was one massive, aging wound, running from withers to croup. Necrotic tissue, black and thickly crusted, oozing serum, was everywhere. It was as if someone had poured a caustic substance all over the dog's back, burning it. An accident surely. She'd gotten under a car, gotten grease or oil on her coat, and some fool had poured on cleaning fluid or the like to try and clean it. Christy closed his eyes for a moment, cursing himself. Here he'd been running around all day poking into things that didn't concern him, and all the time she'd surely been in pain from the vast wound on her back. How could she bounce and act so happy?

"Why didn't you tell me, Agatha?" he whispered. Then he let her down from the table but closed her into the examination room and went to beg Karen's forgiveness.

Dinner was off. Exploring condos was off. He'd have to start immediately removing the dead tissue from poor Agatha's back.

6

AGATHA HAD SHOWN TEETH to Christy when he first clipped her. When he worked around to her rump, she'd swung on him, not biting, but hitting his hand with her muzzle, demonstrating to him that if he kept on bothering her she easily could bite. Yet she lay completely still, with no fussing, while he worked late into the night removing much of the crust of dead tissue from her back. The next morning, when he started on the rest of it, she only trembled but didn't snap. Gala begged for attention, but she got breakfast and a morning-long assignment to an outside run instead. With the two sick cats, Agatha's back, and the morning's slate of patients, Christy was busy. He asked Miss Carroll to put in a call for Agatha's rescuers, then had to keep them waiting while he set a broken ulna for a large white rabbit. Cars came and went. Before Christy could get to the ward for Agatha, he noticed that one car pulled up in the rear, apparently looking for a parking spot. He hurried. He wanted to show Agatha's ladies the wound on her back and confer with them before another patient could claim precedence.

Agatha's back looked ghastly. He'd shaved all surrounding hair to the skin, and the wound was fully revealed. It was no longer black. He'd at least accomplished the removal of the necrotic tissue. But the tissue underneath was like badly butchered meat, and he'd smeared it with a thick layer of bright yellow Furacin.

"I've also started her on a massive course of antibiotics," he explained to the sisters.

Harriet nodded, face stern. "It's like treatment for first-degree burns, isn't it?" she said. "Keep the infection down and hope."

"I think she'll get well," Christy said.

Jean carefully scratched Agatha's ears. "Christy, can't we medicate Agatha's back and give her the pills? We were going to come see you this morning anyway. We've taken the chalet we were thinking about, and we want to keep her with us."

"You might end up buying new carpeting for the chalet," Christy warned. "I applied that Furacin with a pretty heavy trowel, and the moment Agatha brushes something, it's apt to leave a stain. Besides, her bladder's not under very good control. I'd thought it was just a hormone thing. Spayed bitches will sometimes leak urine unless you keep them on a light dose of estrogen. I've had to change her bedding two or three times a day. I figured I'd give her an estrogen shot, but I guess I know the real problem now. With that back, the old girl is apt to exhibit no end of minor symptoms."

"We can keep her in the kitchen. It's not carpeted," Jean said. "There's a nice fenced yard, and we'll take her for walks and just generally be with her. Surely being with people who love her and take care of her will help her get well faster."

"With that shaved back she'll sunburn if she gets too

83

much sun," Christy warned. "I'm afraid she'd be too much trouble for you."

"We'll hold a parasol over her on walks and only let her in the yard in the afternoons. It's shaded then."

"What can I say? Agatha's your dog, and certainly she'd be happier in a home environment. If you're willing to put up with her temporary problems, well, it's not as though she requires hospitalization."

Jean and Harriet both smiled, but there was a grimness in the sisters' expressions. If they ever chanced to meet the former owners who had so neglected Agatha, Christy wouldn't have wanted to be in the people's shoes. The women had brought a new nylon slip-collar and leash for Agatha, at the sight of which the dog began her zany bouncing, liberally smearing Furacin on their double-knit pants suits. Agatha headed for the door, and she cried a little when she had to be held back for a short discussion of diet and when she should be brought in again for Christy to check her back.

But, oh, how she bounded in leaving the clinic. She lunged toward the creek, apparently demanding a walk, and the two women had little choice but to go with her. Christy saw he would have to give them a pointer or two about collaring Agatha high under the ears for better leash control. He turned from the window to meet Miss Carroll's beautiful smile.

"Our patients love leaving us, don't they?" she said.

"Yes. We save their lives, and they still think we're the bad guys."

"Are you keeping both cats over the weekend, or do you want them picked up?" Miss Carroll asked.

"The little guy with the needle is okay, but I'd feel better if I could keep him under observation through tomorrow," Christy said. "The other poor little cat, Mildred, still isn't responding. She'd better stay."

"Leukemia?" Miss Carroll asked softly.

"I'm afraid so. Can you ask the owners for permission to

send off a blood specimen to Fort Collins? I'll keep her on IVs through the weekend. Where's our other patient?"

"We're through for the morning," Miss Carroll said.

"Oh. I thought I saw someone else drive in. Well, I promise I'll get the distilled water this afternoon. Anything else we need?"

They wound down the week's work. Agatha came back from the creek, dragging her new owners, and she went straight to their station wagon, as though she already knew it belonged to her. Christy and Miss Carroll exchanged grins as Agatha was chauffeured away, then it was good-bye. Christy locked the front door of the clinic and luxuriated in the knowledge that he had a whole afternoon to himself and a whole day tomorrow, too. It was too bad Karen had left so early for Colorado Springs. Maybe dinner tonight, though? Christy whistled his way back to Ward Three for a cat check, then went out the back door to get Gala in from her run.

He saw Gala huddled in the rear of her run looking hang-dog. He saw Cletus Knight in the middle of the run leaning over a yellow-green puddle. He saw two of Knight's coddled Dobermans poking their heads out the window of a silver Bentley, ready to bark, which they did upon sighting Christy. He saw red.

"Get the hell away from my dog," Christy shouted. "What do you think you're doing?"

Knight turned with lazy grace. "Get her inside fast," he said. "If this isn't antifreeze, I'll drink it myself. I saw her lapping at it."

Christy's mind churned. Antifreeze. Ethylene glycol, sweet-tasting, pleasant-smelling, so tempting that a cat or a kid would drink it as quickly as a dog, so deadly that a few tablespoons could kill a medium-sized dog, as it seemed to do every fall when people serviced their cars for a cold winter to come. Antifreeze, good Lord, first an emetic if Gala had just drunk the stuff? Then what?

Both mind and body started to work. Christy rushed into

the run, brushing past Knight, and picked up Gala, cradling her in his arms. About sixty, sixty-five pounds, he judged. He'd weigh her to be sure. Gala squirmed, but he held her to his chest and rushed back to the clinic. Knight was right behind him.

Christy was so upset that at first he couldn't find the right buttons to raise the examination table on which he deposited Gala. Knight stepped to the other side to restrain the dog. Christy smelled her breath when he finally got the table up. Chemical smell. She'd obviously swallowed some of the anti-freeze, but how much? She was frightened and tried to jump off the table, and Christy cautioned himself to calm down. Knight held her firmly, one huge hand around her muzzle and one on her back, but fighting against them wouldn't help the dog's condition.

"All right, Gala, you're a good girl," Christy said. "You haven't done anything wrong." Was her mouth slimy? He should have checked the run. She might have started vomiting already. God in heaven, how long ago had she drunk the stuff?

"An emetic," Christy decided. "I'll assume she just drank it. Damn it, why didn't I keep a closer eye on her this morning?"

"Because you were busy all morning," Knight said. "Shall I let her go? Do you give it by mouth?"

"No, an injection. We'll get her into the surgery. It'll be fluid and ethanol therapy after that."

While Knight carried Gala into the surgery, Christy grabbed a syringe, then went into action. After Gala brought up the contents of her stomach, she obviously felt less lively. But nausea was to be expected. She lay quietly while Christy started the IV in the right foreleg. He'd need a lot of fluid. Lactated ringer. Then the ethanol to decrease production of toxic metabolites. He asked Knight to hold Gala's foreleg extended while he looked up the dosage. The level in the IV bottle slowly decreased as Christy double-checked his math on 5.5 ml of twenty-percent ethanol per kilogram of body weight. He would give it intravenously every four hours for five treatments, then every six hours for four more treatments.

As Christy added the ethanol to the IV, Knight asked, "What will this do?"

"Depress the central nervous system, among other things. An unavoidable side effect. But the antifreeze makes them feel drunk. I guess it sort of evens out."

"The antifreeze destroys kidney tissue, doesn't it?"

"Not if I can prevent a buildup of oxalate crystals."

"So you'll monitor kidney function?"

"Among other things. Overhydration could cause pulmonary edema if you don't monitor fluid therapy pretty closely."

"It looks like you're stuck here then," Knight said. "Can you hold on to her for a while? I'll be back soon."

Christy started to call after him. He owed the big man an apology. But Gala stirred uneasily, so Christy stroked her with his free hand, watching her. The eyes closed. Coma? No, certainly not. Nausea, confusion, and feeling darned drunk. There was no way he could count on her having up-chucked all the antifreeze.

How did it get there? Or, rather, since it couldn't possibly have been an accidental spill, who would have deliberately poured an appetizing puddle of poison out for her? Thank God it wasn't strychnine. Of course, strychnine probably wasn't all that easy to get, and you could poison dozens of dogs and cats from the contents of the ordinary kitchen or garage. He ought to call Officer Shannon. Later. He was in for a long wait. If she showed improved clinical signs after twelve to sixteen hours, the prognosis would be favorable. "Come on, girl," he whispered to her. "Come on, make it."

It seemed scarcely fifteen minutes before he heard foot-steps in the back hall. It was Cletus Knight returning with a huge picnic hamper. Christy had cleaned up and put Gala in a recovery cage in the surgery until it was time for her to be dripped again, and it obviously didn't occur to Knight that the dog could be left alone. He took a paper towel and the spray bottle of disinfectant that always sat near the stainless steel operating table, cleaned it without comment, then began pulling bowls and plates from the hamper. There was a gorgeous salad, with artistically arranged tomatoes, green beans, black olives, green pepper, onion slices. There was a hot pot of goulash and noodles. There was French bread and even a large thermos bottle of iced tea.

Knight smiled. "Lunch," he said. "I had everything just about ready at home."

"You cooked all this?"

"Sure. I like to cook. Lucille and Alicia can go out for something low-cal. They're always complaining about gaining weight on my cooking."

He deftly served Christy a plate of salad with a topping of tuna and anchovies.

"Salade Niçoise," Knight said. "It's supposed to be a main dish, I guess, but I get hungry. Figured you were, too. I hope you don't mind the iced tea. When you grow up in the South, you get addicted to it. Would you rather I ran back to the house for a bottle of wine?"

"No. No!" Christy said. They dived in. Knight ate without conversation, but it was a companionable silence, broken only by the clunk of the thermos as he refilled Christy's glass, the rattle of a serving spoon as he reached for more goulash. After two helpings, Christy went to Dr. Potter's office to put on a fresh pot of coffee. The pile of notes Potter had left, he noticed, was taking on the appearance of a trash pile, sliding slowly across the desk, becoming decorated with coffee-cup rings. The uppermost one pleaded, "If you run across an unidentified X ray of a canine femur, please hold it for me. It's Lee's Fanci, but I've misplaced it." Christy had promised himself faithfully to read all of Potter's notes this weekend. With Gala to keep under close observation, it looked as if he'd get his chance.

Back in surgery, Knight was eating his way through the rest of the feast. Gala's head was up, watching the last of the goulash. "Not this time, Gala," Knight told her. "You've got to settle for your good old IV. How about it, Christy? There'a a little salad left."

"Thanks, I couldn't eat another bite. You've saved my life. You saved Gala's, too. I hope you'll forgive me for shouting at you that way. I got confused for a minute there. I didn't understand."

"I did. Don't worry, I would have shouted at you, too. Anyway, I liked what you said. 'Get away from my dog.'"

"Did I say that?"

"Yep. It looks like she's moving in on you."

"If she lives to do it," Christy said worriedly.

"You think it's in question?"

"I hope not."

"You're just acting like an anxious dog owner," Knight said.

"I'll tell you one thing," Christy said. "I'd like to get my hands on whoever did this to her."

"I have nothing against revenge, but you'd probably end up in jail," Knight said. "There might be a better way to go about things."

"You know who it was, don't you?"

"No." Knight's huge hands moved among the empty plates packing things neatly back into the picnic hamper. "I'm just suspicious."

"This guy Jerome?"

"It's a good bet. He's been acting a little oddly, people say. Almost as if he's hiding. It seems that he was out of town for a week or ten days. Then he came back a couple of days ago, picked up his mail, and has promptly disappeared again. That's what I came by to tell you. I knew you were interested in him, so I asked around."

"If it was really Jerome who gave Gala such a nice lunch of antifreeze, I'm not only interested, I'm enthralled."

"You could tell the police if you wanted to," Knight said. "Just leave me out of it, okay?"

"Jerome. Damn it, I can't understand it. She was his own dog, wasn't she?"

"Well, she belonged to him briefly, at least. He took her out of the pound in Littleton a few weeks ago. She'd been abandoned. Some slobs left her locked up in a rented house after they skipped out and left the rent owing. A real estate agent found her. Figured she'd been there alone for four or five days. No food, of course. But she was okay."

"How did you find that out?" Christy asked.

"I made a few phone calls," Knight said.

Knight looked quietly at Christy as if waiting for more questions, but Christy found he had nothing he dared ask this baffling man. Something in Knight's eyes warned that how he had discovered even such innocent if obscure facts as a dog's recent history was his private business. Christy concentrated instead on the dog. "I guess Jerome's got adoption papers on her from the pound," he said. "The rat. Do you suppose he'll turn up wanting her?"

"Maybe not. Maybe he's dead, like his chum Philip Schumacher. More likely he's on the run or staying under cover."

Christy discovered that he was smiling. "Good," he said. "Either way he can't claim Gala."

"There's a possibility he might be somewhere close about," Knight said. "I understand he has a cabin near Notch Mountain. He goes up there once in a while."

"Is it close enough to drive to Vail and try to poison a dog?"

"Easily," Knight said. "Also close enough to drive down and try to shoot one."

Before Christy could stop himself, his sandy eyebrows rose with surprise. He had told only the police, no one else, about Gala's being shot at. But he stuck to the main question. "We can't really be sure it's Jerome who's been trying to kill Gala," he pointed out.

"Too true. But think about it, Christy. That's a Doberman Pinscher you've got, not a pussycat. Oh, sure, anybody could take a potshot at her from a safe distance. But she wouldn't let just anyone in the world walk into a small area with her and stay there long enough to pour out a dose of antifreeze."

Since Knight had somehow learned about the shooting attempt, he might also have learned how Gala ran in back of Christy to hide, but Christy found he was reluctant to say more than "Maybe she's all bark and no bite. Or couldn't somebody have stayed outside the run and just sloshed the antifreeze inside?"

"It's a possibility," Knight said.

"But why try to kill little Gala? What would it accomplish? Oh, I get it. It's like the Vail police think. She's a witness to Philip's murder, and she might give the murderer away."

Now it was Knight's turn to raise an eyebrow, but his expression was skeptical. "It might be simpler than that," he said. "For instance, Jerome would know that a police inquiry would turn up a party-party relationship between him and Philip, but in a party town like Vail that wouldn't mean much. But the dog, that means a closer link. Jerome's not the type to take in a dog just to be bighearted. She was protection. For something. Something that Jerome is trying to disassociate himself from. Like stolen goods. Get rid of the dog, and you get rid of proof of that particular link."

Christy glanced at the black Doberman, lying so still now. "You couldn't give me directions to Jerome's cabin, could you? As soon as I can leave Gala, I'd like to talk to that guy."

"I'll go with you," Knight said.

Christy sat up straight. He might not be as big as Knight, but he didn't need any hand-holding. "That's not necessary," he said.

"You might get lost," Knight said.

He left after inquiring if Christy needed anything. Christy poured another cup of coffee and returned to the surgery to sit with the dog and ponder. If he could just remember what kind of car he'd seen nose toward the back of the clinic that morning. But he'd been distracted, and it was gone from his mind. For that matter, Knight himself could have poisoned Gala. His presence in her run surely demonstrated that he'd had the opportunity. There was a heaviness in Christy's stomach. Lunch? It could have been poisoned, too. No, nonsense, Knight had served himself from the same platter and pots. The heavy feeling just came from eating too well.

Didn't it?

The phone rang lengthily at the reception desk while Christy was giving Gala her IV again at four that afternoon, and he got to it too late to answer it. As evening drew near and the dog seemed to be doing well, Christy decided to move an extra IV stand to the cabin. He could drip her as she lay in her familiar basket for the eight o'clock, midnight, and four A.M. IVs. The phone extension in the cabin was ringing when he entered on his second trip, lugging Dr. Potter's pile of notes, and he grabbed the phone in time to hear crackly static but no voice. The haunting thought of an emergency call that he hadn't answered kept Christy alert for the phone after that, but it didn't ring. He took a wobbly Gala to the cabin and returned to Dr. Potter's office for ice and a new bottle of Scotch he'd bought. Then while he was with the hospitalized cats, the phone bell shrilled, but it was only the owner of the rabbit with the broken ulna reporting that the rabbit refused to eat and asking if it should be force-fed. As the rabbit was severely overweight, Christy explained that a twenty-four-hour fast was to its advantage, but asked that he be phoned the next morning if the rabbit still refused food.

When he returned to the cabin, he found Gala curled up in her basket looking guilty. Scraps of Dr. Potter's notes were scattered everywhere. One of Christy's shoes was in Gala's basket with her, half hidden under her favorite black glove. He knew he ought to scold her, but she was having a hard enough time already. He took back the shoe and spent the rest of the evening looking over the ragged remnants of the notes. "Harry Kyle owes me $155, and if he comes in with that Pit Bull of his, maybe you can collect it." "Can I impose and ask you to mark the no-book-wanted square and mail back any book club notices that come in?" "Tell Miss Carroll . . ." Tell her what? Christy couldn't find the end to that note.

There were additional notes about Dr. Potter's cherished potted plants. Give them all only tepid water. Give one-quarter-strength Miracid with every watering to the Boston fern in his bathroom. Poor Potter, if he only knew that Christy hadn't managed to make it to the condo, he'd be tearing out his hair. The last scraps sounded manic: ". . . a snake." "Salt?" ". . . and help yourself to the lox in . . ." The fragments began to dance in Christy's mind until he was tempted to throw them all in the fireplace, but he kept them carefully. Maybe he'd do better at deciphering them another time.

Gala seemed sober but subdued the next morning. Her central venous pressure and other clinical signs were looking pretty good, and Christy began to feel optimistic about her condition. He moved her gear back to the ward and supervised all her exercise periods that Sunday morning. He had to do it anyway to measure her urine output, but he was also determined to keep her safe. He kept both front and back doors of the clinic locked. The phone brought another emergency shortly after Gala's ten o'clock IV. Two Akita bitches had decided to see which one was the toughest. They belonged to the same family but arrived in separate cars, still trying to get at one another. For both, it was mild anesthesia, Delta Albaplex for possible infection, the clippers to reveal the puncture wounds that had to be cleaned and treated. One Akita preferred a neck grip, the other the juncture of the humerus and ulna, Christy noticed. He kept

them an hour to get over their grogginess from the light anesthesia and was seeing them out the front door to their separate cars when loud knocking began at the back door.

It was Bev Farrell, wearing a dress and looking as though
she'd been to church. "Why did you lock the door?" she
demanded. "I always come in the back. Where's that darling
Old English? Would you believe it, I dreamed about her last
night. O-o-o-h, she's not here. You didn't put her down?
Now, damn you, Christy—"

"No, no, no," he said. "She's an outpatient now. What're
you doing here?"

"Cletus Knight asked me to baby-sit your Doberman. Hi,
Gala. Quiet. I say, quiet! Stop barking this instant, you
gorgeous devil."

From her crate, Gala puffed her cheeks out tentatively, an
unvoiced bark that she suppressed. Bev skipped to her crate
and unlocked it, but at least she had sense enough to let the
dog come out to her, not reach in to pet Gala.

"Here, she's confined to keep her from moving around too
much," Christy scolded.

"Then I'll take her to the cabin. It's not my idea of luxury, but at least the dog can rest more comfortably there
than in your old clinic. We'll wait for you there. Cletus said
bring your Jeep and meet him at his house. Hurry up,
Christy. He's ready. But tell me first what I do with Gala.
Nothing by mouth? Water only? What?"

She barely let him answer before all but pushing him out
the door. Christy turned back with a worried question about
more emergency calls, but Bev told him impatiently she knew
where to refer any if they came, and Christy did well to grab a
jacket before he pulled away in the Jeep. His own Sunday
garb was old jeans and a work shirt, but he knew he wasn't
being summoned to Knight's house for a social event.
Jerome's cabin. Jerome. Dead with six bullets in him maybe?
Nice, if Jerome was Gala's would-be murderer. Or alive and
considerate enough to answer a few questions. Slowly. Very

slowly, so Christy could see how his hands felt around Jerome's throat. Christy thought that dog-poisoning should be a hanging crime.

Knight came out his front door with his big male Doberman and the youngest black bitch. He asked, "How's Gala? Is everything okay?"

"She seems to be doing fine," Christy assured him. "I've still got her on IVs, of course. Her next one's due at four o'clock. Will we be back by then?"

"Easily," Knight said. "When is the IV after that? Eight o'clock?"

"No, ten. She's on a six-hour shift now."

Apparently satisfied, Knight said, "It's a nice day for a ride. You don't mind if a couple of my Dobes go along, do you? I need to get Annie out more. Socializing."

Christy wasn't sure what Knight was talking about, but he liked having the dogs. Both climbed with dignity into the back seat of the Jeep at Knight's command, and the menacing-looking black male leaned forward and slurped the back of Christy's head. The young bitch played follow-the-leader and sniffed Christy's ears thoroughly before giving him a daintier kiss.

"He's Poe. She's Annabel Lee. Annie for short," Knight said. "Head west on Seventy, then take the Minturn exit."

"How far is it?"

"Maybe thirty minutes. We'll have to walk a little at the end."

"I want to thank you very sincerely for doing this," Christy said.

Knight looked him over silently. At length he said, "Well, Christy, I'd do a little favor for the dog, even if I wouldn't do it for you. But if it's a favor to you, too, that's good. My dogs like you. That makes you okay in my books."

Christy grinned. "Do you always take your dogs' word on judging character?"

"Yep," Knight said. "One of the greatest of all Doberman

experts once said that if your Dobes don't like a person, watch him. Chances are he'll turn out to be a rotter. But it looks like you've got their stamp of approval, and you've got mine."

Christy hadn't felt so warmly proud of himself since Jimmy Williamson had presented him with a stick of Juicy Fruit in the third grade and thereby started a lifelong friendship. His newest friend seemed to have nothing more to say, so Christy gave himself over to enjoying the drive. Like so many roadways, it followed water, first little Gore Creek, then, when they turned off, Eagle River. Outside a small town named Minturn they passed a ranger station. Christy caught a glimpse of the road ahead of them snaking steeply up a cliffside, but Knight directed him off at a side road. A sign pointed the way to a pair of public campgrounds, but they went on past them some five or six miles through grave green pines and leafless aspens, climbing, climbing. Christy overshot the next turn and had to back up. It was a two-rut path rather than a road, and no one had been picky when it came to clearing rock out of the way. They banged and scraped their way upward, perhaps two more miles. Christy wondered if he would have to buy Dr. Potter a new Jeep. At the last wriggle of the ruts, they emerged in a flat clearing, and Christy was amazed to see a late-model Chevrolet and a pickup sitting side by side near the trees. How in the world had a city car like the Chevy managed to get up there?

"It looks like Jerome has guests," Knight said. "Just park in the road. We won't outstay anybody." He locked the dogs in the Jeep and told the male, "Poe, look after things." Poe's ears pricked up so tightly they almost touched together. He jumped over the seat and took up a position behind the steering wheel. Annie scrambled over after him, looking interested but puzzled.

"Aren't you going to bring the dogs?"

"Not this time. The cabin shouldn't be far. Jerome's overweight, so he's probably lazy. If you want a really pretty hike sometime, take the campground road a little farther, and there's a trail up Notch Mountain. You ought to go. You can see Holy Cross Mountain at the end of the trail. Big cross of snow. The old-timers said anyone who climbed up to see the cross was cured of anything that ailed them. You could haul your patients up there."

Christy didn't know why Knight was feeling chatty. Surely they should be creeping through the underbrush, tiptoeing, watching for the enemy. Then suddenly the enemy was there, three young men at the bend of the path. One carried a rifle. Knight didn't look worried, but Christy was.

"You, there," Knight called. "Tell Jerome it's Cletus Knight. And don't go pointing rifles at people, son. You might get shot."

"Did you bring a gun?" Christy whispered.

"Yes. But I won't have to use it. Jerome thinks of himself as a pro. His little creeps won't try to shoot anybody unless they get mighty, mighty nervous."

The three youths ahead of them held a brief conference, then one called back, "Jerome's not here. Turn around and go home. No visitors wanted."

Knight said, "In case he is here and you just happened to overlook him, you'd better tell him who I am."

They conferred again, then retreated around the bend in the path. Knight covered the distance swiftly. Christy ran to catch up. From the bend, he could see a log cabin, with another old log structure near it that had apparently been cannibalized to repair the first. The setting was a delight, a sunny meadow, but the cabin was an eyesore. Its two small windows were covered with plastic film, tattered, sagging as badly as the cabin. Yet to one side there was a neat screened-in porch that must have been inviting in summer months. Christy thought he saw movement through one of the film-covered windows. Then four young men came out, minus one rifle. No one was grinning like a Cheshire cat, so

Christy didn't know if the fourth youth was Jerome or just another of his underlings.

"Don't come any farther," the new arrival called.

Knight said, "All right, here's my message for Jerome: The cops know the Doberman he tried to kill belonged to him. So they already know about the connection between him and Philip Schumacher. Don't go after the dog again. There's no point in it. And I take a very personal interest in people who try to kill a dog."

A fifth man, heavily bearded, plump, older than the others, came out of the cabin. He was the man Christy had seen at the post office with a big stack of mail in his arms, staring curiously at Gala. Today he looked apprehensive, but he spoke up boldly.

"I'm not real thrilled to see you, Mr. Knight," he said. "Did you go blabbing to the cops that I'm here?"

Knight laughed, a deep rumble in his chest. "I'll tell you, Jerome, it came to my attention a while ago that you'd been making inquiries about me. I don't know how far down the road you got, but one of the first things anyone might learn is that I'm not much for blabbing, and I'm not much for talking to policemen. I'm only filling you in on how things are going to be about the dog. She's coming along nicely after that antifreeze you gave her. There aren't going to be any more tries at poisoning her. Believe me."

"I didn't poison her," Jerome said.

"You'd be a fool to admit it," Knight said.

"Oh, come on, she's my dog. I wouldn't poison my own dog."

"She's not yours anymore. Let's get that understood. If Dr. Christy can't keep her, she's going to join my gang. You might say I've adopted her. As a sort of godfather."

Jerome looked aggrieved, but obviously Gala the Doberman wasn't the only thing on his mind. "Don't get the wrong idea about any of this," he told Knight. "I don't know what you've heard, and maybe Philip deserved it, but I didn't have a thing to do with killing him. None of my people did."

"That's your business," Knight said. "You've got things straight about the dog now, right?"

"Yeah, right," Jerome said.

"Happy landing," Knight said. He waved and started back down the path.

"Just a minute," Jerome called.

"Forget it," Knight called back. "I'm not interested in your problems." In a lower voice, he said, "How about it, Christy, are you up to a little jogging once we get around the bend? They're going to try to cut us off at the road, and I don't want them disturbing my dogs."

"They're going to attack us?"

"The Three Musketeers and D'Artagnan might, but I expect Cardinal Richelieu will stay at the cabin and wring his hands. Got to be observant. Didn't you see the other trail on the left side of the cabin? Didn't you see how they kept looking at it? Some people get annoyed easily. Okay, ready, set, go!"

They were very high, every bit of ten to eleven thousand feet, and Christy's ears buzzed the moment he started running. Knight loped along more easily, but the four young men might be much better acclimated for foot races at high altitude. Christy listened hard for the roaring barks of a pair of alarmed Dobermans, but he heard only his own heartbeat pounding in his ears and the sound of his labored breathing.

"Here," Knight said. "Very, very quiet now." He swerved off the path, taking them through a grove of thickly growing aspens filled with downed trees that, dead of old age, sagged against their vigorous successors. How to be quiet in such a thicket? Christy climbed and at one point crawled. He was almost twenty feet behind Knight when the big man suddenly crouched. Knight was at the edge of the grove. Poe and Annie started barking.

Footsteps, running? Christy couldn't be sure. He crawled

slowly toward Knight. Two yards closer to Knight. Another yard. Knight sprang to his feet, uncoiling like a spring, and stepped from the trees. There was an "Ooof," and Christy saw that one of the young men had collided with Knight. As though he was breaking a brittle twig from a tree, Knight stripped a rifle from the youth's hands with one movement of his powerful arms. Then he threw the youth away. Just tossed him, a piece of unwanted trash. The youth plummeted into the aspens with a louder "Ooof," then lay silent.

No need for stealth now on Christy's part. He crashed through the edge of the aspen grove and joined Knight on the path, shoulder to shoulder. Knight gave him an approving grin, then turned the grin on the three youths confronting him. They stood frozen, in Indian file, no other firearms in evidence. At the sight of Knight's smile, the first one in line backed into the second.

"Oh?" Knight said. He glanced ostentatiously at the rifle he held casually against his right shoulder. "This?" he said. He threw the rifle well behind him and Christy, and he grinned again, in broad invitation.

The first little Indian accepted, perhaps spurred by humiliation at having backed away from Knight. He lunged at the big man, and Knight's forearm banged against his throat, and the youth sagged to his knees, gagging.

"Two down, two to go," Knight said. He wasn't even breathing hard. "Which one would you like, Christy?"

The two still on their feet turned and ran. They must indeed have been accustomed to the altitude. They made good speed. Knight poked an idle toe at the gagging young man on his knees before him, glanced at the discarded young man in the aspens, and said, "I guess they'll live. If they don't, you'd better by God remember one thing, Christy: You were never here, and maybe you've never even met me."

"Don't worry," Christy said. He turned and picked up the rifle.

"Leave it," Knight said. "We'll be far down the mountain before they decide to come back this way."

"It has your fingerprints on it," Christy said. He took out his handkerchief and started polishing. "Maybe you'd just as soon not leave a gun with your fingerprints in some damned fool's possession."

Knight gave him another look of approval. "Christy, you have a devious mind. That shows promise. Thanks. I owe you one."

"Nope. I owe you several."

Knight trotted to the Jeep to reassure his dogs. Their barking had turned to agonized whines as they pleaded for freedom to join the action. Christy polished the rifle thoroughly and leaned it against the Chevy's fender. Nice .30-30 Savage. He wondered where Jerome and friends had stolen it.

Poe and Annie both growled at Christy when he neared the Jeep. They were excited and ready. Knight quieted them, and Christy jockeyed the Jeep through a country turnaround and started back down the mountain. He said to Knight, "I've got three questions. Okay?"

Annie decided to leap goatlike into the front seat and sit on Knight's lap. He cradled her and scratched her chest delicately and said, "Maybe."

"They're easy ones. First, are you sure now it was Jerome who tried for Gala?"

Knight was silent for several seconds, then admitted, "I'm uneasy about it. I think he did try to shoot her. He started our little conversation with that guilty look. Take my word for it, I'm an expert. But I almost believed him about not trying to poison her. Maybe he assigned the job to one of his underlings, and the underling got bright ideas of his own. Or maybe it was someone else entirely. Second question?"

"Did you really fill in the cops about Gala having belonged to Jerome?"

"No. I kind of thought you might do that. Last question?"

Christy said, "It's about Poe and Annie. What would they have done if they'd been on the path with us when the guys attacked?"

Christy hadn't realized that Knight was tense until he saw the big man relax. Knight smiled and continued scratching. Annie closed her eyes, the better to enjoy it. He said, "Aside from getting shot at, which I'd just as soon avoid, Annie would probably have run back and forth and barked a lot. She's too young to be very sure of herself yet. Poe would have tried to rip somebody's throat out. That's something else I'd just as soon avoid. Say that Poe was a hero and saved both our lives. You'd still get flak about 'vicious Doberman' from 'concerned citizens' with nothing better on their minds than killing a dog for protecting his owner. Dobermans get too much bad publicity. So I left them in the car. Does it seem silly?"

"No, but I have to wonder, do your Dobes protect you, or do you protect them?"

"It works both ways. You're going to keep Gala, aren't you?"

"Hell, yes," said Christy. He stepped a shade harder on the accelerator, suddenly anxious to get home to see how his very own dog was doing.

7

BEV FARRELL REFUSED to leave. She was contentedly ensconced in the cabin with Gala. A small fire crackled in the fireplace, and Gala's basket was in front of it, next to a chair Bev had dragged up. Bev had a glass of Scotch and water in her hand, and Gala had Christy's shoe again. Christy took away the shoe and gave Gala a once-over, then made the mistake of telephoning Nat Shannon at the police station before Bev finished her drink.

Shannon was off-duty. Christy left a brief message: Jerome's whereabouts, how to get to the cabin, Jerome's brief ownership of Gala, and his feeble denial of the charge that he tried to destroy the Vail Police Department's chief witness to the Philip Schumacher shooting. He didn't mention Cletus Knight.

Bev's eyes snapped with interest. "No, no, Mark Niemeyer is meeting me here," she protested when Christy thanked her for dog-sitting as a means of implying that she might leave now. "I've got to wait for him. Did you and

Knight really confront Jerome up in the mountains? Tell me everything he did."

"Forget Knight," Christy warned. "He just came along to bulldoze Jerome and his friends into leaving Gala alone. He's like all the other people I've met recently: They don't want to get mixed up in police matters."

"Nobody does," Bev said. She made a liar out of herself by staying long after Mark Niemeyer knocked at the door of the cabin. At Mark's knock, Gala was out of her basket in an instant, barking, and she barked all the harder when Christy opened the door to reveal Mark, this time wearing magnificent gray tweeds.

"Friend, Gala," Bev told the dog sharply. "Now cut it out. It's a friend. Come on in, Mark. Go to your basket, Gala."

The dog obeyed, but Christy decided it was time to take her outside. He heard the phone ring soon after he went out. Only one ring. Bev apparently grabbed it. She leaned out the cabin door, calling, "Shannon wants to see you in about an hour. I told him you'd be here. So if you have any errands to run, go now. Mark and I will stay here with Gala."

"There's nothing I need."

"Sure there is. Dr. Potter said to pick up fresh blood for his house plant. He said you could get it at Tom Miles's chalet."

"Dr. Potter called?" Christy demanded. "When? What did he want? Why didn't you tell me?"

"I forgot," she said. "Stop frowning, Christy. If you wouldn't rush around so much, people could remember to tell you things. It's nothing crucial, for heaven's sake. He said he forgot to write you a note about the blood for his pothos. It's some crazy idea he got in California. He's experimenting."

Mark appeared at her shoulder. "Blood, uck," he said. "What's wrong with fish emulsion?"

"I didn't ask," Bev said. "Dr. Potter did wonder where

you've been for the last three days, Christy. Or maybe it was two days. He said he's tried for you again and again at the condominium, and yesterday at the clinic, too. I told him you were hard at work helping the police solve a murder, so they'd stop accusing you of it."

Christy's heart didn't sink, but his stomach did. He said, "Come on, you didn't tell him that? I've barely left the clinic. I've been hard at work here. I'd better call him back and explain. What's his number?"

"He didn't leave a number."

"But he told you his hotel? The city?" She kept shaking her head. "The state?"

A final shake. Bev said, "I think I heard surf. If you ask me, it's Acapulco. Beach resorts are where he usually takes his rich widows."

Mark raised his eyebrows. "I suppose surf at Acapulco sounds different than it does anywhere else?" he said sourly. "Bev, you have such an active imagination."

"How can I get in touch with him?" Christy asked plaintively.

Bev folded her arms. "You're frowning again, Christy. Listen, go get your blood. Dr. Potter's blood, if you prefer. Shannon's going to be put out if you aren't back when he gets here. We'll rustle up some lunch, so don't worry about that. On second thought, maybe you should worry. You don't seem to have anything in the clinic refrigerator but hamburger meat. Safeway has a special on pork chops. You could go by there. Get carrots while you're at it. And a stick of butter. Pork chops and buttered carrots. Do you like sauerkraut? We could cook it with the chops, with onion and tomato. Really, Christy, do you ever hurry? I'll give you a list."

"What about Karen?" Mark asked at her shoulder. "Didn't she say she was coming?"

"Oh, that," Bev said. "I forgot. No, she said she couldn't make it for lunch, but she's free for dinner. You'll want an intimate little dinner for her here, Christy, so you won't have to leave Gala. You'd better pick up some steaks while you're shopping. I won't write them down. If the steaks don't look too appealing, frozen sole might do. What do you think, Mark? Can he manage baked fish in a wood-burning stove?"

Christy didn't even ask when Karen Hamilton had called. As a phone-answering service, Bev Farrell was a complete wipeout. Never mind, he'd call Karen when he got a free moment. Free time? He wondered what it was like. He took the grocery list away before it could get even longer. Bev handed him written directions for the weird plant-food pickup. Christy hurried.

He didn't ask where the mayonnaise jar full of blood had come from when handed it by an inoffensive-looking man at the front door of a house exhibiting a full Austrian Alps treatment. He wrote down the pothos's dose and drove quickly on to Safeway.

He paused in the parking lot and added distilled water to Bev's list. At last and at least he could accomplish that small mission for Miss Carroll. He jumped out of the Jeep and thought for a moment that he must have banged its door into the car next to him, for an angry male voice shouted, "Hey, you! Christy, or whatever your name is! Hold it right there!"

Christy's first thought was of Jerome's cohorts. Instead, it was the younger Schumacher son, Peter, bearing down on him.

A young couple pushing sacked groceries in a cart stared at Christy. He thought they should stare at Peter. The youngster stalked directly toward Christy, then stopped four feet away, face working with anger, mouth working so hard that he stuttered.

"L-l-listen, you bastard," he panted. "You stay away from my family."

Christy bridled. "You listen," he snapped. "I don't like being yelled at in public, and I don't like being called names. So knock it off."

"Yeah?" Peter said. "Well, you'd just better be careful who picks up the phone the next time you make your dirty calls. If you want to bug the old man, call him at his office. Don't call my house and bother my mother anymore."

"You're making a mistake," Christy said. "I've never telephoned anyone in your family."

"Sure," the boy scoffed. "I'm warning you. Leave my mother alone."

"I haven't even met your mother," Christy said.

"Yeah, sure, and there's cops nosing all over the place trying to connect my brother with some lousy burglary ring. I suppose you didn't have anything to do with that, either?"

Christy felt a stab of guilt, then told himself he was being ridiculous. "I don't run the police station," he said. "Go bark up another tree."

"I've warned you once. I won't say it again," Peter said darkly. "You just be careful about my mother." He wheeled and walked away.

The young couple with the groceries had stopped two cars down. They still stared. Christy shrugged and did his grocery shopping. Vail on a quiet Sunday afternoon in autumn could be confusing.

A second chair for Mark had joined Bev's in front of the fireplace when Christy got back to the cabin, and Gala had his best navy-blue sweater in her basket this time and was chewing on her black glove. A pot of water, possibly in lieu of anything else, boiled on the wood-burning stove. Mark took the groceries from him and started unsacking them, and Bev reached for a skillet. She had the pork chops browning before Mark reached two rib-eye steaks in the bottom of the sack and clucked his tongue. "You might as well find room for these in the clinic refrigerator," he told Christy. "You won't be needing them tonight. You and Karen are dining with Cletus Knight. A pity. They look like nice steaks. Oh, well, maybe you can cook steak for Karen tomorrow. How many carrots do you want, Bev?"

Christy sighed. "What time?" he asked.

"What time what?"

"What time am I picking up Karen for dinner at Knight's?"

"Oh, I don't know. Seven, wasn't it, Bev? Yes, that sounds right. Seven. Now, Christy, don't take that sweater away from Gala. She told us clearly that you always put it over her when she naps."

Nat Shannon arrived just as lunch was ready. Gala did her barking routine again, and Christy tried the command he had heard earlier from Bev. "Friend, Gala," he told the dog. "Get in your basket." After token fussing, she obeyed. He regarded her thoughtfully.

If Shannon had wanted a private conference with Christy, he gave up the plan in return for a plate, and the four of them sat down to eat. Christy told him of the brief clash with Jerome at the mountain cabin. He left out Cletus Knight's role, which meant he had to edit the heroics on the trail when Jerome's four minions came plowing after them. He did mention Knight once, though, to say that Knight had recognized Gala the Doberman as having been in Jerome's charge before she was found in Philip Schumacher's apartment. It was the only way he could explain his interest in Jerome.

"There's something else," Christy told Shannon. "It isn't necessarily true that Gala knew the person who shot the Schumacher boy, and maybe she's not any kind of a witness after all. Apparently almost any well-trained Doberman will let a stranger in at his master's command. I saw eight Dobermans do it when I talked with Knight. And Gala's been doing it all day."

Bev snorted. "You're a nice pair of amateurs," she said. "Certainly a dog will let strangers in. You can't give up having company just because you have dogs. That doesn't mean the plumber or somebody can just march in while the dogs are by themselves. But it's okay when the owner is there."

Shannon paused with a forkful of sauerkraut en route to his

mouth. "Maybe you're right," he said. "I've met Knight's dogs, too. But I'd never have the nerve to shoot Knight with his dogs standing around. I figure I'd have to shoot all of them as well. And that's a little nutty, too, once you stop to think about it. What kind of person would pump six shots into a kid, even a nasty kid like Philip Schumacher, and not bother to kill the dog while he was at it?"

Mark said simply, "An animal lover." He folded his paper napkin and began to pick up plates.

Bev said, "It didn't have to be an animal lover. Maybe Philip put Gala away in a bedroom. She could easily have gotten out later. She knows how to open doors."

Christy and Shannon both gawked. "She does?" Christy said.

"She opened the closet door to get your sweater," Bev said. "I saw her. It's not so unusual. I knew a Briard once who could even shoot a deadbolt. He did it with his teeth. Now, Nat, it's your turn. Christy has told you everything. You tell us. Was Jerome still there when you got to the cabin?"

Shannon shook his head. "Long gone. I wish you'd called me before you went up there, Christy. We want to talk to that guy."

"Don't blame Christy," Bev said. "He's impulsive. So what did you find at the cabin? More troves of stolen treasure?"

"Doesn't anybody do anything but gossip in this town?" Shannon said. "This is serious business, Bev. It's nothing to spread around."

"Who talks? I just listen," she said innocently. "For instance, I heard you found a whole golf bag full of men's and women's watches at Philip's apartment."

Christy said, "Did you? Why didn't you mention it? Hell, Nat, I never hold anything back on you."

"Uh-huh, sure," Shannon said. "You tell me every little thing, don't you? Like how you drove alone up to Jerome's cabin, a stranger in these parts, but knowing exactly how to find your way? Never mind. I guess there's no harm in telling you we found a warehouse full of cameras and jewelry and stereos stashed at Jerome's cabin. It'll all be in the *Denver Post* tomorrow anyway. How reporters get onto these things I'll never know. They've been calling my office every day since Philip got shot, and today they've already called twice trying to make a connection between the burglaries we've been having and all the stuff that showed up in Denver."

"Denver?" Bev said quickly. "Something showed up in Denver?"

"You might say that. Philip pawned over a thousand dollars' worth of jewelry in Denver the day he was killed. He had the money in his pocket when he died. No pawn tickets, but it wasn't hard to figure out."

Mark stopped rattling plates. "Ah," he said with satisfaction, "he was ripping off Jerome, and Jerome shot him."

Bev said, "It could work. Jerome was the ring's Fagin. That's why he went out of town so often, to fence the stuff they burgled. So Philip waited until Jerome was off on a selling trip, and he did a little selling of his own, and that's why Jerome shot him. Is that it, Nat? Though I can't see why Jerome didn't search Philip's pockets after he shot him."

"When you've got it all backed up with evidence, please let me know," Shannon said. "Good pork chops, Bev, Mark. Thanks for the lunch."

"Sit down, Nat. You've got to tell us. Jerome was behind all the burglaries, wasn't he? He got his friends to steal for him? And paid them off with parties and pot?"

"I have no comment," Shannon said. "Which is precisely how I plan to respond to any conjectures by reporters."

He left, over Bev's and Mark's objections, and they left Christy with the dirty dishes. Christy called Karen and got no answer. He called Knight and found only Alicia on duty, with confirmation that Knight expected him and Karen at seven. Gala was to be brought, to avoid leaving her unattended at home, and her ten o'clock IV was to come with her in case they lingered long at the dinner table. Christy gave up on confusion and dirty dishes, threw two more logs on the fire, and took a nap. Gala joined him on the bed. The closet door was open, and she had his navy-blue sweater in her teeth. Christy muttered, "Shannon was right about you. You are a thief. A member in good standing of a burglary ring." He covered her with the sweater and went back to sleep.

The first snowflakes fell soundlessly, with no wind to warn of their coming. An inch was mounded on the windowsills of the cabin before Christy realized that it was snowing at all. Then the wind came, and huge flakes whispered against the windows. They said, Come out, and Christy did. Gala begged to accompany him. She seemed to be feeling fine, so he let her run unleashed for a few minutes about the cabin. She whirled and bit at the flakes and ran at him repeatedly, leaping into his stomach with front paws stiffly extended, until he laughed and chased her and they fell together in the soft sifting of snow. Christy wrestled with her, but that startled Gala, so he dusted himself off and took a handful of the starkly defined snow crystals into the cabin to wonder at and admire before they melted. He gave Gala a carefully rationed dinner, the first solid food he'd allotted her, and he warmed the Jeep a long time before putting her into it. She looked cold. She looked pathetic. He went back and got his blue sweater and buttoned it around her, and she sat in the front seat beside him looking very proud of herself as he drove into Vail.

Karen lived in an older condominium on Willow Circle, right next to the central village. Christy left Gala and the Jeep at the curb and climbed to Karen's door. She didn't answer his ring right away. As a matter of fact, such silence greeted him that he checked his watch, wondering if he'd made a mistake in time. But, no, the time was right. He rang again. From somewhere far back in her rooms, he heard the quick click of heels as she hurried to the door.

Karen's long hair was pulled back in a bun. She wore no jewelry and, as far as Christy could see, little makeup. But she needed no artifice. She wore a softly draped dress of peach-colored wool, cut just low enough to reveal a gentle curve of breast, and Christy noticed with great satisfaction that Karen had legs. He'd only seen her in pants before. A waste. These were long, beautiful legs. She ruined the effect slightly by plopping down on a leather bench by the door and trading her shoes for snow boots. A greater length of beautiful leg flashed in the process, and Christy looked away politely.

While Karen's building was conventional enough, the decor of her condo was unusual. A Baldwin grand piano vied for attention in the living room with a mellow Bessarabian kilim rug. A cigar-store Indian glared across the room at a twenty-foot Chinese screen. A forest of thorny euphorbias cuddled up to four contemporary chairs upholstered in flame-colored velvet, and everywhere Christy looked there were things. Porcelain things. Copper things. Carved wood things.

"Yes, I know," Karen said, following Christy's gaze on its travels about the crowded room. "Mother collected. Mother had terrible taste. I've always suspected she did the Vail place up with her worst mistakes, hoping an avalanche would happen by. Then with the insurance money she could have started all over again. But I like all the stuff."

"I'll bet every object reminds you of her," Christy said.

"Yes, it all does," Karen said. "I loved her very much, and I like thinking about her."

"You sound breathless," Christy told her. "Did I catch you at a bad time?"

"Oh, no. I was just back in the junk room looking for these snow boots. Can't hear a thing back there. I almost didn't hear the doorbell. Have you been waiting long?"

"No, I just got here," he said. "Well, shall we?"

She handed him a white coat to hold for her. She was ready. She just needed to lock the back door first. Christy waited. When she came back, she confessed hunger. She postponed a guided tour of the condo and its bibelots in favor of prompt arrival at Knight's house, and only the sight of Gala the Doberman sitting in the front seat of Christy's Jeep seemed to give her pause. She even backed up a step or two.

"Oops," Karen said. "It hadn't occurred to me you'd be bringing your dog again. Is she going to Knight's house with us?"

Christy was also given pause. He didn't demand that people love animals, but tolerance seemed little enough to ask. "She's been very sick," he said. "Knight asked me to bring her so she wouldn't be left all by herself."

"Poor dog," Karen said.

She didn't sound very sincere to Christy, and she showed no eagerness to get in the Jeep with Gala. Christy unbuttoned Gala's sweater and instructed her to jump in the back seat. The dog jumped reluctantly. The evening seemed off to a poor start, but once they had circumnavigated the tidal wave of Knight Dobermans and Karen was seated with a margarita in hand in Knight's oversized living room, she looked relaxed and happy. She looked even happier after Knight inquired briefly as to Gala's welfare, then said, "No more dog talk this evening. I promised Lucille. And only one drink before dinner. I'm experimenting with smorgasbord fare, and we're required to drink aquavit and beer with all courses except dessert."

"I love pickled herring," Karen said.

"You might not love mine," Knight told her. "I pickled my own."

It was beautiful. It was plentiful. Christy decided he could live with home-pickled herring, and he was even happier with the shrimp and cheese and a fresh mushroom salad with dark

Danish bread and butter that came with the first course. He also sighed happily over trout in a sour-cream sauce that made up the second course. Icy aquavit kept appearing in the small glass at his elbow, and he was almost sorry to switch to Danish beer when caution dictated that, given many more courses and much more aquavit, he'd be under the table before the end of dinner. Gala was already under it. Privileged guest, she was allowed the house when Knight put away his own dogs, and she stationed herself on Christy's feet so she could nudge him occasionally in mute inquiry as to whether she wasn't going to get a morsel of trout or a bite of roast pork.

The roast pork was Knight's masterpiece. Stuffed with apples and prunes, it was accompanied by red cabbage and caramelized potatoes, and both Knight and his beautiful friend Lucille dug in as though the previous courses hadn't existed. Karen managed to match them through one helping, then fell behind on seconds, as did Christy. Table conversation picked up, with the afternoon's snow as a starting point, moving on to the skiing that would soon follow.

"Not for me," Lucille threatened Knight. "One blizzard, and I'm heading home to New Orleans. I'm a good Southern girl. That ski business is for you snowbirds."

"Do you really prefer the off season?" Karen asked her. "Most people hate it. Skiers have one standard question they just have to ask when they find out someone lives in Vail full-time: 'But what do you do in the summer around here?'"

Knight laughed his low, rumbling laugh. "Well, what do you answer, Karen? What do you do in the summer?"

"Try to keep cool," she said. "Have you ever been through a Texas summer? That's why Texans have been coming to Colorado for generations. Besides, I like Vail the whole year around. I liked it better before Philip got shot, though. I'm a little skittish now about being alone at night in that condo."

"I do believe that's an invitation, Christy," Lucille said. "Accept fast. The lady needs a protector."

Christy tried a leer on for size. "Do you think she meant it that way?"

"Mmm-hummm," Lucille said. "If she did, you'd better take advantage of it while you still can. Once the police pick up this Jerome character I keep hearing about, it looks like your crime wave will be ended."

"I wouldn't be too sure of that," Knight said, pouring another beer.

Christy asked, "Meaning?"

Knight waved off the question and said, "I hear you had a few words today with Philip's little brother, Peter," he said. "Be careful of that youngster, Christy. He looks skinny and lazy, but he's a mean one."

Christy shook his head in wonder. "Does everyone in Vail know everything about everybody else?" he said. "There was practically no one around when he decided to call me out."

"What did he want?" Karen asked. Her face was flushed, though whether it was due to the magnificent food or the gentle accumulation of aquavit and beer Christy couldn't tell.

"Just crazy stuff about phone calls and leaving his mother alone," Christy told her. "He practically threatened me, come to think of it. What's the matter with that kid?"

"Probably dope," Knight said. "Peter's got the monopoly over at the high school. Some people say he samples his own wares a mite too often."

"Are you sure of that?" Christy said.

"I've seen him pass a few dimes from time to time," Knight said. "He's never been very careful about it."

"Do the police know?"

Knight smiled. "This is a resort town, Christy. Full of money and high-powered connections. Resort-town police usually don't exactly condone eccentric pursuits, but they try not to be too pushy if they can help it. Courtesy and tolerance, those are the watchwords. Just so long as no one gets hurt."

"But dope in a high school?"

"Just lightweight stuff. If he ever started dealing dangerous things, our local guys would squat on him fast. It's a workable policy."

"Was Philip Schumacher into dope dealing, too?" Christy asked Karen.

"Heavens, how would I know?" she protested. "He was one of my more casual acquaintances."

"You would have noticed," Knight said. "Hurried conversations on street corners. Money and little goodies changing hands. Did you ever see anything like that?"

"Certainly not. If I had I would have dropped him far faster than I did. My dad would drag me back to Texas quicker than I could scream for help if I got mixed up in anything like that. Philip was just strange, that's all. I figured it was because his father is a psychiatrist. Have you ever noticed that psychiatrists always seem to have the craziest kids, and preachers have the wildest, and teachers the dumbest? Besides, the whole Schumacher family is crazy if you ask me."

Knight asked, "In any specific way?"

"Well . . . here's a for instance: Philip took me by their house once. I think he was putting the touch on his mother for pocket money. Mrs. Schumacher's a funny lady. Cutesy teenager clothes. Hair too long and loose for a middle-aged lady. Little wispy voice. You know the type? She's got a little British-sounding accent, too. Canadian, I think. So I made polite conversation, and I asked her about her accent, where she lived before Vail and all, and she shut up like a clam. Hardly said good-bye to me. I asked Philip about it later, and he only laughed. But he wouldn't talk about where they came from, either. Why would a family be ashamed to say where they're from?"

Christy offered, "Maybe he only wanted to sound mysterious."

"No, it's the whole family," Karen said. "Gosh, when

you're from Texas, you just naturally talk about it. That's why the Schumachers struck me as so strange. No one seems to know where they lived before they got here. I got curious and asked around. They just appeared in town three years or so ago. Even Dr. Schumacher ducks the question. It's as if he has no past. I decided it was just what you'd expect from a nutty psychiatrist and his nutty family."

"Nutty, for sure," Knight agreed.

"I remember something," Christy said. "The Schumacher maid told me relatives were coming in from Maryland for Philip's funeral last week. Maryland? Home state? Could that be the answer to Karen's mystery?"

Knight looked interested. "You've met Miss Sue Teasdale?" he said. "Lucky boy. That little redhead is something to behold. She's nice, too. I really like her."

Lucille punched him. Gala growled under the table. Lucille's punch had been playful, but Gala apparently hadn't been able to discern that. They left the table, and Knight invited Christy to use the den to give Gala her ten o'clock IV. He stuck around to help and chat, then they rejoined Lucille and Karen for fruit and coffee in the living room.

The party broke up soon after. It was still snowing, and Christy was none too sure of his hand with a Jeep on snowy roads. They slithered a bit going downhill. Aquavit bubbled in his veins. A pause to feel less festive wouldn't be a bad idea. The gory fertilizer for Dr. Potter's pothos was still in the Jeep. He suggested to Karen that they finally explore his condo and tend all the plants while they were at it. Gala could surely be sneaked in this one time.

Dr. Potter's building was one of the four-story redwoods that seemed a favorite architectural style of the village. Parking was underneath, and Karen said, "Good, I know this building. It has heated parking. We can leave your Doberman in the car."

"Karen, do you really hate dogs?" Christy asked her.

"Of course not. They scare me, sure, but I think I'm

doing very well for a person who's never been around dogs at all. I guess it's just taking me a little while to get used to her."

Christy felt he could hardly ignore Karen's feelings about the dog. He felt self-conscious about buttoning a sweater around Gala with Karen looking on, so he just told Gala to be good and locked her in the Jeep. Karen took the condo key. "Second floor? The nearest stairway is around that corner," she said. She led the way upstairs and returned the key so Christy could unlock the door, then had no suggestions to make as to where to find a light switch. Christy put his arms around her. She leaned close to him. Her chin came up, and he discovered she liked being kissed. He also discovered that he liked kissing her very much.

When she finally pulled away, Christy was glad he'd left Gala in the Jeep. She'd be severely in the way in Dr. Potter's bedroom, he thought optimistically. He found the switch, then turned quickly as he heard Karen gasp.

The place was a shambles. Leather-covered furniture had been overturned, then ripped open, foam rubber oozing from the camel-colored leather. A big pile of dirt and withering plants held the middle of the floor, along with pots overturned and dropped beside the pile. Paper and trash were everywhere. The walls were intact, and none of the ceramic pots or other glass objects had been broken. Whoever had trashed the rooms had worked quietly.

For a moment, Christy was overturned, too. All those dead plants. What would Dr. Potter say? "Oh, God," he said. Then, "Who? Why?"

"Jerome," Karen breathed. "Or Peter Schumacher. Someone who doesn't like you. Damn whoever did it. They really made a mess."

Christy felt ill. He also felt terribly vulnerable, and he suddenly wished for Gala's taut body and big teeth to be at his side. "They didn't have to kill the plants," he said. "Dr. Potter will skin me alive."

"You'll have to tell the police," Karen said.

Christy took a brief inventory of her face. Pallor had overtaken her usual high, healthy coloring. She looked frightened. He thought he knew the reason why. "There's no point in your getting tarred by someone else's dirty brush," Christy said. "I'll take you home before I call Shannon. I'll tell him I just came up alone to water the plants."

"No, Christy, I'll stay," she said. "I don't want to be a fairweather friend."

"Thanks, but my way is best."

"Are you sure?"

"I'm sure," Christy said. He didn't add that what he was surest of was the fact that Karen wouldn't enjoy getting involved with anything that might look bad to her father.

"Well, okay, then," she said. "I can walk home. It's not far."

Christy was disappointed that she didn't insist on staying, but he wasn't surprised. He said quietly, "I'll walk you downstairs."

"No, don't. I'll scamper off like a little mouse."

"It's no bother. I'm going down for Gala anyway."

If she turned back to wave from the front entrance, Christy didn't see her. He trotted down to the parking garage for a friend he could trust, a four-legged one.

8

THE POLICE STATION was slow to answer its phones that Sunday night. Christy waited impatiently in Dr. Potter's wrecked apartment and listened to six rings before a woman's voice finally cut in. He was put on hold, and he had ample time to curse the day hold buttons were invented, then Officer Lincoln came on.

"Sorry, Christy," Lincoln said briskly, "but we've been tied up on the Schumacher shooting. What's your problem?"

Christy told him in angry detail about the destruction of Potter's apartment, the mess of dead plants on the floor, the ripped furniture, and added that he suspected either Jerome or the youngest Schumacher, both of whom seemed to have it in for him, of being the culprit. "Frankly, if I get my hands on either of them, you may have a second murder to investigate."

"Odd that you should say that," Lincoln said. "I was just about to ask you where you've been all evening."

They sputtered back and forth for a moment, Christy

wanting to know why the police should care, Lincoln insisting on an answer. Christy said, "Since you put it that way, I was at Cletus Knight's house, eating smogasbord."

"Anyone else there?"

"Sure. Knight's girlfriend and Karen Hamilton. I, uh, took Karen home right before I came up to the condo and found all this. Now will you tell me why it's important?"

"What time did you get there? To Knight's house, I mean."

"A little after seven. Why? What is this?"

"Seven, huh? Not good enough. We figure it happened between six and six-forty."

"You figure *what* happened? What are we talking about?"

"Lord, Christy, what's this innocent act? It's been on the radio. Peter Schumacher was shot dead tonight. The youngest Shumacher kid. We got a report that the two of you had a quarrel this afternoon. Ever since the maid found his body, I'm afraid you've been pretty high on our list of people to check."

"Holy God," Christy said. "Hey, we didn't quarrel. He just—"

"Save it, Christy. Shannon will want to talk to you. He'll probably want to see Potter's place, too, to see if he can figure out whether or not it was the Schumacher kid. He's over at the Schumachers' now, waiting for them to come home. Stay there, will you? I'll call him and tell him. Maybe he can run over in the meantime. Is anything missing? Burglary as well as vandalism?"

"I don't know. Tonight's the first time I've been here," Christy said. "Do I have to stay? Your canine witness is with me, and she's tired. I could just lock up and leave the place as it is."

"Not until I talk to Shannon. I'd come out and look things over myself, but we're so busy down here that you may have to wait your turn to be grilled, old son. Just stay put. I'll get back to you." He hung up.

Christy sat quite still, the phone in his hand. The demolished condo now looked menacing as well as ugly. Gala sniffed cautiously through the mess. He put down the phone and called her, and he put one chair on its feet so she'd at least have a place to lie down. She groaned as she crawled into it and made herself comfortable. She put her head down, but she kept her eyes on Christy, as though she, too, felt threatened by the ambiance.

They waited. They waited some more. Christy finally said, "Oh, hell," untangled the plants from the dirt on the floor, and repotted everything that had a root structure intact. He watered them in the kitchen and put them on the counters. Not as much destruction in here. Whoever had done the trashing apparently worried that too much banging of pots and shattering of glass and pottery would bring the neighbors, and they'd left the kitchen pretty much alone.

At least an hour passed. Outside, snow still fell. Much more of this, Christy figured, and he'd be snowed in. He started for the phone to call Lincoln again, and he jumped, heart pounding, when it rang at him first.

It was Dave Lincoln. "Go home, Christy," the young police officer said. "Lock up tight and don't touch anything. We'll have to get to you in the morning. Everything is coming to a head tonight. Jerome was just picked up in Gunnison, and Shannon won't have time for you. He'll be leaving for Gunnison just as soon as Dr. and Mrs. Schumacher manage to make it home."

"Wait," Christy said. "I've already touched some things. I just finished—" But the phone banged again in his ear.

Christy wasted no time in leashing Gala and taking off. He left a light on in the kitchen, forlorn signal that someone was home, no burglars or vandals need apply. Talk about locking the barn after the horse was gone. If he'd been staying in the condo, as Dr. Potter had expected him to, maybe it wouldn't have been broken into and wrecked. Maybe Dr. Potter's cherished plants wouldn't be straggly little sprigs. And, God, all that expensive leather furniture ripped. Dr. Potter would have a fit. Christy could get the place cleaned up, and he could talk to some plant expert, maybe Miss Carroll, to see if his awkward job of repotting the plants could be improved upon, but there wasn't a way in the world he could get the furniture reupholstered before Dr. Potter returned.

Christy knew he was in for it. So much for staying on permanently with Dr. Potter in Vail. He buttoned Gala up in her sweater but was so preoccupied that he didn't worry about the snow, and the Jeep plowed sturdily through some five inches of glistening whiteness as Christy pulled out of the underground garage. On impulse, Christy swung uphill. He'd go home by way of Forest Road and the Schumacher house. He had the restless, helpless feeling one had after a death, wanting to do something, but knowing that nothing could be done. Death, yes, he'd scarcely thought of that. Another youngster dead. Shot, had Lincoln said? Shannon there waiting. Where were the mother and father?

Only one car, a little green Saab, was parked in the Schumacher driveway, and snow had covered the tire tracks it had made in arriving there. Christy could see lights upstairs. Shannon, waiting alone. He could stop and speak to Shannon, tell him how inconsequential his encounter with young Peter had been, maybe sleep better if he didn't fear the police were breathing down his neck. Christy parked in the street, not wanting to be in the driveway in case Dr. and Mrs. Schumacher returned while he was there, and took the chance of leaving the motor running so the heater would stay on. He knew it could be dangerous to Gala. Carbon monoxide poisoning. So he rolled a window down a few inches, told Gala to stay, and slogged through the snow to the second-story deck. He'd stay three minutes at maximum.

Shannon opened the door. Sue Teasdale was in the living room, huddled on a couch, looking gray about the mouth.

"Does she have to stay?" Christy asked Shannon. "I could take her to a friend's house for the night. Or one of the lodges. Or even to Dr. Potter's cabin. I could sleep in the clinic."

"No, I want to stay here," she said in a small voice. "The Schumachers are taking it pretty hard. Mrs. Schumacher will need help."

"They know?"

Shannon said, "I called them. They were visiting friends in Denver. Mrs. Schumacher went into hysterics. I guess that's what's holding them up."

"I heard about Jerome getting caught," Christy said. "Was it him?"

Shannon looked at him oddly. "We have a number of possible suspects," he said, reminding Christy subtly that he was one of them. "But no, it doesn't look like Jerome is our killer. Miss Teasdale was out of the house for about an hour tonight. She found Peter when she got back. The State Patrol picked Jerome up near Gunnison about six o'clock this evening, if we've got the straight of it. Peter was still alive and kicking then."

Christy said to the shivering redhead, "I'm so sorry. What a shock it must have been for you."

"Indeed," she said. "Indeed." She jerked her chin toward the television set, and Christy realized with a thrill of horror that a sheeted body lay within six feet of him on the floor. She said, "Poor little slob, he complained like everything when I went out for dinner. There was nothing interesting on the tube. Nobody ever invited him anywhere. Well, I left him. I guess it's a good thing. They might have pumped six bullets into me, too."

Christy questioned Shannon with a look. "Six bullets? Like the other one?"

"Yeah, a carbon copy," Shannon said. "Six very messy holes in the kid. Only something new has been added this time. They left a black leather glove on his chest."

Through the residue of much aquavit, through the shock of seeing first Dr. Potter's condo and now a sheeted body, intellect worked slowly. Christy knew another black glove. He saw it several times a day, the thumb chewed off, the fur lining scruffy. It was in Gala's basket, with her other treasures, including, from time to time, Christy's best navy-blue sweater. "Gala has a black glove," he said. "Gala the Doberman. She sort of collects things. Some dogs do. You don't suppose she, er, collected it the day the other brother was killed, do you?"

"Holy Christ!" Shannon said. "You've had it all this time?"

Christy almost denied it. Gala had a glove. He had no glove. But protection of dog and man was a two-way street, Knight had said. "That's right," Christy said. "I just left it in her basket with some socks and stuff. I never thought anything of it."

"I want that glove," Shannon said.

"I'll bring it," Christy said. "You want it tonight?"

"Oh, hell, listen to me," Shannon said. "Sorry, Christy, it's turning into a long day. Don't bother. I'll send someone by for it tomorrow. It's at the clinic?"

"Dr. Potter's cabin, actually. I guess I've sort of moved in there."

"Yes. Lincoln told me about the condo getting ripped off. We'll get to that tomorrow, too. All right? But at least take the glove away from the dog and keep it safe somewhere, okay?"

"Of course."

Shannon's head turned. He seemed to be listening. He relaxed after a moment. "Thought I heard a car," he said. "I wish the Schumachers would hurry."

Christy didn't. The last place he wanted to be was Dr. and Mrs. Schumacher's home when they returned and saw their son lying dead on the floor. He mumbled a good night to Sue and assured Shannon he'd be at the clinic or the cabin all the next day. Shannon walked him to the door. Snow no longer fell. Shannon murmured a few weary words about the weather and went back into the warm house. Christy far preferred the crisp, clean bite of the cold. Gala cuddled into her sweater. He drove her home carefully but cautiously and busied himself with lighting a fire.

She jumped into her basket to await its warmth, and he had to disturb her to remove the glove. Real leather, it looked like, although the fur lining was obviously fake. A man's black winter glove, maybe large size or extra-large. The stitching was carefully done, and if it hadn't been covered with dried dog saliva and missing one thumb it might have been handsome. What other stains were on it? Philip Schumacher's blood? Christy saw that Gala's teeth had also been applied to the index finger. He put the glove on the mantel. Then, because the fire was catching well, he moved the glove to the top of a bookshelf across the room. No point in making everyone in Vail mad at him—Dr. Potter for letting his condo get wrecked, the police for letting a valuable piece of evidence go up in flames. The police would be testy enough as it was if they really thought he was a suspect in this newest shooting. He dropped morosely into the chair Bev Farrell had left beside Gala's basket, and the dog tilted her chin and licked his dangling hand. The fire felt warmer. Christy felt better. If he'd gained nothing else from Vail, he at least had gained the love of an animal. He wondered if they allowed dogs to visit their jailed owners on death row.

Gala had her last IV at four o'clock the next morning. She checked out well and said she felt terrific, but Christy feared she might be tired after so much activity the previous night. He let her stay in the cabin instead of bringing her into Ward One. He locked the cabin carefully to keep her safe. He could look in on her occasionally between patients. He tackled promptly the unpleasant chore of telling Miss Carroll of the wreckage at Dr. Potter's condo. Yes, Dr. Potter had insurance, but she didn't know how much. Yes, she'd contact the company. Yes, of course, she'd undertake nursing the wounded plants, the minute the police inspected the condo and said it was all right to go in and start picking up and cleaning up.

The police seemed to have more pressing things to do. The morning passed without Christy's hearing either from Lincoln or Shannon. He took that as a good sign, for if he were a serious suspect surely the police would have come out to talk to him first thing. Wouldn't they?

Afternoon started grimly enough. The owners of the hospitalized cat named Mildred, the one he feared was suffering from leukemia, balked at paying for lab tests, and at their insistence Christy had to put the little lady down. He hated to do it, but even without a lab report he was privately convinced about the leukemia. Chemotherapy was available, but it was so tough on the cat that he felt sure he was saving Mildred suffering. Then Bev Farrell and Mark Niemeyer dropped by, abuzz with talk of murder and a report that Jerome had confessed all to the Gunnison police. They returned an hour later to negate the report. Instead, they had heard that Jerome had tried to commit suicide by hanging himself with Gunnison-jail bedsheets. An hour later they came again. That last report was also false, and Jerome was now in Vail in police custody undergoing questioning, and a number of young men and women were being rocked with rumor as their chums were called in to answer queries about Jerome's burglary ring.

Christy concluded that the third report might have at least some substance, because Dave Lincoln phoned soon afterward and asked that Christy meet him at the condo. Lincoln whistled at what he saw, listened to Christy's story again, then told him to clear out until fingerprints and other spoor could be checked. He was no longer needed, but told to stay available. Dr. Potter's plants looked awful. Christy went back to the clinic, and after Lincoln called with an all-clear on the condo, he held down both reception desk and his own duties while Miss Carroll rushed to the condo for a preliminary meeting with the insurance adjuster and an attempt to administer first aid to the plants. He joined her there after clinic hours, and they vacuumed and scrubbed and straightened while listening for the phone to ring and fruitlessly trying to figure out where Dr. Potter might be at the moment and how Christy could reach him to tell him the dismal news.

After the condo was as rehabilitated as they could get it until the upholsterer could take over, Christy went back to the cabin and waited. At worst, Dr. Potter would phone. Or, not quite as dire, Shannon might call asking about gloves and burglary rings and quarrels with a dead teenager. Next after that, Karen might call to ask if he'd really refrained from mentioning her presence when he phoned the police from the condo. No one phoned at all, and Christy went to bed early with a biography of Lawrence of Arabia. Gala alone seemed charmed by the long, quiet day, and she stayed right beside him.

The next day passed as slowly. Bright sun came out on Tuesday morning and melted the snow, and Bev and Mark complained about the sunshine when they came by with their latest crop of rumors. Christy refused to take them seriously. A boy's two hamsters both died of pneumonia within ten minutes after the weeping boy and his mother brought them to the clinic, and Christy wondered if he would have been happier as an air-conditioning repairman instead of a veterinarian. He lamented to Miss Carroll that pneumonia was wiping out all his rodent patients. It didn't help Christy's feelings at all to hear her gentle revelation that Dr. Potter referred most of the patients of the gerbil, white mice, and hamster ilk to the knowledgeable and experienced owner of a pet-supply shop nearby in a developing area known as Eagle-Vail. Experience could come only with the passage of years, and he regarded even the coming days with foreboding.

But Christy's first patient on Wednesday was Agatha the

Sheepdog, and he was so cheered at the sight of the bouncing dog that he forgot to feel gloomy. Her back looked better, although still not good. The tissue was still open, and the beginnings of a new scab showed the same tendency to slough. A peel was indicated, with general cleaning of the huge wound. That meant anesthesia.

"She'll be a good, reasonably healthy pet for you when we get her healed up," he assured Agatha's ladies. "You'll see."

"Oh, we're not worried about that," Jean said. "We just want to do everything for her that we can."

Harriet's cheeks turned rosy. "Yes, and speaking of doing things for her, there's something we should tell you," she said. "I took her to Dr. Schumacher Sunday morning. He analyzes dogs, you know."

"Why on earth did you do that?" Christy asked.

Harriet looked embarrassed. "She cries so much," she said. "Jean said I was being silly, but I thought she had a problem adjusting to a new life. Dr. Schumacher lives just down the street from the house we took, so I dropped in and asked if he could look at her."

Jean said disapprovingly, "Yes, he told Harriet he always telephones a dog's vet before he accepts the dog as a patient, but he didn't want to bother you since it was a Sunday. He said he'd call you Monday. You must have thought Harriet was terrible, going off to another doctor without telling you."

"I didn't know about it," Christy said. "Dr. Schumacher never called. But then, I guess he's been awfully busy since his son was . . ." The two women looked at each other sadly. They both seemed ill at ease, though whether it was because they had sought an outside opinion without first telling him, or a natural reaction to murder done practically next door, Christy couldn't tell. To switch the subject, he asked, "When does Agatha cry? When you leave her alone? When she needs to go outside?"

"Oh, she cries all the time," Harriet said. "Usually when we take her out for walks. She'll see another dog, and she practically weeps tears. Or children. She always cries when she sees them."

"Maybe she just wants to play," Christy said. He ruffled Agatha's shaggy ears. "How about it, Agatha, did you have children and dogs in your old home? Do you want to play with everyone you see?"

"If that's the case, analysis is definitely indicated, isn't it?" Harriet said. "I suppose we could adopt another dog for her to play with, but children . . ."

The women exchanged another glance. Christy saw that he'd touched a tender spot. Harriet unmarried, Jean childless, perhaps. He changed the subject again. "How did it go? What kind of information does an analyst try to elicit about a dog?"

Harriet said enthusiastically, "It was very interesting. We had to do it all outside, because of his wife's allergies, and he let Agatha just wander around at first, watching her, then he asked me to call her to me and pet her. Then I had to tell her to sit, and then we put her on leash and let her walk with me, then he took the leash, and after that he asked a lot of questions about her physical condition and all. I was supposed to go to his office on Tuesday, but, well, you know. His receptionist called on Monday and canceled all his appointments. Poor man."

Christy hesitated, but since Harriet had brought it up, he decided to be nosy. "Did you see Peter Schumacher while you were there?"

Harriet looked at Christy with bright, excited eyes. "Yes, I saw him. The very morning of the day he was shot. I've been dying to tell someone about it."

"Now, Harriet," Jean warned.

"I don't care," Harriet said. "It's something you don't forget. To see a person only hours before he's murdered. Jean thinks we should be shocked and horrified and too ladylike to speak about it. Well, not me. I'm not the decorous type."

"Did everything seem normal to you?" Christy asked.

"The youngster, I mean. Did he act nervous, or worried about anything?"

"Well, of course I'd never seen him before," Harriet said, "so I don't really have much basis for comparison. But yes, I suppose everything was fairly normal. When I first went in he was just sitting there in front of the television set watching a Sunday morning sermon."

"A sermon?" Christy said. "That doesn't sound like the Peter Schumacher I've been hearing about."

"Exactly," Jean said. "I've been telling Harriet things are not always what they seem."

"I suppose you could be right," Harriet said. "I'm not sure he was watching the program. He could have been deep in thought. He didn't even look up when I came in. As a matter of fact, he didn't look up until after his father asked me who was vetting poor Agatha and I mentioned Dr. Christy. Then he got up rather angrily and left the room."

"You didn't tell me angrily," Jean put in. "You said purposefully. He left the room purposefully."

Christy coughed and again changed the subject, this time quickly. "Well, at least Agatha is getting every possible kind of care. Will you be going back when, uh, when things quiet down?"

"Yes, I suppose so," Harriet said. "If it's all right with you, that is. Meanwhile we're not supposed to pet her until she responds to a command, such as sit or come. We're establishing dominance. Dr. Schumacher says in the canine world it's the subordinate dog that does the petting, or, rather, the licking, and Agatha might get the idea she's the Alpha Wolf, unless we show her different."

"Gracious," Christy said. "And here I've been petting dogs all my life."

Jean smiled. "It does sound pretty silly, doesn't it? As I told Harriet, what's the point in having a dog if you can't touch it?"

"Maybe it makes good sense for an aggressive dog,"

Christy said. "I don't think you're going to have much aggression from Agatha, though. If she's cranky now, well, she's bound to be in pain from that back."

"Yes, but she's terrible to other female dogs," Harriet said. "She seems to like boy dogs, but not girls. So we'll keep her in analysis for a while once Dr. Schumacher starts seeing patients again. Maybe it will help her."

Christy pigeonholed the sisters as the overly doting kind of pet owners. They probably dived as deeply into other hobbies as they were now doing with dogs. He only hoped they both followed Jean's lead about not talking of Harriet's visit to the Schumacher home, especially to the police. If the only thing on Peter Schumacher's mind the morning of the day he died was a certain Gordon Christy, D.V.M., he'd just as soon the police not hear about it.

Agatha cried when they left her behind, surely confirming Harriet's belief that she should be psychoanalyzed, and she showed Christy her teeth when he injected the usual light tranquilizer he preferred before anesthesia, but that seemed perfectly normal dog behavior to Christy. Get left by your mistress or master? Sure, a dog would object. Get punched with a needle? Dogs couldn't enjoy the moment's pain any better than people did, and being uninhibited souls, they showed it.

One male dog with prostate trouble, two shots for cats, one in-season bitch whose careless mistress rushed in for a mismate shot, and Christy was back in the surgery with Agatha sleeping soundly on the stainless steel table, the heart monitor beeping away. He went to work on the dreadful back. It went well. Christy whistled. He found one lone clump of hair follicles alive and well among the dead tissue. Agatha would have a sprig of fur to help cover the scar. His last act was to check her bad eye. It didn't look actively infected, but it showed no improvement. He doubted she had any vision in it at all. Since the sisters balked at nothing in pursuit of their new hobby, he'd suggest they take her to

Denver soon to a fine veterinary ophthalmologist there and get the expert opinion he needed. He popped an antibiotic shot into Agatha's neatly shaved rump to help eye and back, and he decided to take a number-seven blade and the clipper and go over her fur while she was still groggy. Give her a less ragged clip. There was no point in letting her look ridiculous.

The clipper buzzed along to Christy's whistle, and he didn't know anyone had entered the surgery until he saw Cletus Knight laze around the table into his line of view. Knight was dressed in a dark jacket and slacks, complete with tie and white shirt, and Christy yelled, "Hi. Don't get too close to the dog hair, or you'll get it all over you."

"They tell me dog hair brushes off," Knight said. "It looks like you could use a hand."

"Just one, then. Stand at arm's length, and hold Agatha's muzzle. Now that she's coming to, she keeps telling me to leave her marvelous person alone or she'll take a chunk out of me."

"What are you treating her for?"

"Some of everything," Christy said. "I've never seen a dog with more troubles. All non-fatal, thank God. She's another rescue case. Two really dandy ladies have taken her in."

"Miss Carroll said you don't have any surgical cases backed up this afternoon. Want to do me a favor?"

Christy turned off the clipper. "Certainly," he said. "Name it."

"You're very trusting."

"Only sometimes." Agatha stirred and tried to get her feet under her. Christy decided his grooming job was good enough. "Hold her muzzle for another second while I pick her up," Christy said. "How about it, old girl, are you ready for a nice nap in a transport cage? Oof, Agatha, one thing's sure, at least the cruds who abandoned you didn't try to starve you to death. There, all right, let her go now. She's basically gentle. She just likes to remind me she could take my face off if she wanted to."

"Do vets get bitten often?" Knight asked idly.

"Once in a while. Not nearly as often as you'd expect. I've never been bitten myself. Most animals are better behaved than people."

"Dr. Potter's going to like you," Knight said. "He prefers animals to people, too. Excepting, I suppose, the female Homo sapiens. It's surely his favorite of all creatures."

Christy felt the glow go out of the day. "Dr. Potter's going to hate me the minute he hears how I let his condo get wrecked," he said. "I keep waiting for the phone to ring. I guess he won't fire me until he gets back, though."

"Don't borrow trouble," Knight said. "Potter's a pretty understanding old guy."

"What's he like?"

"I guess I'd call him all put together. About that favor. Would you mind looking at Annie's right foreleg for me? I know I'm cutting into your lunch hour with no appointment. I was only going to come by for a fresh tube of Panalog, but I got a little worried about her at the last minute and stuffed her in the car."

"You bet, I'll look at her. What's the trouble?"

"A little bump. I thought she'd just bashed herself, running around the yard, but it won't go away."

"Let's check her out. Where's your car? Out front? If it's nothing much, you needn't even bring her in."

"How could you tell I hate to bring my dogs into the clinic?" Knight asked.

"You seem the type. Clinics. Germs from other patients. Rabies dripping off the ceiling."

"I'm not that bad, Christy," Knight said. "But it's true, I don't like to take them around animals that are sick. Honest Indian, I'm not just trying to beat you out of the bill."

Knight's silver Bentley contained only the one Doberman this time, young Annie, who sat behind the driver's seat looking typically self-important. Knight commanded her to move over, and Christy slid in to look at the foreleg. The bump was only the size of a large pea, but it was swollen and angry. "We'd have to send away tissue to be sure, but it's almost certainly a histiocytoma," Christy said. "They often just go away on their own, if you want to wait and see."

"But 'cytoma,' does that have to do with tumors?" Knight said worriedly. "God, Christy, don't tell me it's malignant."

"Not on a dog. A histiocytoma can pop up after a bug bite. Spider. Bee. The dog's body isolates the venom, to put it simply for an overly worried dog owner, so you get a painful little bump. Come on, now, Knight, it's nothing to be so concerned about. There are three standard ways to treat it: wait, or inject with steroid and see if it goes away, or excise surgically. I prefer an electric needle, if that's what you choose."

"Let's get rid of it. Right away. I'd say right this minute, but I told Sue Teasdale I'd sit with her at that dreary memorial service for Peter Schumacher."

"So that's where you're going all dressed up," Christy said. He meditated a moment. "Would I be barging in if I asked to go with you? Are you supposed to have an invitation to a funeral?"

"I doubt anyone would notice us," Knight said. He leaned out of the car and straightened to his full height, giving the lie to his words. Knight at a wedding or funeral or any occasion in between would be about as inconspicuous as a panther strolling into an ice-cream parlor. "Anyway, it's not a real funeral," he said. "The Schumachers had the body cremated, so there might be an urn or something. The service is at two o'clock in the chapel. We'd have time to grab a sandwich before I meet Sue."

"Why does she want you to come?"

"I didn't ask. She did me a favor once. Dancer got out of the car at the post office, and while everyone else was screaming about loose Dobermans and running in the opposite direction, Sue just reached out and grabbed the collar, right before Dancer could run into the street. So if Sue wants me to go to a memorial service, I go to a memorial service. Dragging you with me. Get a jacket, Doc, and let's take off. I want to pick your brain more about Annie's bug bump."

Christy ducked out to the cabin for a jacket and tie, and on a hunch he picked up the black glove that the Vail police had apparently forgotten. While Knight walked Gala, Christy put the glove into a manila envelope, more than half anticipating seeing Nat Shannon at the service. He could give it to Shannon there. He could also give himself a firsthand view of the Schumachers. Not from ghoulish curiosity. Their double tragedy had touched his own life uncomfortably, and he kept thinking it would be a good idea to do something about it, if he could only figure out what to do.

One turkey and avocado sandwich at a health-food restaurant was all that time allowed. Knight didn't even take time to go by his house to drop Annie. They sat three to the front seat as Knight nosed the Bentley past the firehouse and a bank, then Christy learned a new thing about the foresight of the Vail developers. They had provided the town with an interfaith chapel on the banks of Gore Creek. It was distressingly close to the Schumacher house. Just around the corner and a block down from Forest Road. The family could easily have walked to the services for their second and last son. From Christy's one glimpse of Mrs. Schumacher, he figured the small, vague woman would cringe every time she had to pass the chapel in the future.

Mrs. Schumacher was muffled in black. Poor lady. How dismal to be so well equipped with funereal garb. She was helped to a seat by a stranger in a black suit, and Christy wondered where Dr. Schumacher could possibly be. Ah, in a corner, being consoled by a man who had "M.D." stamped all over him, as clearly as if he wore an Aesculapian staff in his lapel. Schumacher looked as though he hadn't slept. Surely he should be with his wife instead of huddled in a corner. Maybe her grief was too appalling to him.

There, Sue Teasdale was coming into the chapel. She was so pale that Christy could distinctly count eight freckles that he hadn't known she possessed. She had an uncertain look about her that made Knight frown with concern as he stepped over to her. Christy saw Dr. Schumacher's head swing, and his red-rimmed eyes stared in their direction.

"Are you feeling okay, Sue?" Knight asked her quietly.

"I always feel okay," she said in a small voice. "Will you look at all the people who came? More than at Philip's funeral. I wonder how many will come to the next?"

"Shhh," Knight said. He took her hand, and she gripped back tightly.

"Yes," she said, "this whole business is driving me a little crazy. Dr. Schumacher's crazier, though. I think he's gone around the bend. Help me find a new job, will you, Cletus? That's one of the things I wanted to talk to you about. I'm ready for a change."

"Sure," Knight said. "Leave it to me."

The service was ready to begin. Dr. Schumacher went on to sit with his wife. Christy, Knight, and Sue Teasdale sat in the back. Behind them the chapel doors opened several times as latecomers arrived.

For a memorial service, not a standard funeral, the service seemed on the formal side. It was conducted by a young minister whose light tenor voice chimed oddly with the resonant words: "I am the resurrection, and the life: he that believeth in me, though he were dead, yet shall he live. . . ."

Christy saw that few young people were in the chapel. Peter's schoolmates all had classes at that hour, he supposed. Or maybe teenagers shied away from paying last respects to the local drug dealers. When Christy became conscious again of the tenor voice, it was brisk, rapid. The minister was getting on with it: "Behold, thou hast made my days *as* an handbreath; and mine age is nothing before thee. . . ."

Poor Mrs. Schumacher. Her slim shoulders heaved with sobs. Good, Dr. Schumacher was slipping an arm around her and patting her awkwardly. The tenor voice rapped on: "O spare me, that I may recover strength, before I go hence, and be no more." What was that from? Psalms? "Thou turnest man to destruction. . . . Thou carriest them away as with a flood. . . . *they are* like grass. . . . In the morning it flourisheth, and groweth up; in the evening it is cut down, and withereth. . . ."

A half-dozen men sitting together in back of the Schumachers looked like more professional colleagues. Christy suddenly spotted Karen Hamilton sitting across the aisle. As if feeling his gaze, she turned and saw him, too. She smiled, but her smile faltered as her eyes went to Sue Teasdale, sitting next to him. She turned away and looked at the preacher. There were other familiar figures among the mourners. Christy saw at least two patients. The owners of two patients, rather. Jean and Harriet sat quietly at the side of the chapel. Mrs. Read, owner of Dandy the Husky, was beside them. Was she having Dandy psychoanalyzed, like Agatha? Mark Niemeyer sat near them staring at the ceiling. Bev Farrell wasn't with him, which surprised Christy. There was another head near the front that he recognized, Nat Shannon's. Christy felt in his pocket for the manila envelope with the glove. It made him feel a little less of an intruder, as though he had a real reason for being there.

A choir of three men and three women sang a hymn. The choir had sheet music, and no one else seemed to know the words:

> "Day of wrath! O day of mourning!
> See fulfilled the prophet's warning!
> Heaven and earth in ashes burning!"

All through the minister's brief eulogy of whatever admirable qualities he had been able to discover in young Peter, Christy found himself thinking of the parents, not the son. He realized the service was over only when Knight and Sue Teasdale rose. People crowded around the Schumachers.

Christy looked for Karen, but she had already slipped out. So he went over to Nat Shannon.

The police officer looked tired. He looked preoccupied. He gave Christy a weary smile and a shake of the head. "Don't ask me," Shannon said. "Don't mention 'progress.' Don't inquire about 'new leads.' Talk about the weather. It's about all I can stand at the moment."

"I take it things aren't going too well," Christy said.

"Watch it," Shannon said. "You've crammed about six implied questions into one remark. If things were going well, maybe I could get some sleep. Maybe Chief Fellows would even stop asking me when I'm going to have something new to report. Or stop asking questions about you."

"He, uh, he's asking questions about me?"

Shannon nodded grimly. "You still look pretty good to Fellows," he said. "After all, you're new in town and you have a nasty habit of falling out with murder victims just hours before they end up dead."

"I hope that's your idea of a bad joke," Christy said.

"Yeah," Shannon said. "I laugh every time Fellows starts pushing me to look into your background. Maybe I shouldn't tell you this, but Dr. Schumacher phoned Chief Fellows and requested the same kind of inquiry on you. How about it, Christy? Did you know the Schumacher kids sometime in your deep, dark past? Get involved in burglaries and pot pushing with them?"

"My past is about as mysterious as a tube of toothpaste," Christy said defensively. "It's all on record, Shannon. Just call some of my old professors at Colorado State. Or call my mother in New York. Good Lord, don't. I mean, don't call my mother. Come on, Shannon, I've spent just about my whole life going to school, ear-deep in books. I sure haven't had any time to get involved in crime."

"That's about what I expected," Shannon said. "Don't worry about it. Like I told the chief, these shootings of two brothers aren't your run-of-the-mill homicides. Someone is trying to make a point. Not that I think it's beyond a cat-and-dog doctor to make a point now and then, but it seems a little heavy-handed over a simple car mishap and a trashed apartment."

"Thanks for that, anyway," Christy said. "I guess I'll just incriminate myself again if I give you that glove I told you about. Your Chief Fellows will surely think something is dicey about my having it."

"Oh, the glove," Shannon said. "I'd have been over to pick it up by now, but we've had our hands full with Jerome and the Schumacher homicides and matching the loot from the cabin against our swipe sheets and lab tests and all the people who keep coming in to volunteer information or ask questions. Maybe I'll make it out this afternoon. Sorry I've been so slow. We're pretty short-staffed at the moment, it being the off-season."

"I figured as much," Christy said. "So I thought I'd save you the trip."

"You brought it?" Shannon said. The weariness in his eyes evaporated a little as Christy reached for the manila envelope. But Knight interrupted.

Knight said, "Nat, can you spare just a minute? I want to point out someone to you. Sue Teasdale, the Schumacher maid. She has information for you about some anonymous phone calls the Schumachers have been receiving. Dr. Schumacher said not to tell the police, but Sue decided it would be best. She doesn't want to upset Dr. Schumacher by talking to you right under his nose at his son's funeral, so I told her I'd alert you that she'll be calling. She says she'll come by the station this afternoon when she gets a private moment, okay?"

Shannon looked wearier than ever. "I'm not sure I'll be in this afternoon," he said. "Come on, I'll meet her outside, and we'll find a handy bush to skulk behind while she fills me in."

Knight objected and began to explain. The mention of

anonymous phone calls alerted Christy, but Shannon gave him a look that said he was being a busybody, and Christy turned away to give them a little privacy. He knew he could ask Knight all about it later.

People were leaving the chapel. Mrs. Read and Harriet McAfee were occupied in signing one of those forlorn little white guest books that funeral directors later presented to a grieving family, and Jean Ditton seemed to have struck up a conversation with Mark Niemeyer. They walked out of the chapel talking, and Harriet hurried to catch up with them, but Mrs. Read spotted Christy and came over. Upset by the two murders, Mrs. Read was thinking of flying home, and she had just learned that a health certificate was needed for Dandy the Husky.

"That man one of the McAfee sisters was talking to said the air-freight people never think to ask for a health certificate unless you don't have one, then they always ask," Mrs. Read said. "You don't think flying would frighten Dandy, do you? I'd be right on the plane with him, but Mr. Niemeyer said they insist on putting the poor dogs in with the baggage, so Dandy won't know that, would he?"

Christy thought of the big dog. He seemed a stable specimen. "I think he'll be just fine, Mrs. Read," he said. "Especially since he's never flown before. I've known a couple of dogs that seemed to learn fear after they'd been on a plane a few times, but the first time out didn't bother them a bit."

"Perhaps I should drive back after all. I'm just afraid it will decide to snow, and there we'd be, stuck in a blizzard somewhere. And I wouldn't be gone that long. Just until the police catch this crazy murderer. It would be so much easier if I could leave my car here."

"Why go at all?" Christy asked. "You don't think you're in danger, do you?"

"A woman alone is always in danger," Mrs. Read said. "My husband used to make that point continually."

Nat Shannon rejoined Christy, giving Mrs. Read his look of apparently chronic fatigue. Christy thought of introducing Shannon as the local guardian of the law and enticing him into reassuring Mrs. Read as to her safety, but the officer's expression made him think twice. Shannon nodded a bit curtly to Mrs. Read and said, "The glove, Christy? I'll take it now."

Christy handed over the envelope. Shannon opened it and slid the glove out. "They look like an exact match, but damned if they're not both for the left hand," he said. "Now what kind of screwball thing is that?"

"It beats me," Christy said. He smiled guiltily at Mrs. Read, and just as guiltily he said to the police officer, "Now, look, Nat, I don't know whether you can get fingerprints off leather or not, but if you do, you'll have to hang both me and Gala. I guess I've handled it six or seven times, taking it away from her and putting it back in her basket."

"I'm not the expert, but I doubt if this thing will give us any clear prints," Shannon said. "If it does, though, we'll need your prints for comparison. Will you be at the clinic this afternoon if—"

A heavy hand grasped Christy's shoulder and jerked him backward. He struggled for balance. Mrs. Read gasped and Officer Shannon blinked in surprise, offering no help, but another ally must have stepped in, for Cletus Knight's low voice rumbled, "Just a minute, Doctor," and the hand let go of Christy.

Christy turned to see Dr. Schumacher. The man was paler than ever. "Who are you?" Schumacher asked Christy hoarsely. His red eyes turned to Mrs. Read. "Who are *you?* What do you want from me?"

Christy could only stammer. Knight said quietly, "This is Dr. Gordon Christy, Dr. Schumacher. He's filling in for Dr. Potter. I thought the two of you had met. And this lady is . . ."

"My name is Carolyn Read," Mrs. Read said. "I'm vacationing in Vail. I do hope we haven't upset you, Doctor."

Schumacher stared at Christy and Mrs. Read for a moment longer, then looked toward the guest book. Finally his gaze locked on the black glove in Shannon's hand. "I have the right to know," Schumacher said. "Both my boys. Both of my poor boys . . ."

Nat Shannon said, "Yes?"

Schumacher shook his head and took a step backward. "This is not the place," he said. "But I have the right to know."

Shannon gestured with the hand that held the glove. "I believe I understand, Dr. Schumacher," he said. "It has to do with this business of the phone calls, doesn't it? I'll be glad to go over the details with you later, of course, but I think you'll find that Dr. Christy has no involvement of any kind with this. As for this lady—"

"How do you know about the phone calls?" Schumacher asked.

"I'm a policeman," Shannon said. "It's my business to know. If you'd come to me earlier and told me about them, I might have . . ."

The doctor turned away wordlessly. Christy gaped after him. "He's serious, isn't he, Nat?" he said. "He really thinks I'm some sort of spook that murdered his two sons."

"Good heavens!" said Mrs. Read.

"No, he's just grabbing at straws," Shannon said. "I'll straighten him out. Don't worry, Christy."

9

"DON'T WORRY, DON'T WORRY," Christy fretted to Knight as they left the chapel with Mrs. Read. "All Shannon does is worry me, then tell me not to worry." To Mrs. Read, he added, "I hope that business back there didn't distress you."

"No, but really, what could that doctor have been thinking?" Mrs. Read said.

Knight said, "Don't let Schumacher bother you. He's not himself, according to Sue. Those phone calls have just about driven him over the brink."

Having Mrs. Read with them made questioning Knight awkward, but Christy was deeply curious. "What about the phone calls?" he asked. "Who's been calling? What's it about?"

Knight looked around, as if checking for the whereabouts of Officer Shannon or Dr. and Mrs. Schumacher. "Just some crackpot, probably," he said. "You know, the kind of nut who gets his kicks deviling people after a death in the family. Sue says the phone rings three or four times a day, and

when they answer it, all they hear is a whispering voice saying vicious things."

Mrs. Read said, "How awful."

"What kind of things?" Christy asked. "And why didn't
Dr. Schumacher want to tell the police?"

"I don't know," Knight admitted. "Sue didn't tell me any
specifics. Then Shannon took her off to his car to talk to her,
so I didn't get a chance to listen in."

Mrs. Read stayed with Christy and Knight, looking both
disturbed and excited, rather like Harriet McAfee had
looked when she told of seeing Peter Schumacher on the
morning of his death. Apparently a safe brush with crime was
as exciting as a game of bridge. Mrs. Read's bridge buddies,
the McAfee sisters, walked up a moment later, escorted by
Mark Niemeyer. The women asked if they could pick up
Agatha the Sheepdog on their way home, and Christy remembered his manners and introduced Knight to all the
ladies. Knight and Mark Niemeyer already knew each other.
Since they were near Knight's Bentley, Christy also introduced Annie the Doberman, as a small public-relations gesture for the Doberman Pinscher tribe. The two sisters
seemed to have overcome some of their timidity about
Dobermans. They tried to make friends with Annie, but the
young dog was aloof. Mark Niemeyer ignored Annie's
hauteur and scratched her back, at which she promptly
melted and allowed Mrs. Read to scratch her as well.

"She's a beauty, Cletus," Mark said. "Have you put any
points on her yet?"

"No, I haven't even had her in a show ring," Knight said.
"I'm going to wait until she's mature before I start taking her
out. Tell me, Mark, was young Peter an acquaintance, or are
you a family friend?"

Mark's face stiffened slightly. "Neither," he said. "Mine
is a professional relationship with Dr. Schumacher. Oh, I
wasn't a patient. But a good friend was."

"Oh, yes," Knight said, nodding. His questioning gaze wandered to the sisters and Mrs. Read.

"Jean and I are neighbors now," Harriet said. "The chalet we rented after we got Agatha is just two doors away from them. Jean thought it would be proper for us to come, just to show the Schumachers we care."

"I'll bet you took them a loaf of banana bread or the like," Christy said.

"Zucchini bread, actually," Harriet said. "How ever did you know?"

"You seem the good-neighbor type," Christy said. "Miss Teasdale, the Schumacher maid, was sort of lamenting before the, um, first funeral that Vail isn't the kind of place where one has a lot of old friends and neighbors to bring things for the, um, grieving families."

Knight let no one off the hook. The question mark in his eyes was turned lastly upon Mrs. Read, who said she had gone to the sisters' chalet to consult with them as to whether she should temporarily leave Vail to its murderer, and they suggested that she come along with them to the service.

"And I'm not sorry I came," she said stoutly. "Even if Dr. Schumacher did glare at me so. It's a Christian act to go to any church service. Besides, I was feeling very much alone, and now I've seen Jean and Harriet, and you, Dr. Christy, and I've met you, Mr. Knight, and you, Mr. Niemeyer, and it would be silly to feel all alone with so many people around you, wouldn't it?"

The sisters promptly began clamoring that Mrs. Read shouldn't cut her vacation short. Mark politely chimed in, and even Knight rumbled a reassurance, and it was several minutes before Christy could assure the two sisters that he would be back at the clinic promptly to release Agatha to them. Good-byes were said. Once in the Bentley with Knight, Christy said, "I think I'm about to ask you for a pretty heavy favor. Will you be busy this afternoon after I close the clinic?"

"Nope. I'm free right now, for that matter," Knight said. "Alicia took Lucille into Denver shopping, so I'm at loose ends until they decide to come back."

Christy checked his watch. It was a quarter after three. "I guess I'll have to impose on you later, if you don't mind," he said. "I've got a cat with an abscess already waiting. And there are other appointments. You know how it is, everything is a major emergency to pet owners. Is it okay if I bring Gala when I come?"

"Just try to get through the door without her," Knight said. "What's this favor you have in mind? Tell me now, and maybe I can get going on it this afternoon."

"No, I need time to get my thoughts marshaled," Christy said. "I want to make sure I can explain myself."

"Fine," Knight said. "Let's make it for cocktails and dinner, then. And as long as you've got appointments on your mind, put me down for Annie and her bug bump first thing in the morning. Empty stomach, right? No food or water after midnight, right? I guess you couldn't do it at my house, right?"

Knight was indeed right. Christy figured a maximum of five minutes for the minor surgery, but surgery it would be, and Christy liked all the breaks he could get. Completely sterile conditions. Precautions like the heart monitor, since young Annie would have to be anesthetized. Knight began nodding his head long before they arrived at the clinic and asked only that he be allowed to remain with Annie during her small ordeal, which was fine with Christy. It always seemed to reassure an animal to have its owner around.

Christy's afternoon schedule kept him at the clinic later than he intended. Then, in the early darkness after closing hours, Dandy the Husky kept him even later, arriving at the side of his mistress, who rattled and banged at the front door as though impelled by some dire emergency. Christy heard the knocking just as he was going out the back door. He hurried to open the front door, his eyes all for the big dog.

He threw on the light switch and grabbed Dandy's leash. "First examination room on the right," he said quickly. "What's the matter with him, Mrs. Read?"

"I don't know," she said. Her voice was so shaky that Christy stopped looking at the Husky and turned concerned eyes on Mrs. Read instead.

"Are you all right?" he asked.

Mrs. Read smiled with queer triumph, but her voice was still shaky as she answered, "You bet I'm all right. Dandy saw to that. But that man might have hurt him. He kicked him and hit him, trying to get loose. Poor Dandy. As soon as the man ran away, I rushed right here."

"You'd better sit down a minute," Christy said, pulling forward a reception room chair.

"No, if Dandy's hurt, we've got to help him."

"Just sit," Christy commanded. "I can look at him right here." He knelt and gave Dandy a quick once-over, but except that the Husky seemed excited, Christy could spot nothing wrong. He turned his attention back to Mrs. Read. "He seems perfectly fine," Christy said. "Now tell me slowly. What do you think might have happened to him?"

"There was a man," Mrs. Read said. "He must have followed me into the hall when I started back to our room with the ice bucket."

"At your inn?" Christy said.

"Yes, of course. I'd left Dandy in the room. It was just for ice. There's nothing wrong with an evening cocktail, is there? Particularly after something as depressing as a funeral. Even if you're by yourself and do have to drink it alone?"

"No, certainly not," Christy said.

"So just as I was coming back and unlocking the door, a man rushed out of the shadows and pushed me, right into my room," Mrs. Read said breathlessly. "I spilled every cube of ice. Well, I fell down, on top of Dandy, who always waits right inside the door, and Dandy saved my life, Dr. Christy. Can you imagine that?"

"He went for the man?"

"Growling like Satan himself!" Mrs. Read said. The triumph was in her voice now. "It must have been that insane murderer. Or a crazy rapist. Well, I don't care if he was just a mugger, Dandy fixed him good and proper. He must have grabbed the man by the arm or leg or something. From where I was, still on the floor, I could see the man was kicking at him, trying to get away. Please, does he have any broken ribs? And then there was the blood. I saw it when the man ran away, blood flecks on the carpet. Then there was this. What is this, Dr. Christy? The man dropped this."

Christy was distracted. He glanced at the blue plastic cylinder Mrs. Read held out to him without recognizing it, being too busy probing Dandy's ribs. Dandy uttered a warning growl, and Christy sat back respectfully on his heels, although he smiled at the dog.

"Hold his collar good and tight for me, Mrs. Read," he said. "Dandy's still got his blood up."

"Blood? He's really bleeding?"

"Not as far as I can see. Hold him carefully now. I don't want him to try his shiny teeth on me." Christy remained distracted for a few seconds by Dandy's heavy coat, which made a close inspection for any small wounds difficult. But he found nothing, and he sat back on his heels again and asked for the plastic cylinder. Before he could stop himself, he swore softly under his breath.

"Oh, Doctor," Mrs. Read begged, "tell me. What's wrong with him?"

"Nothing. I'm almost sure. It's just . . . No, it's really nothing. Let's just watch him for a few minutes, shall we?" Observation was the only tool he had now. The plastic cylinder was an object Christy saw many times a day—the protective shield for the needle of a disposable syringe. And a needle in a haystack would be nothing to finding one needle prick under all the luxurious thickness of Dandy's coat.

Christy arranged what he hoped was a calm, confident expression on his face, and he drew a chair beside Mrs. Read and sat in it. Dandy watched alertly, then, after a moment, sat in front of them. "How about you, Dandy?" Christy said. "Congratulations, boy. You're a hero."

Mrs. Read leaned forward and hugged the dog. "He surely is. To think, I was going around feeling alone and, well, vulnerable. I'm not alone. Not with Dandy around. And I'm sure as heaven not vulnerable. You should have seen the way he chased that terrible man through the corridor, Dr. Christy. I had to call him three times before I could get him to come back."

"Then you brought him straight here? I think it would be a good idea to call the police now. And tell me, honestly, do you feel a little scared about going back to the inn? Would you like me to help you find another place to stay?"

"Afraid? With Dandy at my side? Not me," Mrs. Read said. She smiled. "It's a lovely inn, and I feel very comfortable there. I'll phone the police if you want me to, but if there's any question about some disgusting criminal being bitten, and they want to cut off Dandy's head for a rabies test, well, no, maybe I won't report it after all."

"There won't be any chance of that," Christy assured her.

Christy had plenty of time to phone Cletus Knight to apologize for running late, and ample time to observe Dandy the Husky for symptoms of having been injected with some substance, poisonous or otherwise. He also had time to realize that injecting a dog while it's going for your throat was an unlikely act, and that the needle cap probably had nothing at all to do with Dandy. By the time he had calmed Mrs. Read's fears about anything the police might do to Dandy, other than congratulate him, Christy had developed fears about Mrs. Read herself. But no, she had felt no pinpricks. No, she had just been pushed down, although only heaven knew what would have happened next without her beloved Dandy. No, she didn't feel queer or nauseated or dizzy. Yes, she'd make a full report to the police, and since it was right on her way back to the inn, she'd stop by and tell them in person. It was nice of Dr. Christy to offer to drive her, but now that she knew Dandy was so naturally protective, she didn't think she'd ever feel afraid of anything again.

"So you see," Christy told Cletus Knight upon sitting down in Knight's den with a Scotch and water in his hand and his own dog by his side, "not every dog runs in back of you to hide when there's trouble." He petted Gala, to let her know that he didn't hold cowardice against her.

"And Mrs. Read never saw the man's face?" Knight said thoughtfully.

"No," Christy said. "All she saw were his heels, departing speedily while being nipped at by Dandy."

"That needle cap, did you pocket it? Or give it back to Mrs. Read to take to the police?"

Christy made a wry face. "I gave it back to her. I even told her what it was. But, yeah, I hated to do it. Anybody can buy syringes, as all good druggies know. Nevertheless, it really screams 'medical man,' doesn't it? Now Chief Fellows will have a new reason to talk about me and mayhem in the same breath. But since I know I wasn't roaming around an inn attacking ladies with a syringe in my hand, I find myself thinking of Dr. Schumacher instead. He gave Mrs. Read a hard look at the service, you know. Could he possibly have done it? What do you think?"

Knight still looked thoughtful as he sipped his Scotch. "I'm not sure what to think, Christy," he said. "I only know I don't like this kind of thing happening in my town. Attempted assault on middle-aged ladies. Two murders. Sure, Vail is a wacky kind of place. So's Aspen. All resort towns are. The occasional woman will shoot her lover, or the occasional kid decide to finance a ski season by having his clothes starched with heroin in Hong Kong and trying to smuggle it in, but deliberate, brutal murder like the two we've had here attracts the kind of attention Vail could do without."

"Don't you think Shannon can handle it?" Christy asked.

"He hasn't done too well so far," Knight said. "I don't mean to cast aspersions on Nat. He's a good man. But this may be outside his experience. Until Jerome came along and organized his band of rip-off artists, serious crime-prevention in Vail meant keeping cars off prohibited streets."

"Do you think Jerome is our killer?"

"No, and neither do the police," Knight said. "Nat wasn't in a very confiding mood today, but I understand that they've got a darned good case against Jerome for heading a burglary ring, and nothing else. He's clear for Peter's death."

"Because the police can't prove that Jerome or any of his people did it?"

"Because they don't think Jerome's people did it in the first place. They've picked up most of his chums, but the word is that the inner circle, at least, are going to face burglary raps. No murder charges."

"I agree with Shannon," Christy said. "I keep coming back to the Schumacher family. Not just the two boys, but the whole family. What did you mean when you asked Mark Niemeyer if he was a family friend or a friend of Peter's?"

Knight looked uncomfortable. "Well, Mark's gay," he said. "Sorry if that sounds discriminatory. I'm the last guy who wants to come on like a bigot. But the whole world knows that sometimes an older guy and a younger kid get it on together, and the older guy might live to regret it."

"Not Mark," Christy said. "Gay or not, he likes animals."

Knight smiled. "And people who like animals never commit murder? That's an interesting theory, Christy."

"Well, what about Bev Farrell?" Christy argued. "She likes Mark. And she's one wise old gal. She'd never be chummy with him if he weren't a good guy."

"Even good guys kill people," Knight said. "And Mark may have had a motive. Remember his mentioning a good friend who was a patient of Schumacher's?"

"Yeah, you acted as if you'd heard about it."

"I had. The guy committed suicide. It created a little stir. That was a couple of years after Schumacher showed up in Vail. It seems Mark's buddy was seeing Schumacher twice a week, and it was right after one of his sessions with the good doctor that he went home and blew his brains out. People gabbed. Wondered just what kind of therapy the doctor was handing out. You know."

"I know I'll ask Mark. Or Bev Farrell. She'd know if Mark had a grudge against Schumacher for anything. But you just put your finger on what worries me about the Schumachers. You said he 'showed up in Vail.' Remember what Karen told us Sunday, that no one seems to know anything about their past? So I'm wondering, where did the Schumachers show up from? Better yet, what happened to make them come here?"

"From the mouths of babes," Knight breathed. He spoke softly but so fervently that all the Dobermans in the room, and there were seven including Gala, sat up and pricked their ears to attention.

"Don't give me any credit," Christy said. "Schumacher himself put me onto the idea. You saw how he reacted at the memorial service when I gave that glove to Shannon. It was like he was scared half to death. He was over there in nothing flat, babbling at us."

"You think it's important?"

"Darn right. Sure, he'd seen another glove like it when Peter was killed, but there was a difference. This one was chewed and slobbered on and wadded. It didn't really look the same unless you were expecting it, like Shannon. But Schumacher, with only the slightest glance from across the room, came flying over to us like gangbusters. I'd like to know why."

"Good question," Knight said.

"Here's something else that Nat pointed out to me: The gloves weren't even a match. I mean, he said they were identical, but both were for the left hand. Left. What could that mean?"

Knight mulled it over. "Left . . . bar sinister . . . bend sinister, to be more precise . . . the mark of bastardy? Or just something sinister? Or just general screwiness? Damn. I thought maybe we were onto something, but what?"

"I don't know."

"Start over. There's a point here somewhere, if we can find it."

Christy said, "Okay, Dr. Schumacher shows up out of nowhere, starts up a practice in a smallish resort town with a mainly transient population. Why? No one seems to know where he's from. Again, why? His two kids get bumped off in exactly the same way, with fancy little curlicues designed to catch attention, one of which, the glove, sends him into instant hysteria. For the third time, why?"

"Is this leading to the favor you wanted to ask?"

Christy ducked his head, staring into his Scotch. He took a deep breath and said, "Yeah. I'd like to know more about the good doctor. I'd like to know where he's from and why he won't talk about it."

"And you think I know the answers?" Knight's tone had an edge to it.

"No, no, I didn't mean that," Christy said. "But you do seem to have access to an awful lot of information. I thought maybe you could find out. You know, check with your, uh, friends, and have them put out some feelers."

"My friends?" Knight said.

Christy sipped his Scotch to avoid looking at Knight. "Yeah, I, uh, was talking to Karen about you, and she said, uh . . . Well, I don't really guess it's any of my business how you get the information as long as you're willing to try. You will try, won't you?"

Knight leaned forward and set his drink on a coaster. He said, "Christy, would you like to know what I do for a living?"

Christy swallowed the last of his Scotch. "Not if you don't want to tell me."

Knight rose and crossed to the huge desk that stood in apparent idleness by the French doors that led to the aviary. Nothing but the same glass paperweight disturbed its surface. Not even a pencil. Knight took a key from his pocket, unlocked a lower drawer, and opened it to reveal that it was stuffed full of files. He chose one, apparently at random, and handed it to Christy. Loose-leaf ledger sheets filled with neat rows of black figures. Correspondence filed in the back.

"Bookkeeping?" Christy said incredulously.

"That's right. I'm just a plain old ordinary certified public accountant," Knight said. "I also do a lot of general financial advising. My clients maybe aren't so plain and ordinary, but that's their affair. Don't you agree?"

Christy nodded mutely.

"No, you don't agree," Knight said. "I can see it in your face. But I happen to be good at what I do, Christy. Maybe my clients aren't all boy scouts, but they trust me, and I work hard to earn that trust. I don't do phony figures, and I don't cheat Uncle Sam, and I never mix in where I'm not wanted. They come to me for one thing, to keep them straight with the Feds. My people may get in scrapes with the law from time to time, but never because of anything I do. And in return, they leave me out of their dealings. I make good money and I live a good life. Not bad for a burned-out jock who wasn't supposed to be smart enough to add anything higher than his point-per-game average."

Christy swirled the ice in his glass and studied the pattern as if it were tea leaves. "You, uh, you played basketball?" he said. A silence fell, and Christy finally looked up to see Knight staring serenely at him.

"Yes," Knight said. "Us black folk is good at that. We also got rhythm."

"Oh, hell, I didn't mean it like that," Christy said. "I

didn't ask because you're black. I asked because you're so damned tall."

Knight laughed, and he really seemed to mean it. "We're into all the minorities tonight, aren't we? First gays. Then blacks. Now the downtrodden tall people of the world. Yes, I played a little pro ball. Three years with New Orleans."

"The Jazz? How come I never heard of you?"

"I got hurt the first year and never played up to strength after that. Besides, I was there when Pistol Pete was still shooting the bottom out of all the baskets. It's hard to get any notice on a court with a run-and-gun guard like Maravich grabbing all the glory. Not that I minded. Without him, we would have stunk up the place."

"You got hurt?"

"Everybody does. Pro ball. College ball. Probably even the peewee leagues these days. You know, the old business of you hurt when you play, and you play when you're hurt. Sprain an ankle, you're supposed to plead for novocaine so you can stay in. That sort of thing. So you get chummy later with an orthopedic surgeon, and you hurt a little for the rest of your life. Then you leave sports, limping a little, or limping a lot, and you start over again. A lot of my friends ended up that way, standing on street corners wondering where the glory days and the money went. But I was one of the wise ones. At least I learned something in college."

"Accounting, right?"

"Yes, I was a pretty good college ball player, and I figured I might make good money with basketball, and I wanted to know how to handle it. Man, you're looking at a partner in five fried chicken stands in New Orleans and two in Denver. Are you impressed?"

"Darn right. All I own is two suits and about three pairs of socks."

"That's okay. You're just starting out. Once you make a few spare bucks, you bring it to old Uncle Cletus, and I'll advise you on a few investments. I'm pretty good." Gently, the big man added, "And, Christy, I meant it about keeping things clean. Anything I do with investments is legitimate."

"I can't wait to get rich," Christy said. "Then you'll make me richer."

"Right. But first let's get this nasty mess cleaned up, okay? You want me to ask some questions, all right, I'll ask. I can't guarantee results, but I have a few acquaintances who owe me favors, and maybe they can talk to friends. Where do we start? How do you find a doctor with no past?"

"That's the point," Christy said. "It isn't easy for a doctor to hide his past. Not if he's still practicing. In the first place, a physician has to apply for a license to the state board of medical examiners. I expect there would be a medical jurisprudence exam that he'd have to pass. At any rate, his credentials are on record somewhere, probably in Denver. Where he got his degree, his course of study, probably where he had his practice before he came here. They'd want to make sure he didn't specialize in malpractice, it seems to me. For all I know, it's a matter of public record. Maybe I could check into it myself."

"No need," Knight said. "If Schumacher had to get a Colorado license in order to practice, I can take it from there. But what if we track Schumacher down and discover he's a nice guy who only came to Colorado to fight his allergies or something?"

"In that case, I guess I'll back off and leave things to Shannon," Christy said. "But I think I'm right. I think there's more to it than just someone with a grudge against a couple of kids."

"If it turns out you're right, does the information go to Shannon?"

"Yes. Certainly. I've got no hangups about playing amateur detective. I just want to get off his most-wanted list. I'll hand everything to Shannon and step away. Nothing could make me happier than keeping my nose in infected cat wounds and sarcoptic mange. Shannon can do the rest."

Knight seemed satisfied and talked skiing after that, over a simple but gargantuan meal of baked ham and potato salad. Christy's mind was still busy, but he fell in with Knight's topic, and they dissected the new Beaver Creek resort next door like two proper Vail chauvinists, then attacked Aspen before Christy took Gala home. It was early enough for Knight to get started on phone calls, but too late for the business Christy had in mind. Given a clear hour or two tomorrow, he would go at it. In spite of his earnest avowal to Knight that he had no interest in playing amateur detective, Christy saw no sense in letting Knight do all the work. He would check with Bev about Mark Niemeyer. And if he could manage a word with Sue Teasdale without running into Dr. Schumacher and risking another scene, he'd like to ask her more about the anonymous phone calls and also about her movements that Sunday when she left Peter Schumacher alone and went out to eat. Not that he thought she was in any way involved, but someone must have known she would be gone, or somehow learned that Peter Schumacher would be alone.

Thinking of Sue led Christy to think of Karen Hamilton, the way she looked at the funeral when she saw Sue, the way she hurried to leave when the service was over. Was there some animosity between the two young women, or was it a simple matter of jealousy? Not jealousy over himself. Christy was too modest to think Karen regarded him as much more than a nice fellow who had an unfortunate habit of associating with scary dogs. But weren't women sometimes jealous of each other just because each suspected the other might be a little prettier, a little more charming? Or was it deeper than that?

At the cabin, Christy ordered Gala to her basket and started to build a fire in the fireplace, but when he went outside for more kindling he saw that he had left a light on earlier in the clinic. There were no patients in residence. No need for lights. He felt in his pocket for the clinic keys, then strolled over and let himself in the back door. The hall was dark. He groped for a light switch, but as he touched it, he froze. He distinctly heard movement in the reception room.

Christy's first thought was of Gala lying in her basket, waiting for him back in the cabin. He wanted her beside him. That reminded him of the man who had gone for Mrs. Read but met Dandy earlier that evening. Then his racing thoughts got really alarming. He thought of Dr. Schumacher's rage at the funeral. If the doctor really believed Christy was responsible for the gruesome deaths of his two sons, might he not hunger for revenge? His last thought was of the unknown murderer himself, someone who obviously felt no compunction about slaughtering people. A large lump jumped up in Christy's throat. Slowly he moved forward. As he moved, the reception-room light went out.

Christy kept going, trying to be completely silent. Half crouching. Blind-man's buff. Listening for sound. Was that a scraping noise? He stopped and listened, endlessly, and when all remained silent he crept forward again, mentally lamenting the barren state of the hall. He wanted a weapon. A chair, a bottle, some kind of club to hit the intruder with. Should he risk detouring into Dr. Potter's office to see what his hands could find in the dark? But stopping seemed more frightening than going on.

He felt his way down the hall until his fingers touched nothingness, and he knew he had arrived at the doorway of the reception room. Should he leap into the darkness crying, "Ah ha?" Instead, he found the light switch and punched it on. Instantly he heard movement behind the reception-room door, and by reflex he slammed his shoulder against it to squash whoever was in back of it. It slammed outward and caught him a hard bump. Christy was off balance. His balance teetered still more, and he sprawled on the floor.

Christy yelped. He heard the sound and had time to feel ashamed of himself for cowardice before he twisted quickly, trying to get to his feet. A silver-tipped cane punched him in the stomach. The man holding the cane peered down at him. He was portly, and his wide, staring eyes looked through heavy trifocals. The man peered a moment longer, then said, "What am I supposed to say? Dr. Christy, I presume?"

"Who are you?" Christy asked.

"Who do you think I am?" the man said. "Who else has a right to be here?"

Christy stammered, "Good Lord, are you Dr. Potter?"

"Who else? It's nice to see you're not in jail. I came as soon as I could, but I had a hard time convincing"—he mumbled a name—"that I absolutely had to put the quietus on my vacation. I thought you were someone trying to break in here. Trying to smash up the place like they did my condo."

Potter had already heard about the condo? Apprehension's icy fingers clutched Christy's intestines. His stomach also was expressing outrage at being punched by Dr. Potter's cane. "If you wouldn't mind letting me up, I'll double-check the clinic," Christy said. "But I suspect there's no one here but us."

"Oh, yes, sorry about knocking you down." A sparkling set of false teeth gleamed. "Knocked you flat, didn't I?"

They migrated naturally into Potter's office. Now that he had a chance to look at Dr. Potter, Christy was amazed that the rotund man had been able to move so forcefully when Christy tried to immobilize him behind the door. He was about five feet ten, but his avoirdupois made him look shorter. Dr. Potter was dressed resplendently in a pale gray suit with a pink waistcoat, pink paisley tie, and pink-and-white striped shirt. A thick fringe of gray hair curled neatly around his balding pate. Wrinkles proclaimed that despite his reputation as a ladies' man, Dr. Potter was sixty or sixty-five years old if he was a day. Maybe older. What name was it that he had swallowed so smoothly? Paddy? More likely a charming widow named Patty who would be reluctant to end her romantic vacation by the sea with Dr. Noah Potter.

Christy plunged in. "You've been told about your condo? It's really wrecked, Dr. Potter, and hardly any of your plants look like they'll survive. I'm very sorry. It was all my fault."

"You have a point," Dr. Potter said. "But I suppose you're not necessarily responsible for all the maniacs in the world."

"I know you expected me to stay there and take care of it."

"True. We'll talk more about it after I have a chance to determine the full loss. I've already been by to take a quick look at the place. I checked in with Miss Carroll, and she told me all. A good thing the bedroom's intact. I wouldn't have a place to sleep tonight. My plants, now, that's a real heartbreaker. Would you believe I'd had that biggest rex begonia for twenty years or more? Coaxing it back to life will be the ultimate challenge to my green thumb. Hmm, I see the office Scotch has disappeared."

"There's plenty at the cabin," Christy said quickly.

"Yes, Miss Carroll said you'd been staying there. Tell you what, I've probably got a swallow or two still on me." Dr. Potter took a silver flask from his back pocket and hefted it. "Yep, just about a swallow apiece. We both could use a boost to our spirits. I don't have anything contagious. I'll go first."

Dr. Potter's thirst was far greater than the contents of his traveling flask. As Christy had left a full bottle of Scotch at the cabin, they locked up tight and moved across the yard. Gala came out of her basket with a rush and a spate of barking at the sight of Potter coming through her door. She charged forward, but she didn't get very close, and Christy could see that the dog was only bluffing. Potter stood still while Christy collared her, then strode onward.

"Got a dog, have you?" he said to Christy. "Get out of the way, girl. It's cold in here. We've got to rustle up a fire."

"Let me do that," Christy said.

"Gladly. Where's the Scotch? Stop that fussing, girl. I'm your host, you know. You're going to have to put up with me. Hurry up, Dr. Christy. If I'm going to extricate you from a murder charge, I'm going to have to know something about it."

Christy paused in the act of going outside for the kindling that he'd started to fetch earlier. "Well, to begin with, I didn't murder anybody," he said.

"Did I ever say you did?" the older man demanded. "No, of course I didn't."

"And I'm just one of the minor suspects they think about when they can't come up with anyone else. The police haven't even come close to charging me. Why, I don't even have a motive."

"From what I gathered from Miss Carroll, nobody does. That makes it all the tougher. Come on, I've got your Scotch poured. Get that fire started. We've got plenty of ground to cover. Lie down, dog. We're going to be here for hours."

10

DR. POTTER PROVED to be a thorough man both in asking questions and in putting away Scotch. Christy felt distinctly jaundiced the next morning when he awoke. He dressed hurriedly, fed and walked Gala, then rushed to the clinic anticipating a quiet session with its electric coffeepot. It was already fully perked and hot. Miss Carroll had arrived early for duty, and so had Dr. Potter, who was in his office, nattily turned out in black slacks, red waistcoat, and a red tie. Christy winced at all that red and looked longingly at the coffeepot. Dr. Potter had Christy's medical charts on his desk and seemed to have other ideas.

"So old Nellie went down," he said by way of greeting. "I'm glad it was you who did it, not me, Dr. Christy."

Christy sidled toward the coffeepot, but Dr. Potter pointed to a chair beside his desk and continued flipping the charts.

"Yes, old Nellie," he said. "I kept her alive at least three years longer than she would otherwise have made it, I suppose. She was a game old bird. Ah, there, Miss Carroll.

Come right in. I'm catching up on things with Dr. Christy. Did the Fischer representative call while I was away? I think I've definitely decided on a new X-ray grouping. And bring the morning schedule when you have time, will you? I want to see what I've got on my plate."

Miss Carroll smiled her lovely smile, looking genuinely pleased to have her employer back. She poured herself a cup of coffee and began answering his questions, and Christy also made it to the pot. He managed to gulp half a mug of hot coffee before Dr. Potter dived back into his discussion of Christy's patients. Miss Carroll brought the day's appointments just as the phone rang, and Dr. Potter grabbed it. "Why, Lisa," he chuckled into the phone, "how did you know I got back early? Sure, bring her in. About ten. I see I've got surgery on a Doberman bitch at nine and a cat at nine-thirty that needs to have his tummy rubbed." He paused. "The male member, my dear, It's always giving problems to senior citizens." Pause. Laughter. "Surely you must have heard that it helps a fellow to have his tummy rubbed. I'm speaking of tomcats, naturally."

When Dr. Potter put down the phone, Christy said, "I'll take the cat and the surgery on Knight's Doberman, Dr. Potter. That'll leave you free for—"

"Nonsense, Dr. Christy. I won't need any assistance. You just concentrate on your murders. No, don't thank me. That's why I rushed home, so you wouldn't be tied up with the practice."

"Well, but, you see—"

"What is it? Speak more clearly."

"I'm no detective, Dr. Potter. I'm a doctor of veterinary medicine. I figured the patients would come before anything else."

"So they do. So they will. And as for your not being a detective, come, come. What are they teaching you young people over at the vet school if not to follow clues and arrive at a solution? It's basic scientific method, Dr. Christy. You collect data and see where they lead you. Now this nine-thirty appointment, a cat with feline urologic syndrome. It so happens that I know the patient but you don't. What would you do before you inititated treatment? You'd evaluate the symptoms. You'd obtain a history, including diet, right? Has the cat dysuria? Hematuria? In your physical exam, you'd determine whether the old boy is obstructed or nonobstructed. You'd collect a urine sample, and you'd keep looking for abnormalities there. Finally you'd arrive at a diagnosis. That's all you have to do to be a detective, Dr. Christy. Isolate your symptoms, evaluate them, and make your diagnosis."

"You make it sound pretty simple."

"No more difficult than veterinary medicine," Dr. Potter said firmly. "Now, as to this surgery you've scheduled. Cletus Knight's youngest bitch, is it? Miss Carroll must have forgotten to bring me her chart."

"No, it's my fault," Christy said. "I guess I didn't think to do more than log it in the appointment book. It's just removal of a histiocytoma."

"Histiocytoma? Where's the tissue analysis?"

"Well, I—"

"Planned to have it analyzed post-surgically, eh? Never mind. I'll go over the little bitch when Knight brings her in. You just run along and see the people we were talking about last night. Bev Farrell's always home in the mornings."

"But, um—"

"As for Dr. Schumacher and his mysterious past, I was thinking about that while I was shaving. Miss Carroll's the one to do a little detective work for us. I think I'll have her call Dr. Avent's receptionist first. What you really want is fellows who have referred patients to Schumacher. Worked with him. They'll know the most about him. Just call in about ten or eleven o'clock, and Miss Carroll can tell you what she's got set up for you."

Christy gave up. "Thank you," he said.

"No thanks necessary." Dr. Potter flipped more charts. He studied one briefly. Craning, Christy saw that it belonged to the warring Akita bitches he'd treated over the weekend. Dr. Potter said, "Can't say I agree with you on Delta Albaplex for bite wounds. In fact, I'd say it was a poor choice."

Christy blinked. "The first doctor I worked with, Dr. Fall, used it for bite wounds," he said defensively. "I thought he knew something I didn't."

"Amoxicillin would be preferable." Potter flipped on to the bottom. "You've taken on some new clients, I see," he said, indicating the last two charts. "What's the idea of giving this Mrs. Read's dog coffee as a stimulant? I must say I never heard of that before."

"Well, Dr. Fall seemed to use it a lot, so I thought—"

"Him again? Did it ever occur to you that he just may have had an oversupply of Delta Albaplex and stale coffee lying around? I'm aware, Dr. Christy, that veterinarians disagree on treatment from time to time, and it must be as perplexing to a newcomer like you as it is to our patients'owners. But when in doubt"—false teeth gleamed—"do it my way. I notice, by the by, that you forgot to record the examination you made of the Husky yesterday evening. Didn't get paid for it, either, I'll bet. Don't worry, I'll ask Miss Carroll to get out a bill this morning. And what about this Old English owned by your Miss McAfee and Mrs. Ditton? I can't imagine how you missed that back. You should have shaved the dog all off when you first started messing with it. I would have."

"I goofed," Christy said glumly. "I started scissoring off the matted coat, and I guess I just kept going with the scissors."

"It's a lot easier to shave a badly matted dog. Take a number-ten or fifteen blade and shear it like a sheep. Hmm, Miss McAfee's obviously single, but what about Mrs. Ditton and Mrs. Read? Grass widows? Well heeled? Any of them good-looking?"

Christy tried to think. Could Agatha the Sheepdog's middle-aged rescuers be considered pretty? Could Mrs. Read? Why not? "Yes," he told Dr. Potter, "they're all three attractive women. I guess they're pretty well-off, too. At least Miss McAfee and Mrs. Ditton were wealthy enough to be staying at the Lodge at Vail before they moved out and rented a chalet so their dog could have a yard. They're sisters. They look a lot alike, and they're both, um, well-filled out."

"Stacked, eh?" Dr. Potter said. "What type are they? Double-knit or après ski?"

"Definitely double-knit. Does that make a difference?"

"It probably means Mrs. Ditton's a widow, not a divorcée," Dr. Potter said. "You develop a sense for these things, Dr. Christy. Well, now, I know you've got a busy morning, and here I'm holding you up. You just go on about your business."

Before hearing from Dr. Potter how badly he'd mishandled his cases, Christy had thought that helping sick animals was his business. He told Gala about it when he moved her from the cabin to a crate in Ward One. She looked at him mournfully. Christy felt the same way. "Sorry, Gala," he told her in a whisper. "I guess I know a good chewing-out when I hear one. Dr. Potter wants me to stay on with him just about as much as you want to grow two tails. I'm afraid Vail isn't in our future, girl. That's all right. We'll stick together wherever we go, won't we?"

Gala cried when he left, and Christy sighed as he decided his relationship with Potter's Jeep was also over. He climbed into his own old car and had to spend five minutes coaxing it to start. The Jeep always roared into life. Then he had to decide what to do first. After Potter's loquacity, he wasn't sure he could take Bev's similar conversational mode without a break. He decided to swing up the hill and do a drive-by of the Schumacher house. If there were no cars around, maybe the Schumachers would be out, and he could get in a quiet word with Sue.

The thought perked Christy up so much that he didn't even mind when his car almost refused the grade and had to toil uphill toward the Schumacher house in low gear. He turned onto Forest Road and did a slow pass by the house, scouting the garage. Sure enough, no cars. He turned at the end of the street and came back, then parked and trotted up the stairs to the second-story deck and rang the bell. He waited one minute. Two. Then, deciding Sue must also be out, he turned to leave. The door opened, and vague, grief-laden Mrs. Schumacher stood before him.

It hadn't occurred to Christy that he might encounter the sorrowing mother of the two dead youths. He felt tongue-tied. What did you say to someone so overladen with suffering? He blurted, "I'm very sorry, Mrs. Schumacher. I just came by to talk to Sue Teasdale for a minute. I didn't know you were home."

Christy felt even more awkward, having said all the wrong things, but Mrs. Schumacher only opened the door wider and said, "Come in. You're Dr. Christy, aren't you? I'm Rosamund Schumacher."

"Yes, I know," Christy said.

She led him into the breakfast room. In a breathy little voice with a subtly clipped accent, she said, "Sue is still asleep. Poor baby, this has all been so hard on her. I told her I'd get Elliott to give her some sleeping pills, but she just won't, so she's awake until all hours. I'll go call her now."

"No, don't. I can talk to her another time."

"It'll be good for her to see you. Dr. Christy, I do want to apologize for the way my husband behaved yesterday. You were so thoughtful to come to Peter's service, then Elliott made such a scene. Officer Shannon came by and talked to him yesterday afternoon, or I wouldn't have known about it. I'm sure Elliott understands now that you're just an innocent bystander."

"Honestly, I didn't think a thing of it," Christy lied.

"How nice you are. It was just that Elliott's been so upset.

Who can blame him? Dr. Christy, no matter what the police said, neither my Phil nor my Pete were members of some burglary ring. Phil found out about it, don't you see? He was going to turn them in, and they killed him."

"Yes. I see," Christy said.

"Well, here I stand chitchatting, keeping you waiting," the woman said incongruously. She tried to smile. Her lips were brightly painted, which made her smile all the more pitiful to Christy. "You have a cup of coffee, Dr. Christy. There's plenty in the pot. And try some of that nice zucchini bread. Sue dresses faster than you'd dream possible. That girl, she's like a daughter to me. Thank God she's here. You wouldn't believe how empty the house seems now."

She left him in the breakfast room in bright sunshine, staring unhappily at the zucchini bread. Christy felt like a crude interloper. He would willingly have sneaked away, but if vague little Mrs. Schumacher was able to face up to death and try to find ways to live with it, Christy figured that he at least could face up to a civilized encounter with her. And Sue didn't keep him waiting long. Within ten minutes she came into the breakfast room with Mrs. Schumacher, looking a little puffy-eyed but otherwise gorgeous. "Hi, Christy," she said. "What are you doing up and about so early in the morning?"

She poured coffee and Christy joined her after mumbling about Dr. Potter's unexpected return, and how he'd been cut loose for the morning to run errands and visit friends. Sue drank as efficiently as she dressed, and when she put down her empty cup, Mrs. Schumacher said, "Now, Sue, you run along with your young man. You needn't mope around here just to keep me company. Take her for a drive, Dr. Christy. She needs to get away from the house."

Sue seemed reluctant to leave Mrs. Schumacher by herself, but the lady was firm, in a motherly sort of a way. Christy found himself outside with Sue, not knowing quite what to do with her. Give her breakfast somewhere? She solved the problem by saying, "Sorry you got stuck with me, Christy. You just had some questions, I'll bet. So did Shannon, after I told him about those phone calls. Where were you off to? Maybe I could ride along with you."

"I was going by Bev Farrell's," Christy said.

"Sure, the dog lady. Will she mind if I come with you? Mrs. Schumacher was right. It is nice to be out."

"Bev won't mind. Neither will I."

Sue said, "Is this your car? You go the unpretentious route, don't you, Christy? That's refreshing in a money town like this. I'm going to have to buy one, but my ambitions rise a little higher."

She opened the car door for herself before Christy could reach for it. "Okay, ask away," she said when he got in. "We'll get your questions over with, then enjoy the morning. What do you want to know? The phone calls?"

Christy put the car in gear. It only died once before it started moving. "Yes, I was talking to Cletus Knight after the service yesterday, and he told me about the calls. He seemed to think they might be from some crackpot."

"Maybe," she said, "I suppose there are nuts who get their jollies that way, but it sounded too ugly to me. And the way Dr. Schumacher has been reacting, I'm not sure you can chalk it off to crazies."

"Was it a man's voice or a woman's?"

"I haven't the foggiest," Sue said, "How can you tell when someone's whispering? That's all it ever is, whispers."

"When did the calls start?"

"Right after Philip's death," she said. "The Maryland relatives were still here, and the uncle answered the first call, I remember. Poor souls, they couldn't get away for the second funeral. It really upset Mrs. Schumacher."

"And what do the whispers say?"

She frowned. "Mean stuff. Just a word or two, and then they hang up. If I or Mrs. Schumacher answer the phone, they don't say anything. They hang up right in our ears. But if it's Dr. Schumacher or Peter . . ." She gulped and tried again. "If it's Dr. Schumacher, then a voice whispers, 'Murderer,' or 'How does it feel?' and nasty things like that."

"Good God," Christy said.

Sue nodded. "Once the whisper was 'How do you like having your first-born die like a dog?'" she said. "Poor Mrs. Schumacher picked up the extension that time, after Peter answered, and she heard it. Well, it was scream-and-sob time, and Dr. Schumacher had to give her a sedative. I finally got to thinking the police should know. Shannon says I did the right thing."

Die like a dog. Dog. Dog doctor? Vet? Dr. Gordon Christy? Was that the chain of reasoning, Christy wondered, that made Peter challenge him the previous Sunday? Or was it something else? He said, "Why didn't Dr. Schumacher want to tell the police?"

"I don't know. At first I think he really believed they were just nuisance calls, some sickie at work. But the calls kept coming, and then Peter . . . the second . . . second shooting . . . and the glove. Dr. Schumacher went a little crazy when he saw that glove. He didn't say anything to Shannon, but I could tell. After that he started taking the calls more seriously."

"And the voice just whispers, 'Murderer,' and short stuff like that, and hangs up?"

"Yes, that's the favorite," Sue said. "It was nearly always that at first. Just 'Murderer.' They didn't start getting fancy until after Peter. They had a new twist last night. 'You tried to kill the wrong person, you murderer.' God knows what they'll think up next."

"The whispers are still coming?"

"Yes. I try to grab the phone first so they'll hang up, but sometimes Dr. Schumacher beats me to it, then he gets the whispers. He glares at me like a fiend when I beat him to the phone, but he hasn't chewed me out."

"Does he try to talk to them?"

"Sometimes. He goes sheet-white every time they call. Sometimes he just stands there holding the phone. A couple of times I heard him say, 'Who are you?' But they always hang up."

"Why are we saying 'they'?"

"I don't know. He? She? It?"

Christy turned east on the frontage road. "What do you know about the Schumachers?" he asked. "Have you any idea where they lived before Vail?"

"No, not really," she said. "Mrs. Schumacher is a friendly old gal, but we don't spend that much time chatting. She knows I'm only there for the bed and board, and she tries to make things easy for me, but it's not as though we're bosom buddies. Why, do you have something special in mind, Christy?"

"Not exactly," he said. "I've just noticed the doctor is close-mouthed about his past. I was wondering if these odd calls might have something to do with that. What about his mail? Surely he gets letters from friends. Have you ever noticed any postmarks or return addresses?"

"The Schumachers don't get much mail," she said. "Just the occasional note from relatives and the usual circulars."

"That's a little odd, don't you think?"

"Not really. The doctor isn't a very outgoing person. I doubt he has many friends."

"Maybe not, but what about Mrs. Schumacher? And the two sons? You'd think they might keep in touch with old friends. People don't just cut themselves off when they move to a new town. Not unless they're trying to hide something, or disappear."

Sue had no theories, and not a great deal of interest in the Schumacher family's mail. Looking out the car window seemed to appeal to her more. Bev Farrell lived near the golf course. The house wasn't large, but it looked like prime property. Christy didn't have to look hard for the address. Bev's red pickup and Mark Niemeyer's Mercedes were parked in the driveway, and Christy winced at the sight of the Mercedes when he pulled up. So much for talking with Bev about Mark privately. From the house, dogs began to bark. Christy stalled for a moment to ask Sue, "Was Dr. Schumacher at home last evening about six o'clock or a little earlier?"

"I don't think so. No, he left the house right after he talked to Shannon and he didn't come back until about seven. Why?"

"First let me ask another question: does he keep syringes around the house? You know, needles, for medical injections?"

"Hmm . . . Yes, when Mrs. Schumacher had hysterics that time about the anonymous phone calls, he injected her with something, so I guess he has syringes around. He must keep them in his study or somewhere, though. Probably in a drawer. I see everything that's lying out when I dust. Why do you want to know, Christy?"

"Mrs. Read, the lady who was standing with me after the memorial service yesterday, had a pretty unpleasant experience around six o'clock. Some man attacked her at her motel. She was pushed down on her face, and her dog got into the act, a big Husky. The guy may have had a syringe with him. She found a needle cap. The guy may also have been bitten. I don't suppose Dr. Schumacher was wearing a bandage or limping or anything this morning, was he?"

"I haven't seen him this morning," she said, "but he looked okay last night. Gee, Christy, you don't think Dr. Schumacher would do a thing like attacking some woman, do you? Why should he?"

"I don't know," Christy admitted. "It's just that syringes automatically make me think of medical people, like Schumacher, or me, or Dr. Potter. I know I didn't do it, and Dr. Potter's been out of town, so I just started wondering."

"I thought you said Potter was back? How do you know he wasn't back in time to visit your Mrs. Read?"

"Well, sure, I guess he could have come back a few hours earlier, but he surely didn't have anything to do with any of this. He hasn't even been in town."

"How convenient for him," she said pointedly.

Christy looked at her, wondering what she was trying to suggest, but Bev Farrell's gruff voice kept him from asking. "Who's out there?" Bev hollered through the door. "Come in if you're coming in, or go away."

Christy and Sue hurried to obey, and the barking got louder as they started up the walk. Then it stopped completely. They heard sounds of activity inside, someone rushing around closing doors to back rooms. Bev finally opened the front door, and a large black cat rushed out of it, a raw chicken neck clutched in its teeth.

"Kate, get back here!" Bev shouted.

Christy had never known a cat before that paid the slightest attention to a command. But Kate the cat halted instantly, reversed herself, and rushed back into the house, still carrying her chicken neck. She put it down in the middle of the living-room carpet. Raw chicken necks went perfectly with Bev's decor. Three were no dogs in sight, and the place was quite clean, but everywhere there were evidences that animals lived here. A floor-to-ceiling cat scratching pole dominated the room, and rubber dog toys lay all around the place. A green alligator and a yellow centipede with long black eyelashes cozied up to an orange porcupine on a sofa, and Christy stepped on a brown camel with a loud squeaker as he entered the room. Three well-chewed nylon bones were scattered by a brown plastic drinking bowl, and a length of shank bone, meatless but still very fresh, had been laid on top of a television set. The cat sat down by her chicken neck and began to devour it while Christy introduced Sue and embarked on the fib that he'd come by hoping to catch Mark Niemeyer.

"Sue Teasdale?" Bev said. "You're the one Knight was telling me about, the one looking for a new job?"

174

"Not really a job," Sue said. "More like room and board. I'm willing to work for it, of course, but I don't really need money or salary. Just a roof."

"You should take what you can get, honey," Bev said. "Vail's full of rich old men and women begging for help, and practically no one who's willing to work for a living." She looked past Sue and Christy and said, "You two come alone?"

"Just the two of us," Christy said.

"Good," Bev said. She raised her voice and called, "It's okay, Mark. You can come out now. It isn't the law."

"The law?" Christy said. He glanced at Sue.

"Yeah, the animal-control people," Bev said. "Mark's back in my bedroom with some of the dogs, keeping them quiet. I always put them away when someone comes to the door. Never know when it'll be some busybody trying to count dog noses. I'm not exactly legal, you know."

Christy cocked his head. "Why do you let that bother you? Knight's over the limit, too, and he never seems to worry."

"No one comes to Knight's door without an invitation," Bev said. "My house is different. I get Bible thumpers and encyclopedia salesmen and neighbors and all sorts of riffraff knocking at my door. Even veterinary doctors. So I hide dogs. It's safer."

Mark Niemeyer came into the room, a loaded syringe in his hand. He said, "For crying out loud, Christy, you've made me lose track. Now I don't know if it was Clyde and Classy that I shot, or Bonny and Brio."

Christy stared at the syringe. "I beg your pardon?" he said.

"It was Bonny and Brio," Bev said. She looked guiltily at Christy and said, "We're shooting my whole pack for parvo this morning. Don't you look daggers at me. Why should I pay you or Dr. Potter fifteen bucks for a parvo shot when I can do it myself for about two?"

"I wasn't looking daggers," Christy said.

"Well, you sure as hell shouldn't," she said. "Not with the prices Potter charges. We still have Clyde and Classy and Freckles to go. Maybe you should do it. For free, of course. After all, you're the one who made Mark lose count." She lowered her voice. "Mark always acts like it's killing him to give a simple sub-cu shot."

Mark heard her, of course. Even with a lowered voice, Bev spoke too loudly. "You should talk," Mark said to her. "You close your eyes every time you even see a needle."

"I can't help it," Bev said. "It's a phobia. Well, how about it, Christy? You going to shoot up the rest of my dogs?"

Christy saw an opportunity. "I'll be glad to do it," he said. "Without charge, naturally. Boosters? What are you using?"

"One cc of Duramune" Mark said. "It's out in the kitchen. We boost them every three months, since everyone but Freckles and Penny gets exposure at dog shows, and Bev figures Freckles and Penny get exposed to the show dogs. I do my brood of Whippets the same way. Do you think we're overdoing it?"

"Probably not. Better to vaccinate too often rather than too infrequently, at least until we know a heck of a lot more about parvovirus. The kitchen? We'll keep the needles away from Bev so she won't faint."

"Don't worry about me," Bev said. "You just tend to my dogs."

Christy took the syringe from Mark and followed him into the kitchen, while Bev and Sue went back to the bedrooms to fetch selected dogs. Kate the cat galloped in with the remains of her chicken neck and leaped up on the kitchen counter. She watched Christy and Mark, then eyed two aristocratic German Shorthaired Pointers with open challenge as they were led into the room. Christy checked the syringe for air bubbles and found it clear. Kate the cat abandoned her chicken neck and jumped down to trot between the two dogs, her tail held sideways and waving like a flag. One of the Shorthairs nudged her curiously, and Kate sat on her haunches and clasped the dog's neck with her forepaws, then began licking its ear.

"Don't mind the cat," Bev said. "She thinks she's a dog." She tightened the lead on a female Shorthair and dragged her to a kitchen table on which alcohol, cotton balls, and two other loaded syringes waited. "This is Classy," Bev said. "Watch her. She hates needles."

Classy was a young bitch, just out of puppydom. Liver and white, with smooth, well-rounded muscles, she nosed Christy's hand and tried to nose the syringe. Christy stooped and lifted a fold of skin in back of Classy's shoulder, cleansed it with alcohol, and popped the vaccine in, then rubbed the spot a moment while Classy regarded him tranquilly.

Mark laughed wryly. "She always growls at me," he said. "Maybe I should ask you for a few lessons, Christy. How come you're running around this morning, anyway? No patients at the clinic? Drumming up trade?"

"Not exactly," Christy said. He took a fresh wad of cotton and soaked it with alcohol, then repeated the process with the dog Sue was holding, a male Shorthair. "Dr. Potter is back, and he just didn't seem to need me anymore."

Bev looked up sharply. "You mean he canned you?" she demanded.

"How vile," Mark said. "You can never tell about people, can you? And Potter always seemed like such a nice old boy."

"No, I'm not fired. Not yet, anyway. I guess I'm just unnecessary."

"That's terrible," Bev said. "I'll talk to him for you. Or better yet, there's a clinic over at Eagle-Vail. Mark and I know the partners pretty well. We'll call them and see if they can't use a bright young man."

"No, please," Christy said. "Thanks anyway, but I'll just wait and see what Potter wants to do."

"Well, he better damned sure do the right thing," Bev said. She murmured at Sue and the two of them took their dogs back toward the bedroom to exchange them for more vaccination victims.

"Bev's right," Mark said. "I'm sure we can get you connected with someone if Potter falls through. If not the Eagle-Vail clinic, surely in Denver. Bev knows a lot of dog people in Denver. Some in Colorado Springs, too."

"That's very kind," Christy said. "But . . . Listen, I have a confession. I didn't come to talk about Dr. Potter and my future. I came by to ask Bev about you, because I was too chicken to ask you myself. It's about your friend who was Dr. Schumacher's patient. The one who killed himself."

Mark's face lost all trace of friendliness. "Put that syringe down," he ordered. "You're not giving any more shots here." He called, "Bev? Bev, what do you think of this? Christy has come over this morning to accuse me of murdering those two young Schumacher creeps!"

"No, honestly," Christy said. "I didn't mean anything like that. I just wanted to ask—"

Bev roared back into the kitchen, followed by an Afghan, two more Shorthairs, and a bewildered Sue Teasdale. Mark repeated himself to Bev, who looked surprised, then deeply indignant. Sue looked intimidated. The dogs romped clownishly underfoot until they realized Bev was angry, then they, too, began to give Christy unfriendly glances.

"Look, I'm sorry," Christy said. "I never thought for a minute Mark had anything to do with the Schumacher shootings. It's Dr. Schumacher's past I'm trying to find out about, not Mark's. I mean, not his friend's. I mean . . . oh hell. Now I've insulted everybody. I apologize to you all. Including you, Sue."

Bev questioned Mark with a raised eyebrow. Looking mollified, he nodded. Bev said, "What about Schumacher's past? Why is that important?"

"Because I've got the crackpot idea the whole Schumacher family had been hiding something. Something that might have started all this grief."

"Something they did?"

"Maybe. Or maybe just something that happened to them."

Bev still looked suspicious. "What makes you think Mark can tell you anything about Schumacher's past?"

"I don't know that he can," Christy said. "I guess I hoped his friend might have mentioned something in passing. You know, anything odd that Schumacher might have let drop during treatments."

Mark said, "I'm afraid I can't help you there. Larry never said much at all about Dr. Schumacher. They always talked about Larry's past during analysis, not the doctor's. That's the way it's supposed to be, isn't it?"

"But your friend did . . . Excuse me, there isn't any delicate way to put this. Your friend did kill himself. Was it because of anything, anything at all, that took place during his treatment?"

Sue's social antennae were sensitive. She interrupted to ask if Bev's back yard was fenced and if it was okay to take the three kitchen dogs outside, then excused herself. She gathered the dogs and led them away expertly. Mark didn't rush to answer Christy's question. He seemed to be thinking it over. Bev decided to talk about Sue, perhaps giving Mark time. "That's one nice girl," she said. "Good with dogs, too. She just might fit very neatly into this household."

Mark looked at the clutter in the kitchen. "As a maid?" he said.

"No, of course not. I don't need a maid. Besides, we talked about that in the bedroom. Sue says Knight has already turned up about three new maids' jobs for her, but she's not sure she wants any of them. All she really needs is a room. She could work in some shop or one of the boutiques for ski-lift money. Just think, Mark, a built-in dog-sitter, for when we're off to the shows."

"Hmm," Mark said interestedly.

"We wouldn't have to take the whole gang every time."

"Mine like to go," he argued. "I wouldn't dare leave any-one at home."

"Aw, come on, Mark," Bev said impatiently, "are you going to tell Christy about Larry or not?"

"I don't know what to tell," Mark said quietly. He gazed at Christy. "It's fairly common knowledge that I'm . . . at-tracted to an alternate lifestyle. Bev knows about it. All of my friends know. I don't make a big thing of it, but I don't try to hide it, either."

Christy said. "Would it bother you to tell me about your friend's suicide?"

"No. I've had plenty of time to get used to that. It de-stroys you at first, you know. You think, What did I do? If I hadn't said this, would he have done that? But Larry wasn't suicidal because he was gay. Believe it or not Christy, some people like being gay. He just had these depressions. They were pretty regular. He could be the happiest guy on earth, then about every three months he'd start getting quiet, and a week later he was in the dumps. God, that's a nice bit of phraseology, isn't it? A manic-depressive gay?"

"Was he really manic-depressive? Is that what Schumacher diagnosed?"

"I don't know. Larry never talked about it. He just got depressed. Then he came home one day about a year ago after a session with Schumacher and shot himself. He was very considerate. He went out into the garage. We'd just put in new carpeting."

Bev said, "Hey, come on, now. You'll get depressed your-self, thinking about it."

Mark said, "No, Bev. You have to come to terms with things. You can't just put it out of your mind and forget be-cause you can't stand thinking about something terrible that happened. If you don't remember, you'll force yourself to forget all the happy times, too. Then you end up with nothing. Christy, I think you're on the wrong track about Schumacher. Being a psychiatrist is a high-risk profession, I guess. Just a couple of weeks after Larry shot himself, one of Schumacher's other patients committed suicide. Maybe it just comes with the trade."

"Two suicides, that close together? Didn't the town decide Schumacher was at fault somehow?"

"Not really," Mark said. "The second man was only a tourist. Hung himself in his hotel room. There was a story about it in one of the papers, just a few days after we shipped Larry's body home, but no one blamed Dr. Schumacher. The man had only been to see him once or twice."

"I don't remember any newspaper story," Bev said.

"You wouldn't," Mark told her. "It was only a couple of paragraphs on one of the inside pages. I might not have noticed it either if it hadn't been for Larry."

Christy said, "And there was nothing odd that Larry ever mentioned about Schumacher? Nothing fishy?"

"Not that I remember. It was all straight couch-and-chatter stuff. I did ask Larry not to bring me into his discussions with Schumacher. I think the right to privacy includes that much. But heavens, we were very happy together. What was there to talk about?"

There was nothing, as far as Christy could see. He gave the last two dogs their parvo boosters and took Sue away soon afterward, finding himself a washout as a detective. It was nearly eleven o'clock, too early to suggest lunch. Sue wanted to go back to the Schumacher house anyway, and Christy figured Dr. Potter might at least allow him to drop by the clinic instead of just calling in. He drove Sue through the village, half listening to her chatter about the possibilities of moving in with Bev Farrell and becoming Bev's resident dog-sitter, and half pondering the meager results of his morning's nosiness. There were new people on his syringe list, for whatever that was worth. Schumacher, Bev Farrell, Mark Niemeyer. Not Potter, no matter what Sue had said earlier. Certainly not Potter. No, that was impossible. Wasn't it? And yet . . . who else had left town so abruptly on the very day of the first death? Who else was so conveniently absent, supposedly in the company of some unnamed person who might or might not exist, when the second Schumacher boy was shot? Who else had turned up unexpectedly in Vail in plenty of time to have attacked Mrs. Read? Who else had such ready access to syringes? Who else but the dapper Dr. Potter?

He urged the car up the hill to Sue's street, still thinking ghastly thoughts. The look on his face must have matched the darkness in his mind, for Sue nudged him and said, "What are you fretting about, Christy?"

He pushed his disloyal thoughts into the background and tried to compose his face. "Nothing," he said. "I was just thinking. It's rotten, isn't it? Ugly things happen, then you can feel ugly yourself trying to find out about it."

Sue reached to the steering wheel and patted his hand. Silently. At least she didn't tell him not to worry. As they rounded the corner, two female voices and an outbreak of doggy yapping hailed him. Harriet, Jean, and Agatha the Sheepdog trotted toward his car, Agatha in the lead. Christy pulled over to the curb.

"How nice of you to stop," Harriet said. She smiled. "And here's Agatha, feeling all too energetic this morning, as you can see. She looks good, doesn't she?"

"She looks fine," Christy murmured, smiling at the big dog. Then he turned to Sue and said, "Sue Teasdale, this is Miss Harriet McAfee, one of your new neighbors."

"We've already met," Sue said cheerfully. "This is the nice lady who brought the zucchini bread."

"Oh, of course," Christy said, "And her sister? Have you met Mrs.—"

"Jean," the other sister said, leaning close to the car window. "Everybody just calls me Jean. Nice to meet you, Sue. Agatha, stop jumping on Christy's car. You're getting mud all over it. But, really, Harriet's right, Christy. Agatha feels just fine today. Her back hardly seems to be hurting her at all. She's been naughty, though, haven't you, you naughty girl? Come see. She dug up a whole bed of tulip bulbs, and she couldn't have been out in the yard more than fifteen minutes."

Nothing would do but that Christy and Sue see the vandalized flower bed. While they were there, Christy checked Agatha over, worrying to himself that her ladies might be allowing her shaved back to get sunburned. Then the ladies seemed confident that as long as he and Sue had come to see Agatha's tulip bed, they would like to see the rented chalet. Agatha romped in, leaving muddy footprints all over the kitchen floor, and complained loudly at being locked into a spacious utility room while Christy and Sue were dragged away for a house tour. If the kitchen was muddy, the rest of the place was immaculate. It seemed an odd setting, though, for the two very proper sisters. A bar dominated the living room. Both bedrooms had king-sized waterbeds, and the one huge bathroom sported not only a small bar of its own but a large hot tub. It had a walled patio outside that seemed obviously designed for nude sunbathing.

"I love it," Sue said, clasping her hands.

Christy also made appropriate noises. Very nice. How different. What a view. Harriet, the more talkative of the two sisters, said, "It sort of out-California's California, doesn't it? I assure you we don't have a hot tub at home." She winked at Sue and whispered, "Nor waterbeds."

Christy, still feeling guilty about his momentary loyalty lapse and the unthinkable things he had been thinking about Dr. Potter, decided to do a little probing on Potter's behalf. "That's right, you're from California. What part?"

"North Hollywood," Jean said. "Believe me, that's not nearly as exotic as it sounds."

"Dr. Potter was asking about you," Christy said. Jean's eyebrows rose, and Christy lied a little. "He was very impressed by how kind you've been to an injured stray. It sounded as if he'd like to get to know you both. Are you by any chance a widow?"

"Why, yes," she said. "Why do you ask?"

"It was Dr. Potter who asked. He's a widower, I believe. Or maybe a bachelor."

The two sisters exchanged smiling glances, and Christy realized that he'd been right, they were attractive women.

"We'd be charmed to meet Dr. Potter," Harriet said. "Would you two like a cup of coffee? Jean, don't we still have some of that zucchini bread you baked?"

Christy made their excuses, saying that Sue was due back at the Schumacher house.

"Oh, please don't go," Harriet said. "You can surely stay at least for the coffee, can't you?"

Jean said, "Now Harriet, don't insist. These young people have other things to do than visit with us." To Christy, she said, "You'll have to excuse us. We're both a little nervous today, and not much in the mood to be alone. Carolyn Read phoned us last night and told us about that mugger trying to rob her. What a thing to happen. And here's poor Mrs. Read, just trying to enjoy a vacation, like Harriet and me. I'll bet she never comes to Vail again."

"I talked to her, too," Christy said. "She seemed just fine. You really shouldn't worry about her."

"Well, she did seem more excited about Dandy biting the man than about being attacked. What a pity she didn't see who did it." To Sue, Jean added, "The man pushed her to the floor, you know, and she couldn't see a thing. Except her dog chasing the man down the hall. Is that typical of dogs, Christy? Do you think Agatha would defend us if we were assaulted?"

Christy said, a little reluctantly, "Just using common sense about keeping your doors locked and not wandering around by yourself at night would be the best idea."

"But surely Agatha would bark at a burglar," Harriet said. "Why, she barks any time people ring the doorbell."

"Oh, sure. She might even get in a bite or two between bounces if she caught a burglar prowling around. That's enough to chase most people away."

"But she wouldn't attack, like Dandy?"

"If Dandy had really attacked seriously, Harriet, the man wouldn't have still been on his feet to run away. A lot of dogs will threaten. Bark. Snarl. Even charge and, like Dandy, show what their teeth are for. But they can quit pretty fast if they're threatened in return. So the best idea is just to keep your doors locked if you're at all worried. And if you hear funny sounds call the cops."

Sue said as they pulled away waving, "You're putting the fear into me, Christy. All this talk about assaults. I wish I had a dog."

"I'd loan you Gala, if it weren't for Mrs. Schumacher's dog-allergy," Christy said, "But, really, don't worry about anything."

Then he caught himself. He was giving the same nonsensical advice people gave to him. The sooner Sue was out of the Schumacher house, the better she'd feel, he knew. He gave her a hearty pep talk about the joys of dog-sitting and the virtues of Bev Farrell before he delivered her back to the gloom of the empty house and Mrs. Schumacher, and he drove back to the clinic hoping she'd act quickly and take his advice.

11

GALA MET CHRISTY at the clinic with cries of joy, and Dr. Potter met him with a puzzled stare. When Christy encountered Dr. Potter in the hall, the older vet had on the standard green jacket, concealing much of the splendor of his togs, and he apparently had a patient waiting, because he only said, "Miss Carroll didn't get very far along setting you up with physicians to talk to. She has a couple of messages for you that she thought might take precedence. Oh, yeah, and your dog cried all the time you were gone. Why didn't you just leave her in the cabin? She seemed comfortable there last night."

"I thought you might want the cabin, Dr. Potter," Christy said.

"What for?" Dr. Potter said. He regarded Christy for a moment, still looking puzzled, then turned and went down the hall. Christy stared after him. Dr. Potter definitely was limping. On the other hand, the rotund man carried a cane when he was off-duty, and maybe it wasn't just for show.

Gala's cries from Ward One had turned to moans again, and Christy stole a few minutes to walk her and put her back in the cabin before he reported to Miss Carroll. The dog grabbed her old sock from her basket and leaped onto the bed, then shook the sock so hard that if it had been the rat she apparently pretended to think it was, she would have broken its back. She was showing off for him, Christy realized. He took another two minutes to pet her and talk to her, then he decided the cabin felt a little cold, and he got his blue sweater for her from the closet before locking her in and going back to the clinic.

The day was taking on a gray look. Two chickadees in one of the tall pines in back of the cabin talked excitedly. About the weather? Was there snow on the wind? Christy wasn't sure he welcomed it. Snow could be depressing if you weren't in the mood for it. In the reception room, Miss Carroll was on the phone, and an elderly lady sat waiting for Dr. Potter, holding a smart green cat carrier in which napped an obviously ancient Russian Blue. A standard patient, not one of Dr. Potter's glamorous widows, Christy assumed. Already the practice seemed alien to him, someone else's responsibility. He waited patiently for Miss Carroll to finish a discussion about the desirability of vaccinating one's dog for parvo and distemper, lepto, and the rest while bringing the dog in for its annual rabies shot, then received her sweet smile as she put down the phone.

"I'm so glad you're here, Dr. Christy," she said. She nodded at the ancient cat and lowered her voice. "Mickey's got a perineal hernia. And Mickey's seventeen years old, you see. The surgery is scheduled for noon. Dr. Potter hoped you'd be back in time to help with it."

"He did?" Christy said. He beamed at Miss Carroll.

She registered a shading of the puzzlement with which Dr. Potter had looked at Christy earlier, but she beamed back before continuing: "Then Mr. Knight has called twice, once at ten o'clock and once about fifteen minutes ago. He's very eager to talk to you. He said he'd phone back."

"But the surgery on Annie went all right, didn't it?" Christy said anxiously. "Everything's okay, isn't it?"

"Oh, Mr. Knight didn't have the cytoma removed this morning," Miss Carroll said calmly. "He said he'd rather wait for you."

"He *did*?" Christy said. He beamed again, blessing friendship and loyalty, then wiped off the smile to ask, "How did Dr. Potter take that? Was he upset?"

"No-o," Miss Carroll said judgmentally. "He seemed a little surprised. Mr. Knight's so picky that he'd only let Dr. Potter touch his dogs before, but now that you've joined the practice, I suppose that's changing."

"I don't know that I've really joined the practice, Miss Carroll," Christy said. "Dr. Potter doesn't seem to have much need for me."

"Did he say that?" She looked affronted, and Christy saw that he had another friend.

"No, I just got that impression. Any other messages? Anything I'm supposed to attend to before Mickey's surgery?"

"Yes, Karen Hamilton called. She seemed eager to reach you, too. She asked that you get in touch with her when you have a chance. Oh, dear, I'm afraid you won't have time to eat anything before Mickey's hernia. But you'll probably take Miss Hamilton to lunch afterward, won't you? You can call her from Dr. Potter's office. He's seeing Miss Alexander's Red now. Chronic seborrhea. It shouldn't take much more time, so try not to talk to Miss Hamilton too long, all right?"

Christy trotted back to Dr. Potter's office. There was a note propped against the coffeepot reading, "What do you know about correcting the calcium level in the diet of a zinc-responsive dermatosis case? Or is this just some hogwash theory? Be sure and see me about this." Christy also saw that the office Scotch bottle had been replaced, and he shook his head, wondering at Dr. Potter's hyperactivity as he looked up Knight's and Karen Hamilton's numbers.

Knight's line was busy. Karen's phone rang four times. Five. Remembering Karen's "junk room" and the time it took her to make it from front to back of the apartment, Christy let the phone go a full ten rings, but there was no answer. He stifled a pang of disappointment, a little surprised at himself for feeling that way. Karen thought too much of her dear daddy and too little of dogs to suit Christy. But she was a delightful girl in other ways. He found that he had looked forward to seeing her or at least talking to her and sliding in mention that Sue Teasdale had been at Peter's memorial service by arrangement with Cletus Knight, not Gordon Christy. But maybe it wouldn't matter to Karen. He listened to Knight's busy line twice more and raided the coffeepot before Mickey the Russian Blue's surgery, and he still had plenty of time to don surgical gown, scrub up carefully, and have tracheal tube, surgeon's gloves, a second gown, and other accouterments of surgery ready for Dr. Potter when Mickey awoke from his nap and was brought in for the deeper, anesthetized sleep.

Dr. Potter was chatty during the tricky surgery on a very old cat, but he didn't say a word about Knight's refusal to allow anyone but Christy to remove one small tumor from his dog. He wanted to know all about Christy's findings that morning, if any. He interrupted himself occasionally. "Now, let me get my optical loop here. . . . I'll need a sterile gauze pad. . . ."

He nevertheless worked fast, Christy assisting. Dr. Potter paused once in a while to listen to the slow song of the heart monitor. Within a few minutes, the heart monitor picked up speed. Mickey's heart was beating faster now as the anesthesia began to wear off. Dr. Potter didn't call for more. He neatly finished sewing up Mickey just as the aged cat's limp little body twitched the first time. By the time the ears and whiskers twitched once each, Dr. Potter slipped off the rubber band with which Christy had loosely anchored the tracheal tube to Mickey's muzzle and started to remove the tube, but then he looked closely at the mouth and said, "Hmm. Plenty of tartar. Let's scrape it off while he's still under. And reach me down the cautery, please, Dr. Christy." He replaced the rubber band.

"What did you find?" Christy asked.

"Nothing much. Benign hyperplasia, I expect. A little proliferation of tissue from irritation. We'll just touch it up with the cautery. . . . Thank you. . . . There, that should take care of it. Now to clean him up. You'd think there would be some way to tell if a whisper is a man's voice or a woman's. Whisper to me, Dr. Christy. Let me listen."

But he continued chatting while cleaning the cat's teeth and didn't listen at all. A couple of minutes more, and he slipped off the rubber band and eased out the tracheal tube. "Handy things," he said, holding up the rubber band. "However, I prefer gauze myself. It's easy to get a rubber band too tight. Go tell Mrs. Nichols that Mickey is just fine, and she can sit with him if she wants to until he decides to wake up. No talking to him or petting him, though. I'm sure you've noticed that it's better just to let the patient feel you're there, but let him come to at his own speed. Sorry to rush, Dr. Christy, but I've got an engagement with the insurance adjuster. Tell Miss Carroll I'll be back promptly at three."

Dr. Potter limped away, and Christy gazed after him, this time with disquietude, but also with admiration. The portly man had a deft hand. Christy went obediently to the reception room to deliver the message to Mickey's owner, and he found both Cletus Knight and Karen Hamilton waiting for him.

Karen greeted Christy with a wary smile and Knight with a nod. Had they come together? Separately? Christy glanced out the window while reassuring Mickey's owner as to his condition and saw both Karen's black MG and Knight's silver Bentley, which answered his question. As soon as he took the cat's owner to Mickey and got her settled in a chair next to the sleeping cat, he hustled back to the reception room and found only Knight still waiting.

"What's with Karen?" Christy asked. "Was she in some kind of hurry?"

"I'm not sure," Knight said. "She said she had something to tell you, then she claimed it wasn't important and she left. Said she'd catch you another time. I've got some preliminary information for you, Christy. If you're clear for a while, maybe we should go over it privately."

"Sure. The cabin? But I'm afraid all I can offer you for lunch is a grilled cheese and bologna sandwich."

Knight claimed he'd already eaten, and Christy settled for cold bologna. He was eager to hear what Knight had come up with. Gala greeted them with such frenzied enthusiasm that he had to wait. She wagged her stub of a tail at Knight as energetically as she'd ever wagged it at Christy, and she jumped up on Knight like an ill-trained puppy. The cabin was chilly by now. The day was definitely getting colder. Christy built a fire while Knight told Gala how glad he was to see her, and the big man finally coaxed her to her basket in front of the fire and dropped into a chair beside Christy.

"Ready?" Christy asked through bites of his sandwich.

"Yeah. Eat fast. It's kind of an ugly story, and you're going to lose your appetite."

"Go on."

"First of all, Schumacher went to medical school in Washington, then he went to work for the mental health department."

"Washington, eh? That explains the Maryland relatives."

"No, not D.C. The state of Washington."

"The state? Good Lord, Mrs. Read's from Washington. Seattle, I think. Do you suppose that means anything?"

"Will you stop interrupting? Listen. Then we'll see what we come up with. All right, so Schumacher got in pretty big trouble nearly four years ago for releasing a psychopath from a state psychiatric hospital because he decided the guy was no longer certifiable. The guy promptly went home and killed his wife and kid. His name was Lloyd Glover. Glove. Glover. Get it?"

"Wow," Christy breathed.

"I guess one of the nastiest parts of the whole thing was that the wife managed to dial the police emergency number when Glover was breaking in the back door, and they got it all on tape. Patricia Glover screaming and frightened, begging the cops to hurry. Then the pistol shots started. The tape kept picking up her voice for a while: 'Becky, Becky, run! Oh, God, he's killing me.' Then it was the little girl crying and begging, 'No, Daddy. Please, Daddy. Stop, Daddy.' And hell's own noise from more pistol shots. He emptied a revolver into both the wife and the little girl. Six shots each. Very bloody. Very gory. Follow?"

"Jesus," Christy said. "Yes, I follow." He looked at the remains of his sandwich and gave it to Gala.

"All right, so everything came down on Schumacher, including an order from the governor to review all cases of serious violent acts committed by mentally ill people after they were discharged from state mental hospitals. Schumacher only got suspended, not run out of town on a rail, but the newspapers raked him over pretty good. Glover had previously been arrested a half-dozen times for trying to attack the wife, and he'd been in the loony bin four times. If he wasn't certifiable, I don't know who would qualify. The wife was the focus of his delusions. He thought she was trying to poison him. God only knows what he thought about his little daughter. But, overall, he had a pretty good history of paranoid behavior."

"There was more?" Christy asked.

"Be calm. It's nothing to throw up about. Glover just appeared to believe that his father was Joseph, his mother was Mary, and he was Jesus Christ. He hated cops, because they were radiating his feet. More than a little strange, I would have thought. He also believed he had stopped nuclear war from breaking out in Seattle and that George Bush was a Communist who was trying to take over the United States government. The year he shot the wife, he'd been in close confinement twice. The first time, Mrs. Glover signed the commitment papers. She filed for divorce after that. The second time, Glover committed himself, after making endless public threats to kill Patricia. I guess nobody believed him. I don't know. Mental patients have civil rights and all that, and Schumacher's clinical judgment seemed to have been that Glover had made marked improvement. No more emotional frenzies. No longer delusional about his wife. At least, not that Glover talked about. So Schumacher let him out."

"My God, and Schumacher was allowed to go on practicing?"

"Yeah. I guess he hadn't done anything illegal. Just showed rotten judgment. He had a private practice on the side, and he continued that for a while, but maybe it didn't work out, since he moved to Vail."

"What happened to Glover?"

"The courts declared him incompetent. He's back in a psychiatric ward. He'll probably never be brought to trial."

"But he's definitely locked up? He couldn't have been let out again and have come to Vail?"

"I don't know yet, Christy. I thought of that, too, and I'm trying to have it checked out. I left this number. Alicia will call if the information comes. I'm also trying to have the dead wife checked through. She married young. She was still in her early twenties, twenty-three or twenty-four, I think. She'd filed for a divorce. I got to wondering, what about any young men in her life? Did she have a steady, and did he brood a few years and then decide to go after Dr. Schumacher? I'm trying to get a line on her private life, but stuff like that is harder to check."

"That would figure. Darn, it would even be nice to know if she had any close girlfriends, or any other close friend who had a liking for guns. Relatives, too. So far, you've pinned it down only to someone who knows about the Glover tragedy. Surely the gloves tell us that much."

"I'll get everything I can on Patricia Glover. Anything else occur to you? Anything else I should try to check out?"

Christy said, "It only occurs to me that Nat Shannon should know about this. But I can't figure out how to pretend that it was me who came up with all this brilliant information. I don't suppose you'd . . ."

"God, Christy, I'd really rather not. Let's see. Maybe I can set up a connection for you. Someone to call. A news reporter would be good. Someone from a Seattle paper. Then you could have a legitimate source and ask all the right questions and get the same basic info to give to Shannon. What do you think?"

They were probing the plan when a light tapping at the door brought Gala roaring out of her basket. The door opened. Dr. Potter's voice said, "Quiet, girl, it's only me. Dr. Christy, I finished with the insurance adjuster early. Can I come in? Cletus, how are you this afternoon?"

Dr. Potter joined them by the fire, offering his hands to the flames. He seemed uneasy, and Christy decided he'd better get any bad news about the condo over with. He asked, "How did things go with the insurance adjuster?"

Dr. Potter shrugged. "The company says it will take right at thirty-four hundred dollars to fix the place, but I've got an eight-hundred-dollar deductible, so they'll only pay twenty-six hundred."

Christy gulped and said, "I'll pay the other eight hundred. It's the least I can do."

"We'll see," Dr. Potter said. "I'm not interrupting anything, am I? What have you got here, a council of war about that little histiocytoma on Annie?"

Knight said, "No, I'm not worried about Annie."

"No?" Potter said. "You seemed worried this morning."

"Now, Dr. Potter," Knight said, "the only reason I wanted to wait for Christy is because Annie knows him better than she does you. Annie's a little timid. With Christy, she'll get less excited. What we're talking about is something more serious by far."

Knight proceeded to fill Dr. Potter in on the Glover tragedy. Christy saw that Dr. Potter had recovered his self-assurance. His eyes blinked wisely behind the thick glasses. Had Dr. Potter been worried because Knight preferred Christy for a job of minor surgery? It was a flattering but foolish decision of Knight's, because Potter was obviously a master. And what about Knight, so quickly and efficiently summarizing information for Potter relating to a double murder that Potter himself could have committed? Knight obviously didn't regard him as a suspect. Knight's Dobermans must have given Dr. Potter their stamp of approval. Even Gala didn't seem to mind the older man. She lay quite serenely in her basket, eyes half closed, obviously finding the company congenial.

After Dr. Potter heard the tale through, he mused, "But even if someone thinks he has cause to get Dr. Schumacher, what kind of monster would go after the two boys first? Maybe they weren't so sweet and innocent, but one was just a teenager, and the other just about old enough to vote, wasn't he?"

"The sins of the father?" Knight offered.

Dr. Potter said, "It seems to me you'd better find out all you can about this Patricia Glover's family. Find out her maiden name while you're at it. I'd vote for family, not some young friend, when it comes to revenge."

"Why?" Christy asked.

"Because of the timing," Dr. Potter said. "Would a young person wait four years before declaring war on everybody named Schumacher? Never. Young people are impatient, always in a hurry. You have to mellow a bit before you realize that patience can be useful. And speaking about declaring war on the Schumachers, what about Mrs. Schumacher? Isn't she in danger? Given the pattern, it seems to me she might be next."

"You might have something there," Knight said.

"Jesus, yes," Christy said. "Why didn't I think of that?"

Dr. Potter looked smug. "Seems to me I've heard two heads are better than one," he said. "In our case, three heads."

Christy said, "Gentlemen, if you'll pardon me, I'm going to make a quick phone call. Nat Shannon can surely spare a man to keep an eye on Mrs. Schumacher."

Knight asked, "Are you going to tell him about Glover?"

"Not yet," Christy said. "But try to get me that information source fast, okay? We're coming up with too many good ideas. I'd feel more comfortable if the police were let in on it."

Christy dialed from the cabin and got the usual hold-button treatment from the police station. Then he discovered that Shannon was out, asked for Dave Lincoln, and floated into the never-never land called hold again. Knight checked his watch, pantomimed a telephone to his own ear, and left, and Dr. Potter waved and left with him. The wait finally ended, and Lincoln's voice came on. He listened quietly while Christy, giving due credit to Dr. Potter, repeated the theory that Mrs. Schumacher could be in line for the next six bullets.

"Well, she's safe at the moment," Lincoln said. "Shannon's over at the Schumachers'. Why don't you give him a call over there?"

"Nothing's happened, has it?" Christy said quickly.

"Nothing fatal. Shannon will tell you about it if he wants to. Give him a call, Christy. While we officially welcome assistance from the general public, I'm not too keen on interrupting him just to pass on some theory."

"Chicken," said Christy. He rang off and discovered that

he, too, felt less than keen. Was he just interfering in official business that didn't concern him? Then he remembered Mrs. Schumacher's wan face trying to smile, and he dialed the Schumacher house. But he wasn't at all displeased when it was Sue who answered and reported that Shannon was busy outside with a fingerprint man.

"What on earth is going on over there?" Christy asked.

Sue said, "Just the usual spook stuff. I hope."

"The phantom phone-caller?"

"No, this time they left a note on the door. The classic kind, with all the letters cut out of a newspaper. And, Christy, they left a noose, too. At least I guess that's what it's supposed to be. Mrs. Schumacher found it dangling from the carriage light, the one outside the downstairs door, right in broad daylight. It looked just like an electric light cord to me, tied kind of sloppy, but I called the cops before anyone could tell me not to."

"What did the note say?"

"The usual. 'Murderer.'"

"Nothing else?"

"Yes, 'Murderer. It wasn't suicide.'"

"You sound pretty upset. More hysteria from Mrs. Schumacher?"

"No, Dr. Schumacher. He practically yanked the carriage light off, trying to pull the noose down. He was grunting and sort of choking and literally grinding his teeth. Oh, here's Officer Shannon. I'll let you talk to him."

Shannon was brisk. Shannon was busy. Shannon all but sighed with impatience as Christy stammered through a censored explanation that Mrs. Schumacher might be in danger. Then there was a silence, after which Shannon said, "How can you do this, Christy? Didn't I tell you we're short-handed? But, damn it, you could be right. I don't like the feel of this. Any of this. I'll get Dave Lincoln over here to baby-sit Mrs. Schumacher. Damnation, there goes more overtime."

Shannon hung up abruptly, and Christy winced and removed the phone from his ear. He hung it up, and the phone rang instantly, but he knew Miss Carroll would catch it in the office. Gala said she would like out, please. She had to ask three times in the customary canine way, trotting to the door, then looking pointedly at Christy, before he came out of his reverie and let her out. She loitered, checking dry grass for imagined scent. The afternoon had become very still, Christy noticed. The sky was uniformly gray, with low-hanging clouds. Hanging. A noose, Sue had said. A sloppily tied electric cord and a note on the door. *It wasn't suicide.* What wasn't suicide? The death of Mark Niemeyer's friend? No, Mark's friend had shot himself. But Mark had mentioned someone else, hadn't he? A patient of Dr. Schumacher's who hanged himself in his hotel room, a tourist? Were he and Knight on the wrong track entirely? What did a suicide/non-suicide have to do with a homicidal maniac named Lloyd Glover? It was all too complicated. Christy couldn't make a connection between the one bit of nasty devilment and the other, but neither could he stop puzzling over it.

Miss Carroll came out the back door of the clinic. As she encountered the chilly air of the afternoon, she glanced up at the sky and gave it the approving smile she seemed to lavish on much of the world. Gala ran toward Miss Carroll, cheeks puffed out, ready to bark as usual, but she caught Miss Carroll's scent and laid her ears back in greeting. "Snow," Miss Carroll called to Christy. "I'm absolutely sure of it."

"A big blow?" Christy asked.

"I'd lay odds. Would you call Miss Hamilton at home, Dr. Christy? She says she'll wait there until you have a moment."

"Sure," he said. Then, thinking again of the note and the noose, he wondered if a look at last year's newspapers might not be useful. Mark Niemeyer had mentioned a brief story about the tourist who hanged himself. Perhaps there were bound copies of the local papers at the Vail library. "Anything on for me this afternoon? Does Dr. Potter need me?"

"No, you were to have the whole day off, until Mickey's hernia interfered. You're clear for the rest of the day. You'll be going out, I take it?"

"Out" may have been the key word. Or "going." Gala heard one or the other joyfully and rushed over to Christy and swatted him on the bottom with her snout. Being an intelligent dog, she apparently concluded she was already out, in a way, so she then rushed to Dr. Potter's Jeep and ran two circles around it. She came back reluctantly when Christy called her back to the cabin, and she sat and stared at him while he phoned Karen back. Karen answered on one ring. She must have been sitting right by the phone.

"Christy?" Karen's voice said breathlessly.

"Yes, indeed. How are you? You've gotten to be quite a stranger."

She ignored that. "I want to see you," she said. "It's important. Can I come over?"

"Well, I was going over to the library, but, sure, I'll wait for you here. I'm at the cabin behind the clinic. Why did you leave this afternoon?"

"I'll tell you when I see you. The public library? That's okay, I can meet you in the parking lot. Are you leaving right away?"

"I can. Sure."

"And Christy," she said, sounding breathless again, "will you please bring your Doberman?"

"Gala?" he said.

"She's the only Doberman you have, isn't she? I wouldn't ask it, but it's really important to me."

She said good-bye, sounding excited and somewhat resolute. Christy was more puzzled than ever. He said to Gala, "All right, it looks like you're going to go with me after all. Want to go? Want to go in the car?"

He grabbed her sweater and a heavier jacket for himself

and picked up her leash. This time the dog ran circles around Christy, bucking and making playful lunges at him, threatening to bite but not quite connecting. She abandoned him only for Dr. Potter's Jeep, but charged happily over to Christy's own car when he opened the door and rattled the keys. She jumped in, then leaped wildly back and forth from seat to seat, all but saying, What's keeping you? The gray afternoon was too chilly for an open window to be comfortable, so Gala settled for looking out the front windshield, against which she pressed her nose repeatedly. It was getting hard to see through the nose smears by the time Christy reached the Municipal Building, which, until Vail finished a new library building, contained the town's library.

The library side of the building was right across from the post office. Karen's black MG was already parked to the side of the entrance, top up, windows up, heater obviously working, but she jumped out as soon as Christy pulled in beside her. He got out and braced himself. He didn't know what to expect, but his heart sank when Karen's first words were "Dr. Schumacher."

"Dr. Schumacher isn't taking patients at the moment, Christy, but he talked to me on the phone last week," Karen said nervously. "He told me all about exposure therapy and said I might benefit from it, and when he couldn't see me, well, I just started it myself. What do you think of that?" Karen smiled at Christy brilliantly.

He had no idea what to think. He settled for "Great, terrific. Uh, what's exposure therapy?"

"It's something you can do for phobias. Dr. Schumacher said he exposes patients to their phobia stimulus while they're under deep relaxation, and I guess I haven't been very relaxed about it, but I've sure been exposed."

"Exposed to what?"

"Dogs, you ninny. Big dogs. I wasn't going to spend the rest of my life being scared to touch them if I could help it. So I started imagining dogs. Then I looked at a lot of pic-

tures of big dogs. That's what I was doing in the back room
last Sunday when you came to take me to Cletus's house—
looking at pictures, trying to get my nerve up to touch one of
his Dobermans. Well, now I'm ready, Christy. I'm sorry I
lost my nerve earlier at the clinic and disappeared, but I've
been looking at the pictures ever since without feeling a bit
of panic. So now I need to touch a Doberman."

Christy laughed and hugged her. "You've worked at it that
hard?" he said. "Congratulations. That's wonderful."

She hugged him back, holding him closely for a moment,
then pulled away laughing. "Don't start thinking I did it just
for you," she said. "I was just tired of being Miss Milque-
toast. Oh, God. Hi, Gala. Gala, you're not growling, are
you?"

Christy glanced around. A woman in a tan-and-blue parka
was going into the library, and Gala was apparently trying to
decide whether to bark. He interrupted the dog by opening
the car door a crack and reaching her leash off the dashboard.
"She's not growling at us," Christy said. "I'll just get her out
now, shall I? We'll walk her away from the foot traffic, and
she'll calm down right away when she's just with her friends."

"That's right, she knows I'm her friend, doesn't she?" Karen said. A gust of chill wind whipped her hair across her
face, which looked a trifle desperate. "Where shall we walk
her? In front of the building?"

It was the best choice available. Small snowflakes began to
fall as they led Gala onto a grassy area in front of the prettily
landscaped building. Gala inspected a handful of trans-
planted aspens. No more than a dozen leaves still clung to
the barren trees. The leaves were quite black. Christy spotted no keep-off-the-grass signs, and when Gala lunged toward a frost-blasted flower bed to one side of the lawn, he let
her tug him along. The brown remnants of flowers interested
the dog. Karen stepped forward and said, "I guess I'd better
take her leash now. Hadn't I?"

Wet snowflakes melted in her hair. She looked anxious.

Christy said, "I can hold Gala. Then you can just pat her once or twice. That would do it, wouldn't it?"

"Nope, it's gotta be total exposure," Karen said. She reached for the leather leash.

Gala paid no attention whatever to the change of hands on her lead. She plunged toward the opposite end of the circular flower bed, and Karen plunged with her, talking desperately all the time. "Good old Gala, nice big dog, you like walks, don't you, Gala? That's right, that's good, now you just stop pulling a minute and let me pet you." With a hesitant hand, she reached for Gala's head, but Gala ducked toward a dried columbine, and Karen jerked the hand back. She tightened her mouth and tried again. This time she connected, although only with Gala's back. Karen flashed a smile at Christy. Gala condescended to look at Karen, and the girl faltered again, then boldly reached forward and gave her hand to Gala to sniff. She wiped melting snowflakes from Gala's head and patted her. "Well," Karen sighed. "Well!"

Gala cast a questioning look at Christy. What was going on here? What was she supposed to do? Christy stepped forward to help Karen pat the dog, and Gala endured their attentions for a while, then wanted to continue her walk.

But Karen handed over her lead, laughing nervously. "Maybe that's enough for one day," she said. "Thank you, Christy. Thank you, Gala. What do you think, Christy? Can I come around sometime and give her her dinner?"

"We'd love to have you," Christy assured her. "Tonight? She usually eats around six."

Karen backed away, still laughing. "No, not tonight. Once when I was twelve, I climbed up on the highest diving tower, and it took me forty-five minutes to get up courage to jump, and I was so thrilled with myself that I climbed right back up again. That time it took me over an hour before I could get my courage up. Maybe I'm the type that shouldn't rush things."

Christy and Gala walked Karen back to her car. She managed a good-bye pat before she left them. Christy told the dog, "How about that, Gala, you're a friend to humankind. Good thing I didn't tell Karen you're not half as big and fierce as you pretend to be. She thought she was patting a toughie, and you're only a cream puff."

Christy put Gala back into his car, smiling to himself about Karen's homemade exposure therapy. He sweatered the dog, then trotted downstairs into the library whistling. A proper although pretty librarian looked up from her desk and only smiled, but Christy knocked off the noise and asked about back files of local newspapers. He was still thinking about Karen as he leafed through. He'd misjudged her badly, not only about dogs but about jumping to the conclusion that she was afraid of her father's reaction to a police investigation of a vandalized condo, when she'd probably been just plain scared by the nastiness the wreckage represented. He'd been apprehensive, too, about being in the condo. Thinking now about finding eight hundred bucks to pay Dr. Potter's insurance deductible didn't do much for his tranquillity, either.

Christy had to remind himself of his business. About this time last year, Mark had said. Three community newspapers had been serving Vail at the time, all weeklies but all fairly fat, and it took a while to find what he was looking for. Christy finally spotted it in the *Vail Trail*, in a little roundup of news reports on page twenty-four called "From the Sheriff's Blotter." The Convenient Shoppe Liquor Store in Eagle had been robbed of some eighteen hundred dollars. A duel with beer bottles at Bernice's Bar had left one man with thirty-seven stitches and his opponent under arrest for first-degree felony assault. Paramedics of the Eagle-Vail Fire Department had tried unsuccessfully to resuscitate an apparent suicide victim at an Eagle-Vail hotel Sunday after the man was found hanging off his balcony. Willis Ditton, age fifty-three, of North Hollywood, California, was found by a maid, hanging from the balcony railing with an electric-light cord tied around his neck. Ditton was . . . Ditton. *Ditton*.

Christy wasn't just jumping to conclusions now. It had to be more than coincidence. A woman in a hooded parka and a man in a yellow sweater turned to stare at him as he charged past the card-catalog file to the librarian. Yes, there was a phone and a directory. Yes, of course he could use the phone, if it was a real emergency. Christy dialed the Schumacher house and listened to the rings. At three, Sue picked it up.

"Sue, this is Christy," he said. "Now, listen, this could be very important. Is Mrs. Schumacher there?"

"Yes. She's playing gin rummy with Officer Lincoln."

"Thank God," Christy said. "Tell Dr. Schumacher I might know who's been causing his problems. I'm going to pop next door to the police department and get Shannon, and we'll be right out."

"Dr. Schumacher isn't here, Christy," Sue said. She sounded odd. Disturbed. "He came up from his study and said he thought he'd eat something. The poor man has barely eaten since Peter's service yesterday, you know. So I was making him roast beef sandwiches and coffee, and he was leafing through the mail, and he got all excited and went diving back down the stairs. I took his sandwiches down a little later, and he was gone. He must have left the house."

"What was in the mail to upset him?" Christy asked.

"I don't know. It's right here by the phone. I already looked through it, and it's mainly just condolence cards. Here's one with white lilies on it from Louise Howard. She's a patient. And one from Dr. and Mrs. Leslie. I think he's in the medical complex. And here's an old-fashioned one from Harriet and Jean down the street. It's got a black border around it."

"Harriet and Jean?" Christy said. "What does it say? Read it to me."

"It's just a little quotation: 'What's gone and what's past

help should be past grief.' Then their names, Harriet McAfee and Jean McAfee Ditton."

"Je-e-e-sus," Christy said under his breath.

"What's this about, Christy? Is there anything I can do?"

"Yes. Tell Lincoln to stay close to Mrs. Schumacher. I'm going right now for Shannon."

12

GUSTING WIND and its load of snow had taken full possession of the valley with the approach of darkness. Snow was thick on the windshield of Christy's car, and Gala shivered slightly under her sweater. Christy hit the lights, the windshield wiper, and the heater switches while pulling around to the other side of the Municipal Building to the police department. Shannon's green Saab wasn't there. None of the police Saabs was there. A lone bicycle, apparently a permanent fixture, leaned against a bike rack, perhaps forgotten outside in the wet snow. Christy cursed and pulled back onto the frontage road. He headed through the village, sliding a little. The streets weren't iced over yet, but they were wet and snowy, and he knew his old car would have trouble on the hill up to the Schumacher house.

Ditton, he thought. Not Glover at all, but a certain Mrs. Jean McAfee Ditton and a Mr. Willis Ditton, deceased. Mr. Ditton, briefly a Schumacher patient. Could Dr. Schumacher have been involved in any way in the death of Mr. Ditton?

Or did Jean just think he was? "Murderer," the note had said. "Murderer. It wasn't suicide."

The necessity to do something was urgent, but Christy was still unsure just what he should do. Could do. Mrs. Jean McAfee Ditton, signing her name with Harriet McAfee on a condolence card. Ditton, right there for Schumacher to see. Ditton, the name of a patient who had died in a noose.

Christy hit the hill. As he had expected and dreaded, he began to slide. He straightened the skew of the wheel and let the car roll gently back down the hill. He'd have to get a running start. Thank heaven there was little traffic out.

Below the foot of the hill, Christy braked. Gala decided to crawl over and sit close beside him, and he had to coax her back out of his way. The wet snow was so heavy it clogged the windshield wipers. He rolled down the window and leaned out to clean the driver's side with his bare hand. Ready. Feed the car a careful ration of gas and approach the hill again. Not too fast. Keep it in second. But steadily, steadily. Don't stop, no matter what. One little hill and he'd be on Forest Road, where Dr. Schumacher and the sisters lived.

Symptoms. Isolate the symptoms, analyze them, and the disease could be diagnosed. Dr. Potter was right, he had to follow the symptoms. In a casual town, no one would think much about two women going by their first names. Nice Jean and nice Harriet, the McAfee sisters, as people seemed to call them. But Jean made no real secret that she was a widow named Jean McAfee Ditton. She didn't hide her married name. Nor did she advertise it. But why use it at all if she was somehow connected to the Schumacher killings?

There was another symptom. Around Schumacher, hadn't Jean consistently maintained a low profile? Only Harriet, not both sisters, had taken Agatha to Dr. Schumacher for that bizarre doggy analysis. Only Harriet had delivered the zucchini bread as a neighborly gesture to the bereft family. And only Harriet and Mrs. Read had signed the guest book yesterday at the memorial service. Not Jean. She was there but apparently not ready then to put her full name in writing. He'd seen her walk past the book without signing, but he hadn't thought anything about it.

But if he started thinking about it, wasn't he in effect suggesting to himself that the sisters were actively involved in the murders? Two nice ladies pumping bullets into living flesh? Was he willing even to consider such a thing? Perhaps not. Yet that was surely what Dr. Schumacher might assume.

Christy was going into the ditch. The top of the hill was just ahead of him, but the rear end of the car slid sideways. He swung into the skid, keeping an even pressure on the gas pedal. The car continued to slide for a moment, then it righted itself and slithered upward, over the crest. He breathed easier and reached out to unstick the windshield wiper again as he steered onto Forest Road.

Why now? Why would Jean deliberately give Dr. Schumacher her name on the condolence card? Schumacher would recognize it. The whispers and the noose had primed him for it. Why would the sisters give the game away? What had changed?

Don't stall, car. The Schumacher house was just ahead. Dr. Schumacher had fled after reading the card. Where to? Out in this weather? Or was he safely back home now, grieving, furious. . . . Oh, Lord, skidding again. Right in front of the sisters' chalet. One light on in the kitchen. Footprints, filling in with new snow, leading from the street to the house. Footprints.

Christy braked so suddenly that the car did a complete turn-around in the road, then shuddered against the curb, facing the wrong way. Christy told Gala to stay. He leaped out, slipped, warned himself to take it easier, then headed in a skidding, sliding run, not to the Schumacher house, but into the yard of the sisters' chalet. If Schumacher thought he knew with certainty who was behind his grief, wouldn't he try to do something about it? Was he creeping up on them even now?

The footprints led to a window, then circled around the corner of the house. Christy bounded up three broad steps to the front door and tried the knob. Locked. The house was quiet. Too quiet. He looked frantically at the footprints, following them with his eyes. The kitchen. He had seen a dim light from the kitchen. He dropped back to the snow-covered ground and ran around toward the kitchen door. What was that sound? So anguished, so pitiful. One of the sisters crying out in pain? No, Agatha. Just Agatha the Sheepdog, complaining, locked away in some inner room. Where were the sisters then? Alive? Dead? Where was Schumacher? Finished with his grisly retribution and already gone?

Shattered glass lay in the snow outside the kitchen storm door. It was one of those wood-at-the-bottom, glass-at-the-top jobs. The solid inner door stood ajar, and Christy saw that both doors were jammed open slightly with more glass. He yanked the storm door back and pushed the inner door wide, and glass tinkled. Christy slammed through. He almost ran into Dr. Elliott Schumacher, whose back was toward the door.

"Stop!" Christy yelled. He grabbed Schumacher's arm and spun him around.

"Oh, dear," a woman's voice said. It sounded quietly woeful, disappointed somehow.

Christy's head jerked briefly toward the voice. His widening eyes took in incongruous details. Odd, how Schumacher was dressed in black. Black sweater, black pants, black gloves. Odd, the two syringes he had apparently deposited on the kitchen counter. Odd also, the red-and-orange can beside the doctor's feet. Odd, though not unusual. Its mate could be found in almost anyone's garage. The dim light came from a frosted panel over the kitchen range, atop which bubbled some savory-smelling stew. But the light was bright enough for Christy to read the can: ONE U.S. GALLON. GASOLINE. DANGER. EXTREMELY FLAMMABLE. It was also bright enough for Christy to see Harriet and Jean standing side by side in the alcove separating the kitchen from the living room. A cozy fire flickered in the living room fireplace behind them. Against the soft glow of flames he saw the revolver in Harriet's hand pointing steadily at Dr. Schumacher.

Christy nodded to the two women and Dr. Schumacher and said in a voice he was pleased to notice sounded calm, "Sorry to barge in like this. I seem to have gotten things a little confused."

Agatha whined behind the door of the utility room and pawed at it. She wanted out. Then there was a moment's silence, and Christy could hear the embers settling in the fireplace.

Harriet said, "Thank God you're here, Christy. This man has gone completely crazy. He broke in here and tried to kill us."

Jean looked hesitantly at her sister as Harriet continued, her voice squeezed a little. "Look what I just made him put down. Syringes. Probably like the one he had when he attacked Mrs. Read. And gasoline. He actually brought gasoline. He was going to inject us with something and burn the house down with us in it, to make it look like an accident."

The sisters' backs were to the fireplace, and Christy couldn't see their faces as clearly as he wanted. He had only Harriet's voice to go on. Harriet sounded frightened. Harriet sounded sincere. Had he read the symptoms wrong? He chose a direction and started to speak, but he had to clear his throat and try again. "You don't know that Dr. Schumacher attacked Mrs. Read," he said.

Harriet gestured with the gun. "Roll his sleeves up," she said. "Or his trouser legs. I'm sure you'll find toothmarks where Dandy got him. That will prove it."

Christy turned to Dr. Schumacher. The man flinched and backed away a step, as though to protect himself from prying hands. Schumacher didn't look frightened. His eyes looked sorrowful, as though tears were almost ready to well. But his face held a second expression, a wary one.

Christy said to Dr. Schumacher, "Did you? Did you really attack Mrs. Read?"

The tears of self-pity overcame at least part of Schumacher's wariness. "I only wanted to talk to her," he said. "I wasn't going to hurt her. She wrote down in the funeral register that she was from Seattle, and I thought it was her way of telling me she harmed my poor boys. Why, she might have tried to harm my wife, too. I had to do something."

"So you took a syringe along?" Christy said. "You just wanted to talk to her, but you pushed her into her room and knocked her down? Sorry, Dr. Schumacher, I'm afraid it doesn't look too good."

"There!" Harriet said.

To diagnose disease, a good starting point was case history. Christy said, "We're not quite there yet, Harriet. I've got a couple of questions for you, too. Such as, is that why you took Mrs. Read to the funeral? Because she was from the state Dr. Schumacher ran away from and you hoped it would spook him?"

"Ridiculous," Harriet said. "Why would we want to get Mrs. Read hurt? Christy, would you mind calling the police for us?"

Jean's face jerked toward her sister, but Harriet said, "It's all right, Jean." To Christy, she said, "The only phones in this silly house are in the bedrooms, but don't worry about us. I've got a gun to protect us. If he moves, I'll shoot."

"Don't leave me alone with them, Dr. Christy!" Schumacher said. "They'll shoot me whether I move or not. That's what they were planning all the time."

"Ridiculous," Harriet said again. "Please, Christy, hurry. Call the police."

"I don't think I'd better," Christy said. "Harriet, let it go. Attempted murder is something the police can get their teeth into. Let them have him. Alive."

Agatha whined again, made miserable by hearing voices

outside her door. Harriet waited until the dog was quiet before saying, "I'm not sure what you mean."

Christy felt so tired that he wished they could all go in the living room and sit down and at least accuse one another in comfort. He said, "What I mean is that I thought I came here to protect you from Dr. Schumacher. Now it looks like I'm going to have to protect him from you. I may be just a plain dog-and-cat doctor, and veterinarians don't take Hippocratic oaths, but I guess I can't just stand aside and let a person be killed, no matter how much he might deserve it. You see, I know about Mr. Ditton. And I know about Lloyd Glover."

Both sisters turned shadowed stares on Christy. The flames flickered in the fireplace, and the leaping shadows brought a mad thought, a bad thought, of the mythical Furies. Avengers pursuing a murderer, driving him out of his mind. How appropriate for a vet. Didn't the Furies have dogs' heads, bats' wings, and serpents for hair? But some of the myths portrayed them as august matrons. That seemed a better fit to Christy for the two middle-aged, double-knit women he saw before him.

Jean spoke for the first time, very calmly, very quietly. "What do you know about Lloyd Glover?" she said.

Christy's thoughts tumbled over themselves for yet another moment. How much should he say? So many of his would-be symptoms were pure conjecture. How could he talk his way out the door with Dr. Schumacher beside him, safely away from that revolver? He decided persuasion lay in his speaking fully and frankly. He said, "I know that Dr. Schumacher made a bad mistake and that Lloyd Glover was let loose to kill his wife and child. I don't know precisely what it had to do with you, but I imagine there's a family connection. If the police check Patricia Glover's maiden name, I'm willing to bet it will be Ditton. I know that Dr. Schumacher left Washington pretty abruptly, as though he was trying to put the Glover scandal behind him. I also know about Mr. Willis Ditton's death in Vail a year ago. The police would make that connection too, you know. A man dies, a suicide. A year later his wife and sister-in-law show up and kill Dr. Schumacher, the man who supposedly acted as psychiatrist for the dead husband. The cops wouldn't let it go as just two ladies defending themselves against a grief-crazed intruder."

A shadow moved on Jean's face, but it was Harriet who spoke. "Of course the police will make a connection," she said. "Of course Jean came here. Willis died in this town. We had to save a long time for this trip, but it's only natural that she would make a pilgrimage to honor his memory and that I, as her sister, would come with her. We can't be responsible for the guilt feelings of a man like Schumacher."

"Maybe he's not as guilty as you think," Christy said. "That note and noose you left make it clear you think Mr. Ditton's death wasn't a suicide. But that's what the police said, and, believe me, they're thorough."

"The police didn't know about Dr. Schumacher's syringes then," Harriet said. "He killed Willis. He shot Willis full of something that knocked him out, and he hanged him."

The doctor protested, "No, no, never. I never killed anyone. I didn't inject him with anything at all. If you don't believe me, have the body exhumed."

"Exhuming poor Willis's body wouldn't mean a thing," Harriet said. She addressed her words to Christy, as if she couldn't tolerate speaking directly to Shumacher. "He must have used something that wouldn't show up, especially after a year."

"I deny it utterly," Schumacher said. The self-pity choked his voice again. "The man tried to ruin me. I had to leave Washington to get away from him. When he finally followed me here, he threatened to do it all over again, stand outside my home and my office and talk to everyone who came and went: patients, salesmen, even other *doctors*. And of course everything he might tell them about Lloyd Glover would be

213

completely one-sided. But I didn't do anything. I only talked to him. I tried to make him understand, so he would go away and leave me alone. I'm terribly sorry about Lloyd Glover, but I wasn't to blame. Glover fooled a whole panel of psychiatrists. I kept trying to make Mr. Ditton understand that. In the end, I think he believed me. I've always felt it had a bearing on his suicide."

"Don't believe him, Christy," Harriet said. "He's a self-serving hypocrite."

Christy said, "I'm afraid I do believe him. Dr. Schumacher doesn't strike me as dumb. If there had been anything fishy about Mr. Ditton's death, Dr. Schumacher would have known he was too obvious a suspect. Use your head. Can't you see that you've landed yourself in the same position? If you'd just wanted to kill Schumacher, you should have waited around until he'd gone hiking or fishing or something and popped him off in private with a rifle. But no. He's right here in your house. And Jean can't pass herself off to the police as the innocent Miss Jean McAfee who doesn't have a motive in the world. She's used her real name. Several times. The same thing that brought Schumacher to your door will bring the police. You've got to turn Schumacher over to the cops and let him get whatever's coming to him. You can't afford to shoot him. You've left too many tracks."

There was another silence, the longest yet, then Jean, in a perfect imitation of a patient schoolmarm, corrected Christy. "Selected tracks. Of course I used my real name. Think how it would look for the police to discover I had been using a phony name once they make the inevitable connection between Willis and Dr. Schumacher. Very suspicious, I assure you. I must admit we'd rather hoped no one would learn of Lloyd Glover. Dr. Schumacher was most considerate about keeping his past a secret. But we're prepared for that, too."

"Jean, shut up," Harriet said.

"No, Harriet. Dr. Christy thinks he knows it all anyway."

Jean and Harriet exchanged glances. Harriet said, "Yes, he does, doesn't he?"

Both looked speculatively at Christy, and he saw with sudden alarm that Harriet moved her hand slightly, and the revolver now seemed to be pointing midway between him and Schumacher. He had wanted to drive them into a corner. He should have remembered that cornered animals often turn and show their fangs.

When he was silent, Harriet said matter-of-factly, "When you were talking about all those so-called tracks we left behind, Dr. Christy, you neglected to mention the gloves. Well, certainly they were a risk, but you can understand that we wanted Dr. Schumacher to know why his sons died."

Schumacher gasped. "You admit it? You really did kill my poor boys?"

As before, Harriet refused to speak to Schumacher. She went on: "I'd have been perfectly happy to take your advice about shooting him with a rifle, but he doesn't hike, you see. Nor fish. So it was a matter of waiting for a quiet moment when he was within pistol range. And here he is. And here you are."

"The police—" Christy said.

"Oh, pooh on the police," Harriet said. "They can suspect anything they please, but just because one has a motive doesn't mean one has committed a crime. They'll never be able to prove we had anything to do with the deaths of those two young thugs or that we did anything more than shoot a deranged man who came here to try to murder us. They might even charge us with manslaughter for defending ourselves against Dr. Schumacher. Two or three years in prison at the most. What a pity. It's a good thing both Jean and I know how to knit. It passes the time, you know."

Agatha suddenly barked in the utility room. Everyone jumped. Christy jumped higher than anyone, because he couldn't be sure, staring at Harriet, if the middle-sized revolver in her hand wasn't now pointed more toward himself than toward Schumacher. Christy heard the solid threat in the sisters' voices, and he also heard something else: soft footfalls outside brushing through snow. Someone was coming? Hope quickened as he tried to remember if he'd been in too much of a rush to turn off his car headlights. Officer Dave Lincoln was only two doors away at the Schumacher house. He could have seen headlights, come to investigate a possible wreck on snowy roads. Emboldened, Christy said rapidly and loudly, "And I suppose I walked in at the wrong time and just got shot in the confusion. Believe me, it'll never work. The police will uncover the whole Glover tragedy. You've stacked too many cards against yourself."

Jean parroted, "'The Glover tragedy.' You make it sound very simple. A tragedy. A mistake. There was a tape recording, did you know? Patricia saw him coming and called the police before he got in. They put it all on tape automatically. The way Patricia begged him not to hurt her. The gunshots. The screams. Then little Becky."

Dr. Schumacher groaned. He said, "My God, haven't you ever made a terrible mistake?"

Harriet finally spoke to the man. "No," she said flatly. "We've made little mistakes. But not hideous, stupid mistakes. I have a theory, Dr. Schumacher. If I were running the world, mistakes would be like traffic violations. You make a little one, and you get a warning. You make two mistakes, and your license to make mistakes is revoked. You make a big mistake that hurts someone else, and you go to jail. But a mistake that kills a beautiful girl and a lovely little four-year-old child, why, you get executed for that, Dr. Schumacher."

"But why my poor boys?" Schumacher said. "Why not just me?"

Jean laughed. She sounded genuinely amused. "Indeed, you are a fool, Dr. Schumacher," she said. "Here we've gone to all this trouble to inform you, but you can't even count, can you? Let me help." She held up three fingers and ticked them off. "Patricia. Becky. Willis."

While she spoke, the kitchen door squeaked on its hinges, and there was a soft tinkle of glass. Christy couldn't turn around. He had nerve enough to look at the revolver but not to look away from it. Then something touched him from behind, and he involuntarily sucked in his breath. A cold nose lightly touched his hand.

Gala. No rescue after all. She looked up at him guiltily, the whites of her eyes showing. She had been bad, very bad, her look said. She had disobeyed his command to stay in the car. She had had enough of the cold and had leaped through the window he had so inconsiderately left open after scraping snow off the windshield, and she had followed him, and here she was peeping at him from the corners of her eyes. Distracted by guilt as much as she was, she seemed to take a second before the presence of other people fully registered on her. She looked warily at Schumacher, then trained her eyes on the sisters. She growled low in her throat.

"Control your dog, Dr. Christy," Harriet snapped.

Christy stooped quickly and grabbed Gala's collar. "You tried to kill her, didn't you?" he blurted. "It must have been you who gave her that antifreeze."

Harriet actually looked ashamed. "Jean was worried about the dog giving us away to the police. I kept telling her it didn't matter if the dog acted hostile toward us. Heavens, we learned quickly enough that she barked at everyone, so it was just a matter of degree. It's a good thing your dog is such a coward, or now I'd have to shoot her, too, and I really wouldn't care to spare the bullet. Do you know what she did that day in the older boy's apartment? She just turned tail and ran away."

Christy said, "I'll put her outside." He moved a few inches backward, dragging Gala with him.

There was no question of it. This time Harriet swung the revolver directly to cover him. "Don't," she said. "I'm quite good with this. I practiced a long time before we made this trip."

Christy felt as though a hand had pushed hard on his heart. He hadn't known before that moment how afraid he

217

was. He said desperately, "I'm sure you're good. But you can't use that gun. The police will match the bullets. They'll know it was the same gun that killed the two boys."

Harriet said, "Please, Dr. Christy, give us some credit. That revolver is long gone, deep in the mountains. This is an entirely different revolver."

"You'll never be able to explain my body away," Christy said. "You talk of stupid mistakes—don't make one."

Harriet said, "But we don't even know what you and your vicious dog are doing here. How did you put it? You just walked in right on the heels of a maniac who was trying to kill us, and you got shot in the confusion. True, it might not be as tidy, but don't overlook our secret weapon. Boring middle-aged women don't commit crimes. We might get hysterical and shoot you by mistake, thinking you were helping Dr. Schumacher attack us, but I think I can promise you that no one will ever believe we did it on purpose. It won't even occur to anyone."

Jean Ditton said, "Don't forget to use all the bullets, Harriet. I'm convinced it's always better if it looks like a woman just shut her eyes and fired until the gun was empty. I'd think a single head shot for Dr. Christy, if you can manage it, then several in the torso for Dr. Schumacher, including the heart, of course. Then if you have any bullets you don't absolutely need, one in the refrigerator? Or maybe the ceiling? Just don't hit the stew. I still say it's a good touch to have a nice little dinner cooking when the intruder broke in."

Christy gazed at the two women with horror as they argued briefly in tones of habitual sisterly quarreling over how many bullets to shoot where. He hated to think it, but Harriet could be right. Even now the sisters looked so everyday, so unexciting, that anyone might overlook them unless they had the opportunity so unfortunately given him to see the iron patience in their eyes and hear the determination in their voices. Dog-headed Furies.

The dog whose collar he held suddenly squirmed in his grasp as his fear transmitted itself to her. With a snakelike movement, Gala twisted her collar from Christy's grasp.

"Gala, no!" Christy said. "Come here!" He took a step forward.

Harriet thumbed back the hammer of the revolver. It still pointed steadily at Christy. At the sound of the hammer, Gala tensed. Then, with no hesitation at all, Gala leaped straight at the revolver and the woman. There was no warning growl. A black demon, white teeth bared, simply surged up at the woman. The attack was so swift, so savage, that Harriet missed her one chance to lower the revolver. She screamed and threw her arms in front of her face to ward off Gala, cocked revolver swinging skyward, as Gala hit her full in the chest and bounced to the floor and tensed to spring again. Christy tried to grab for gun and dog simultaneously. He felt sixty-five pounds of furious dog slam into him and knock both him and Harriet to the floor.

"Don't," Harriet cried. She twisted strongly under Christy as he grappled for the gun in her right hand. He managed to grab the cylinder tightly. Gala came in again, snarling now, and it was Christy who cried out this time, commanding, "Gala, enough! Down!"

The Doberman backed away, but only a foot. She turned red gums and forty-two teeth on Jean Ditton and Dr. Elliot Schumacher indiscriminately, daring them to move as Christy kept his hold on the cylinder of Harriet McAfee's revolver so she wouldn't be able to fire it. He succeeded in wrestling it from her hand and pushed backward, trying to scoot away from the woman. He bumped into Gala. Gala jerked her head, teeth bared at his ear, but she knew her master and she knew her target. She stood steady, her chest against his shoulder, ready to take on the world.

It was hard for Christy to get to his feet. He was trembling. When he made it up, he leaned a shoulder against the refrigerator and drew in breath in a gulping mouthful. He gestured with the revolver and said to the two sisters, "Into the kitchen, please. Carefully. That's good. Stand against the stove, if you will. No, facing it. Your stew might start burning if you don't watch the pot. Dr. Schumacher, I believe Miss McAfee said the phones are in the bedrooms. I don't know where in hell Nat Shannon is, but I know one police officer is at your house. Tell him to come right over."

Would the sisters have obeyed him if it hadn't been for Gala? Once they had edged into the kitchen, giving Gala a wide berth, they both looked over their shoulders. They eyed the revolver in Christy's hand with seeming indifference, but the looks they gave the dog were full of fear. Jean pressed even closer to the stove. The dog disapproved of her moving at all and growled, hackles springing up. Dr. Schumacher paused, jerking his hand back from the syringes on the counter, for which he had just started to reach.

Christy wagged the gun at him. "None of that, Dr. Schumacher," he said.

"I was only going to—"

"Yes, I know. Try to remove part of the incriminating evidence. If you want to get yourself shot instead of calling the police, that's up to you. I'm not much good with a gun, but I'll try just to wing you."

Schumacher went toward the bedrooms. He went quickly. Christy checked the revolver in his hand, wondering how to lower the hammer without firing the thing by accident. Then he looked at the sisters. Harriet, shuddering, still looked over her shoulder at the dog, but Jean seemed to be studying the stew pot. Something in the stiffness of her back, the set of her shoulders, alerted Christy. Mourning double death at the hands of a psychopath, these women had been through hellfire. It seemed to have burned away much that was human. An inhuman Fury would have no hesitation in charring her hands to pick up a mere stew pot, hurling the boiling contents at him and Gala.

Christy said, "Turn to face me. Instantly. Now both of you put your hands on top of your heads."

They looked meek and distressed as they stood with their hands atop their heads. Harriet moved a shoulder, as though it hurt her, and Christy discovered that he was studying Harriet with concern, worrying about whether or not she had been bitten in the melee. He thought it over for a second. That was all it took to decide he didn't give a damn.

Waiting for the police, Christy talked to Gala. He also called over and over to Agatha through the utility-room door, trying to reassure both of them. Poor Agatha. For the full three or four minutes that they waited, he could hear the dog scratching furiously at her door, wanting to know what in the world was going on. When Christy finally heard voices outside, he realized that he was still shaking. It didn't bother him. Just because something was frightening didn't mean you couldn't handle it. Gala had taught him that. Gala growled, a growl that he now knew meant serious business, but a deep voice from the kitchen door called, "Gala, good girl. Gala, come."

The voice was Cletus Knight's. Nat Shannon's voice said, "Hold that dog, Knight. All right, ladies, stay exactly where you are. You, too, Dr. Schumacher. Jerry, get some lights on in here and close that door."

Christy wanted two things. He accomplished the first by stopping Shannon and handing him the revolver. He said, "Be careful. Miss McAfee cocked it before I grabbed it, and I didn't know how to uncock it."

"My God, and it didn't go off?" Shannon said. "You're lucky to be alive."

"Oh, I got a good grip on the cylinder. I knew it couldn't fire."

Shannon said, "Couldn't fire? Christy, you damned fool, a cocked revolver can be fired no matter what!"

Shannon's information didn't help Christy's shakes in the least, but another matter had priority. It was grand to hear Shannon sputter, and it was grand to see a strange police officer, and it was grand to see Knight, and Christy knew that in a minute or two he would ask how they had all managed to get there so quickly. But his real thought was for his dog. His hands finally free of the revolver, he limped over to Knight and Gala, feeling as though he'd been run over by a bulldozer when the Doberman had slammed into him. He knelt beside Gala.

"Gala, girl," he said. "Little Gal." He looked up at Knight wonderingly. "She went," he explained haltingly. "She just went right for a double-knit Fury. What in the name of heaven made her do that?"

Knight raised an eyebrow at the oddness of Christy's terminology, but he said happily, "I'd assume her master was in jeopardy, and she knew it. I guess she was just holding up her end of the bargain."

"I'll be darned," Christy said. He patted Gala's chest and stroked her head. At first she didn't want to look at him, perhaps still feeling guilty for being disobedient and following him into the house, perhaps just generally feeling guilty about having attacked a human being, but Christy kept crooning until he got what he wanted—the dog's wide-eyed look of happiness and the beginnings of a doggy smile.

13

THE LOUD WHINE OF A SNOWMOBILE outside the cabin interrupted Christy's question. He and Knight both glanced out the window over the sink in time to see that the driver of the snowmobile was a very young boy. He curved expertly past the pine trees near the clinic, then careened on toward Gore Creek. The youngster was grinning as he guided the snowmobile. Speed and noise obviously suited him just fine, even if the noise might lessen other people's pleasure in the hush of the great mountains and the white splendor of the snow. Knight laughed at the face Christy made, and he said, "The next sound will be the thud of ski boots in the streets. Face it, Christy. Winter's here. Vail's back in business again."

Christy said wistfully, "Yes, but I sort of liked it the way it was. Off-season. Quiet."

"It's good both ways," Knight said. "Especially when all the beautiful ski people start floating in. They can be amusing."

"Yeah, I'll be one of them. When you've got a decent base I'll be back for a visit."

"What are you talking about?" Knight said. "You're not planning to leave, are you?"

"I haven't had much time for plans yet," Christy said. "But, yes, I'll probably head on into Denver later this week. There's a big clinic that's always looking for new D.V.M.'s to work the holiday and night shifts, and that'll give me a little time to decide where I'd like to go next."

"Why does there have to be a next? Why not stay here? Hell, has Dr. Potter canned you? Why, he's—"

"Shh," Christy said. He looked over his shoulder at the other people in the cabin. Dr. Potter was in the most comfortable chair nearest the fireplace listening to Mark Niemeyer. "Dr. Potter hasn't said anything at all," Christy told Knight, "but, heck, I was just relief pitcher while he was on vacation. There was never anything definite about my staying on. Let's talk about it later, okay? Now, about that base I'll be counting on, how much snow did we get last night, anyway?"

Knight looked troubled, but he said, "Only a little over two feet. But don't worry. It's going to snow some more."

Christy chose a triangle of buttered toast spread with a deviled sardine mixture from the platter of canapés that Knight had just taken from the warming oven of the wood-burning stove. When Knight had realized that a party was abuilding, he'd gone home to make canapés, declaring that a boyhood spent eating sandwiches had left him with little taste for cold bologna. He'd returned within a half-hour with hot stuffed mushrooms, crabmeat in ramekins, a dozen kinds of cheeses, and a roquefort and cognac dip with homemade caraway bread sticks. Christy had given interested thought to learning how to cook.

Bev Farrell's booming voice rose over the din of conversation by the fireplace, drowning out everyone else. Knight ignored her and picked up the thread of Christy's original question: "Anyway, as soon as I learned the dead girl's maiden name was Ditton, I knew we had something. I remembered the lady you introduced me to at the memorial service, so I tried to call you. I guess you were at the library. I was afraid to wait any longer, so I called Shannon. He said to meet him at the Schumachers' house, and we both must have been on the way there when you drove by the police station looking for him. Bad timing all the way around. I tell you, boy, you came mighty close to getting yourself shot."

"Yeah, that's what I was about to decide when Gala went into action," Christy said. "How come you told Shannon about Lloyd Glover? I thought you wanted to establish an 'information source' to take credit for everything?"

Knight glanced at his friend Lucille and lowered his voice. "Oh, I had that all set up. Cute-sounding girl on the *Seattle Times*. A reporter. But then the last piece of the puzzle came in, and I didn't think it could wait." Christy took another sardine canapé, and Knight frowned pointedly and started to turn away with the platter. Then he turned back smiling. "Actually, I might have done myself a favor by not involving the Seattle source. She's got one of those sexy voices. She's black, lucky me, and she says she's crazy about soul food and skiing. When Lucille goes home, maybe she'll come out. She insists she'll stay at a hotel, but who knows? I've got plenty of guest rooms, although you and Gala will be filling one instead of going to Denver this week. No, no back chat. It's occurred to me that I desperately need a resident veterinarian. I'll introduce you to my new Seattle friend, so you can see what you missed. Maybe I'll even introduce you to blackeyed peas and smothered chicken with rice, if you can stand the culture shock."

He took the canapés away, heading for Dr. Potter, Nat Shannon and Gala the Doberman. Christy picked up a plate of cocktail sausages wrapped in bacon and, playing host, let himself through the temporary barricade Mark Niemeyer had set up in the cabin. To keep Gala and Agatha the Sheepdog apart, Mark had unfolded a galvanized-iron exercise pen and strung it across the room. Agatha couldn't be left out of the party, Bev had insisted, so here she was, bouncing on Miss Carroll and getting gingerly pats from Karen Hamilton. Karen carefully tested the temperature of Christy's sausages, then offered one to Agatha, who opened her vast mouth like a baby bird and allowed it to be dropped in before contentedly chewing it.

"All those teeth" Karen sighed. "But I love her. Maybe she's just what I need—a big dog of my very own. Do you think there's any chance that Bev would let me have her?"

Bev heard. Christy was learning that no matter how loudly Bev was talking about something else, she could be relied upon to hear anything of interest to her. "Not on your life," Bev boomed to Karen. "I've always wanted an Old English. Agatha stays with me."

"But you've already got so many dogs," Karen said.

"That's just it," Bev said. "When you already have a houseful, one more doesn't matter. You wait until you're married or otherwise settled down. Get a house and a fenced yard, and then we'll find you a nice puppy."

Christy handed his sausages back across the temporary fence. Knight called for more firewood, and as Christy stepped outside to get it, Karen followed. She stamped her feet happily in the snow outside the door, packing it down with her snow boots, and Christy made a mental note to get the snow shovel back from wherever Miss Carroll had put it and dig a path from cabin to clinic. He'd only cleared the walks around the clinic of last night's heavy snow and put in two hours answering more of Nat Shannon's questions at the police station before afternoon and the party had begun. He felt tired, having been up so late the previous night, but Karen positively bubbled with energy.

"I've been wanting a minute alone with you," she said. "I have something for you."

Christy claimed one light, quick kiss from her smiling lips. "You do?" he said. "What is it?"

"You'll think it's silly."

"No, I won't."

But Karen stalled. She stamped the snow some more and said, "We ought to go for a hike before they mess up all the snow. You don't have to stay here, do you?"

"I guess not," Christy said. "There don't seem to be any patients this afternoon."

"It's always like that with the first good snow. Everyone stays home to play in it," Karen said. She looked back at the cabin door. "I'm glad you invited me to your celebration party, instead of your redheaded girlfriend."

"Sue's just a friend, but you were both invited," Christy said. "She couldn't come. She felt she should stay with Mrs. Schumacher. Mrs. Schumacher's all alone now."

"Oh," Karen said. Then, "They're not going to keep Dr. Schumacher in jail, are they? They can't really prove he did anything, can they?"

Nat Shannon came out after them, murmuring thanks for the drink, time to get back downtown, and Christy held him up to repeat Karen's question.

"Come on, there Schumacher was, with two syringes full of sodium pentothal and a can of gasoline," Shannon pointed out. "He tried to claim he brought the pentothal because it's a standard hypnotic and that his intention was only to try to get the ladies to talk, but when we started zeroing in on why the gasoline, he clammed up, long before his lawyer came."

Sodium pentothal. Christy used it himself as a fast-acting anesthesia. Had used it last on old Nellie the Collie when her day came, to give her easeful sleep before a gentle death. He asked Shannon if the police thought Schumacher would have to take his chances in front of a jury, but Shannon claimed complete ignorance.

"You're talking way over my head, Christy," he said. "Chief Fellows and the district attorney are the men with the answers now. Just whether they can make a case against any of the parties is open to doubt, to my eye, but figuring out the kind of evidence that will stand up in a court is among the many things on which I'm not remotely expert."

"You're always so innocent," Karen chided. "Just like the two ladies."

"Were Miss McAfee and Mrs. Ditton still denying everything this afternoon?" Christy asked.

"Everything, plus. We had one tiny connection that looked solid for a while. It's about the dog that the sisters took in so they could get close to Dr. Schumacher. It may have been Philip Schumacher who sideswiped it. But I think Miss McAfee figured out where Chief Fellows was heading, and she started denying that they really saw the car or anything but an injured dog. But he'll keep working on it. Fellows is good at that. His newest theory is that seeing Philip hit a dog sort of tipped the sisters over the brink. Made them decide to follow through on their plan, on the grounds that the kids were both too lousy to live. But my private theory is that they would have done it anyway."

Karen said, "Did the two ladies really ask for their knitting? That's too much, to think of them sitting there so innocently just knitting while the chief goes wild."

"We didn't give it to them," Shannon said. "Knitting needles are sharp. So knitting's out, unless they end up knitting away at some funny farm. If things get too hot, I figure them both for an insanity plea."

"Just like Lloyd Glover," Christy said.

"Yeah. Maybe Dr. Schumacher, too. They can all become certified nuts together. Although, come to think of it, I guess none of it is anything to laugh about. Speaking of unfunny things, Christy, are you sure you've got it straight now about single action and double action when it comes to revolvers? Any time you want to drop by the station for a little demonstration, I'll be glad to give you one."

"Thanks, Nat," Christy said, "but I never want to have anything to do with another revolver."

Shannon grinned widely and mushed on to his small green Saab. Karen asked Christy, "What was that about revolvers?"